AN OBSTINATE WITCH

WITCH KIN CHRONICLES, BOOK 4

E M GRAHAM

An Obstinate Witch

EBOOK ISBN: 978-1-7773212-4-6

PRINT ISBN: 978-1-7773212-5-3

CHAPTER 1

Tomorrow would be my birthday. Despised by my peers and far from the comforts of home, there would be no special cake in my honour. It might be the worst birthday ever, except that I didn't care about any of that.

Maybe because I was now officially an adult, or maybe it was because the power of the almost-full moon was entrancing me, calling to me, running crystal clear through my veins and I felt fabulous and full of life and ready to take on the world. I was invincible, or near enough.

Through the window of my dorm room that evening, I watched it rise over the hills of Scarp, the silver light reflecting in the calm sea surrounding the island. Was it just under a month ago that I'd been tricked into carrying the magical lode stone of the Kin through the tunnel? It felt like longer, yet the moon was only now coming into full again. Another two nights and it would be a perfect circle hanging in the dark blue sky. I breathed deeply through the open window, soaking up the energy of this strange Scottish moonlight that surged through me like a tide.

Hugh had promised to return before the moon was completely full, so he should be back tomorrow. I closed my eyes and let myself dream a little, of Hugh and me, and of rescuing my mother from the Ice King's grasp.

·········

My first inkling that things were not okay was the next morning when Fergie left the island. She wasn't at breakfast, but I thought nothing of it because she'd been mopey and sleeping in a lot lately. I wouldn't have even found out till later except I went to our shared room to get a book I'd forgotten and found her bundled up in her too-tight lilac puffy coat with her battered old suitcase. Her normally bouncy curls were lank as if she hadn't bothered to wash that day. Her side of the room was empty, our small table was bare of her makeup and hair products.

'Hey, what's going on?' I blocked the doorway instinctively as my mind tried to catch up with the shock of the evidence before my eyes. 'You're all packed up? Where you going?'

Even as I said It, I realized, guiltily and a little too late, that she hadn't been herself for a while. Since the incident of the Crystal Charm Stone, if I was truly honest with myself. She'd been quiet, withdrawn, and I'd been so wrapped up in my own head that I hadn't really wondered about it.

A lot of things had changed since the night that Willem had escaped across the channel. On the surface, everyone pretended things were normal on Scarp, except that they weren't and we all knew it. Sandy wasn't with us, for one. I missed him and his calming presence, even though he'd turned out to be such a shite at the end of it, conspiring with Willem as he had to steal the magical lodestone of the Kin.

All the other students no longer taunted me, or sneered at me. In fact, they only acknowledged my presence by avoiding me. If they couldn't pretend I wasn't there, they averted their eyes and refused to sit by me or talk to me. I'd known at the time that my proximity to the Crystal Charm Stone had done something odd to me that night, made me glow as I was infused with its magical energy, but that had only been a temporary thing. I couldn't understand why I was suddenly the social pariah, and no one was talking to me to explain it. Even Fergie had simply shrugged when I asked her, only telling me that she regretted her part in the whole thing, and that she didn't want to talk about it and it was all my fault. I put her touchiness down to her starting her period, and left it alone for I figured she'd come round.

Now I really, really wished I'd revisited the matter with her, because it sure looked like she was preparing to leave the island and walk out of my life.

'What's going on, Fergie?' I asked again as I grabbed her arm and forced her back into our shared room. She winced and quickly stepped away from me as I let go. I hadn't realized my grasp was so strong.

'Sorry, Dara,' she began, then stopped and shrugged.

'Sorry for what?' I wanted to shake her but didn't dare. Besides, I wasn't angry at her, I was angry at myself for not picking up on the clues. She was my only friend here on the island, the only one who would even speak to me after the incident of the Stone. All the other students shunned my presence like I was a plague dog or something.

And looking back, I know there were other things that should have been waving red flags to me. Not about Fergie, but about me. The seasons of the moon were slowly shifting by then, and I could feel something rising in my blood, like ripples of energy, like the inexorable ocean tide.

The good energies inside me grew slowly so I didn't notice the change until suddenly one day, I was feeling on the top of the world, in a wonderful good mood with loads of vitality to spare all the time. I could have gone hiking in the mountains from morning till night and not broken a sweat. In class, all my spells were spot on and my ideas were absolutely brilliant; I had confidence to spare and felt no fear and I always had the right answer. If I noticed that the others were looking at me suspiciously, I just put it down to professional jealousy, for the Kin kids were a competitive bunch.

The strangest thing, which is why I didn't realize it at the time, was that these good feelings felt entirely normal and right, like I was simply becoming the witch I was supposed to be, as if my potential had finally blossomed overnight. To me, there was nothing amiss about the state of affairs so I didn't dwell on the whys or hows, I just soaked up this good energy and assumed it was naturally me.

Over the past couple of days, I'd found that I could see the shimmerings of auras surrounding other people. This talent had crept up on me, and made itself known as I sat alone in the back of the classroom, looking at the other student's heads. I was bored that day for I'd already picked up the more intricate points of aiming ice balls towards a target, the subject of the day. It was simple – I formed the idea of ice in my mind, the knowledge of how the crystal structure would not release the energy, thus giving the quality of coldness – and with a flick of my finger to help propel the missile in the right direction, hit the target every time. I didn't see why these Kin kids, all of them trained from a young age, could not master this easy action spell.

As I sat there, I realized the auras of my classmates were visible to me, and I could instinctively interpret the rainbows of colors. The green and yellow burning lights of Win and her competitiveness, the drawling blue that was Timothy's.

I smiled kindly at Pauline when she darted a hate-filled glance at me, feeling sorry for her and the dreary brown that surrounded her, it was a grasping, fearful subdued aura no doubt stemming from her nasty father, Elder Cromwell. It was obvious to me that her rottenness was a result of her upbringing, that if she'd been given a bit of love and kindness, she too could have been a likeable person. Perhaps even as fabulous as me.

I'd never felt so full or sure of myself before. I was riding high.

Not just the aura perception, but, all my senses were heightened. Without the use of binoculars, I could see the Scottish flag flown by the little fishing vessel two miles out at sea, and could make out the tiny figures of the crew in their yellow oilskins. A raven landed twenty feet away from me one day, each black feather glistening with iridescence, and I watched my reflection in his obsidian eye. And the smells which now assailed me – well, that wasn't so great. I could hardly bear to go to the dining room, for it smelled like every meal ever eaten there had lingered, imprinting itself on the air, centuries of mutton stew and days-old oatmeal were adhered to the very walls. Even the butter had a rancid miasma hovering about it. I existed on bread and cheese and water snatched from the sideboard as I quickly ran in and out, holding my breath.

And today Fergie's aura was tarnished; what should have been lovely russet and forest green tones had dulled except for the hint of deep blue and purple around the edges like day-old bruises. When had this happened? And more to the point, why hadn't I noticed it happening?

'Fergie, is there anything I can do to help?' Too little too late, perhaps, but I had to say something.

She gave a deep sigh and looked me in the eye. 'I just can't handle this anymore. I feel like I'm in over my head, and this is not what I want,' she said, then gestured with her hand. 'All this – Scarp, the Kin hierarchy – all this isn't for me. It's not for my life.'

'But you worked to get here – you worked your ass off! How can you just throw it away?' It was a mystery to me, especially full of the moon's rising energy as I was. I couldn't think of a better place to be than on Scarp with its fresh air and salt water and green hills. The educational environment was exactly what I needed, and I intended to go through every last book in the extensive library before I left.

'And what – Johanna's just letting you leave?' I found that hard to believe. Johanna, the Master of Scarp, had picked Fergie out especially from her small local Hedge Witchery afterschool program in Glasgow. She'd seen my friend's potential – there was no way she'd let the young woman leave without a struggle.

'She can't keep me here, not if I decide to go.' I saw a flash of the old Fergie as she lifted her chin defiantly in the air, even if it was quivering a little.

'But what about me? What am I going to do? You're my only friend here...'

She laughed bitterly. 'You don't need me, Dara. You've changed since that night.' She looked like she wanted to say more, but instead she set her lips firmly together and looked away.

'What? No, I'm me, just a better me.' A fantastic me, actually, I felt like I was really coming into my own. How could she not want to stick around to watch? 'Can't you see?'

Fergie shook her head and looked up at me again. 'You're not you, not anymore. You... you scare me. It's too much like the stories of Auld Meg.' She paused and gave me a significant look. 'I have a bad feeling about this, and I don't want to be a part of it.'

'What are you going to do with yourself? Don't tell me you'll just go back to Glasgow and be a plain old Hedge Witch!' I couldn't believe it. She'd had such big plans when we'd arrived on Scarp. The first of her family to have a proper magic education.

And who the hell was Auld Meg?

'No,' she replied. She looked out the window to the ocean in the distance. 'Not Glasgow for me. I can't go back there. I'm going to try something different. Something completely different and not related to the Kin at all.'

She stared at me intently, and spoke slowly with emphasis, the only bit of life I'd seen in her for ages. 'I advise you to leave now, too. Quit while you're ahead. It's not too late to go back to your old life, Dara. There are bad things coming your way, and it's all because of the Stone and that night. I'm afraid for you.'

And that was that. No further explanation as to her visions and precognitions about me, and she was hell-bent on running away to wherever it was she was headed, to the future that didn't include me. She gave a half-hearted promise to email me, but only after I pressed her. I didn't expect to hear from her ever again.

I was the only one to see Fergie off the island that chill spring day. Down by the water, the mist covered everything like a wet blanket, muffling all sound except for the endless susurration of the waves on the stones of the shore. I sat down heavily on the rocky beach as the ferryman silently rowed his boat to the other side, and she didn't wave good-bye to me. She hadn't even hugged me before climbing onto the boat. My friend just abandoned me to this terrible future she'd predicted for me.

Long after she'd disappeared into the swirling mist, I sat staring after her, never minding the sea damp of the pebbles soaking into my jeans. I was truly on my own now here on this island so far from home. I told myself that this bothered me less than it might have just mere months ago, for today I felt strong and confident and unbeatable, my future was now, I had potentiated my potential, and I was coming into the power that was rightfully mine.

A solitary gull swept across the seascape, its mournful cry echoing off the stone walls of the castle and the cliffs and I knew if I let myself, I could so easily have gotten inside its head, seen what it saw, felt what it felt. I could leave behind this whole lonely island and just soar through the gull's mind, enjoying the freedom of flight. The only thing on his mind was the search for his next meal before his rivals found it.

Fergie didn't even know it was my birthday that day.

CHAPTER 2

Yet strangely, the sadness didn't last with me, as if the hours that passed created a buffer for the loss, and her leaving became a mere fact in my memory. The energies in my body called to me, I was flying on top of the world and could do no wrong, and I felt like I would live forever. I was untouchable.

The mania had almost fully sprung in my blood that evening when the elders appeared on Scarp, brought in by the Kin private 'copter late in the evening just as the moon was rising over the hill, one day from full.

My head and body were buzzing, I couldn't sleep and from my bedroom window I watched the black robed figures walking over the hill from the helipad, talking amongst themselves. Elder Cromwell was with them, and all the others who had stood at my judgement in Inverness.

And Hugh. I could have picked him out a mile away, the tall figure with his broad shoulders and oh yes, his aura of the purest clarity I'd ever seen. Not perfectly white, for there were all sorts of interesting flickers of the rainbow woven within, with a lot of gold and equal amounts of darkness, but it burned a pretty steady clear light all the same. He was easy on my eyes.

I couldn't wait to see him, to talk with him, to tell him how good I was feeling, and there was no doubt in my mind he'd be ecstatic for me too. I lurked in the shadows of the Great Hall as they were all ushered into Johanna's office. At the top of the stairs across from the room, I waited and lurked some more, sure that Hugh would find some excuse to come out in search for me. And I was right! Not a half hour after they'd arrived, the office door opened again and he stepped out.

He'd barely shut the door behind him when I lightly skipped out of the shadows and jumped into his arms, my arms around his neck.

His whole body tensed at the impact and went into defensive mode, flinging me away against the stone wall of the corridor. Fortunately, I hit one of the wool tapestries hung at regular intervals. It softened the blow but I still needed a moment to regroup as I sat coughing amid the clouds of dust stirred up from the ancient material.

'What the...?' He stepped forward to get a closer look at his assailant. 'Dara? What's going on?'

'I thought I'd surprise you,' I said and shook my head clear. 'Not such a great idea, perhaps, I forgot who I was sneaking up on.' I looked back up at him. 'Aren't you happy to see me?'

'Yes, but...' He reached down his hand to help me up. I didn't need assistance but I took it anyway, letting my hand linger in the warmth of his grasp.

'But what?' I grinned as I looked up at him. My five and a half feet were a perfect match for his six feet plus, I'd always thought.

He looked at the air around my head before his eyes settled on mine. 'Wow, you're... you're practically glowing.'

'You can see auras too? I've just begun to see them. Scarp is doing my powers the world of good.' I was babbling – there was so much I wanted to tell him.

He shifted away from me. 'I have to ask, were you listening through the door?' He nodded his head toward Johanna's office.

'That solid oak? Believe me, you can't hear a thing through that, I know from experience,' I said before the meaning of his words hit me and stemmed my flow. I looked across the distance between us. 'What are you saying?'

He glanced over his shoulder at the door before turning his gaze back on me.

'I'm not a snoop, you know,' I told him, looking at him uncertainly.

His face cleared and he laughed, but he kept his voice low. 'I would never think you would pry,' he said, that familiar smile returning to his eyes. I could see the small glints of gold in the green even in the dark, my eyes had become so super sharp. 'But we're discussing you.'

Hugh tried to suppress the excitement in his voice so I stayed quiet and let him speak. 'You're going to Edinburgh,' he continued. 'This may be the best thing to ever happen to you. And me.'

Edinburgh, where Hugh was based most of the time. Off this island where no one would speak to me now that Fergie had left. To be in the big city where life happened, and to get away from the sour pusses who were presently on Scarp? Oh yeah, I was onboard.

'Will I get to see you there?'

He took a deep breath and let it out slowly. 'You'll see me every day. If we can get Cromwell to agree, that is.'

I opened my mouth – I didn't know if I was going to squeal with excitement or what, but he laid his finger lightly on my lips and brought his mouth closer to my ear.

'Not so fast. We're still hammering out the terms with the Covenanters who, as you know, have never been on your side.'

His whisper tickled the skin of my neck and I shivered with a secret delight. We were going to be in Edinburgh. Never mind the Cromwell and his Covenanters, we were going to be together. My life was getting better and better.

'I'll meet you in the walled garden after breakfast.' This last was barely spoken under his breath as if he feared the very walls had ears. After placing his finger on my lips again to make sure I understood, he nodded and slipped away into the shadows of the hall.

Could I ever have received a better birthday present? Looking back, I should have known to look this gift horse in the mouth, especially when the Kin were involved.

·····•·····

I could hardly sleep that night, the room was so quiet. Even though I'd never shared a room in my life before coming to Scarp, I'd quickly gotten used to Fergie's comforting snore six feet away from me. Besides the weird silence, I was too excited to sleep, my energy was buzzing and my thoughts were focused on my future in Edinburgh. With Hugh.

I skipped breakfast, for the thought of entering the stinky dining hall was enough to make me urge. Instead, I waited at our appointed meeting place in the fresh air, the courtyard garden walled on three sides and overlooking the sea. Sandy had shown this secret place to me. It was quiet here, and private. The breeze coming off the water was welcomingly cool on my skin, for I felt as though I had a furnace stoked inside me.

He appeared from the side entrance, his hair still damp from his morning shower yet he was dressed in a suit and tie even this early in the morning. I liked this much better than the formal black silk robe worn during Kin business. The fine wool fabric of the suit hugged his body and showed off his broad shoulders, tapering to his trim hips. It must have been tailor made for him, or perhaps he just looked good in everything he wore.

The grin on his face matched mine, and this time I ran and jumped in his arms and he didn't put me down. We stayed like that for a long moment while I gloried in that spicy sandalwood smell of him, the warmth of his body, my feeling of security within those strong arms.

Finally he let me down gently and we walked back to my stone bench in the sun. I nestled into his arm as we gazed out to the sea and watched the gulls and waves.

'How are you feeling?' I loved how his deep voice rumbled through his chest.

'Number one, now.'

'I mean, how are you feeling?' He emphasized the last word.

I turned my neck to squint up at him. 'I feel good. Great actually, fantastic, never felt better in my life.'

'The past few days?'

'Yeah, I guess so,' I said as I snuggled back into his arm and smiled. 'You're right, come to think of it, just lately. Even though Fergie left, I know I should probably be feeling sad, and none of the others will have anything to do with me, but I feel like I've risen above all that.' I gave a deep sigh of pure pleasure.

He coughed slightly. I knew that sound, that reflex of his. It was the harbinger of a difficult conversation.

I sighed again as I sat up straight. 'Alright, what is it? Out with it. Don't spare me the bad news. I'm a big girl, I can take it. Have they changed their minds about Edinburgh already?'

Hugh gave a surprised laugh. 'No, not at all. That's definitely on the cards, and the move will be very soon. It's just the other stuff we need to discuss.'

I screwed up my face in query.

It was his turn to sigh as he marshalled his thoughts. 'Look, you agree you feel different in the past few days, don't you?'

'Different? No, not really. I feel great, just fabulous,' I said. 'I'm on the top of the world, never felt better in my life. As if all those things I'd wished for myself have come true, and now here I am!'

And that's when Hugh told me the truth. 'This good feeling you have,' he began. 'You say you've never felt so well in your life. Have you given any thought as to why that might be?'

I shrugged, impatient with his mysteriousness. 'Clean fresh air, lots of exercise,' I said. 'Lots of food, well, the cheese is good anyway. Probably just a combination of that and... and maybe hormones.'

Even as the words came out of my mouth, my logic sounded weak, and it started me wondering. What was making me feel so good?

'You know the full moon is upon us.'

'You're saying it's hormonal, then?'

'I'm saying the moon is exerting an influence on you, waking something up inside you.'

'What, I'm becoming some sort of werewolf or something?' I tried to make a joke, to lighten his seriousness. He was worrying me, and I didn't like that uncomfortable feeling breaking into my high. What he was hinting at was ridiculous. My good feelings had nothing to do with anything external. I was coming to be the person I always knew I should be. Nothing to do with cycles of nature. And I loved how my mind was quick and racing.

'Not a werewolf, no.'

'What, then?'

'We don't know, but it's entirely possible,' he said. His eyes were boring into mine now, and no matter how much I fidgeted, I couldn't look away. 'That night with the Crystal Charm Stone? Your contact with it will have had an effect on you, on your body. We fear it might even have caused damage deep within your DNA structure. The Kin are concerned.'

'But how I'm feeling, it's not a bad thing.' Even to my ears, that sounded like a pathetic protest. Sure, I was feeling great, which come to think of it, was perhaps not such a normal thing for me. And a tiny voice of reason piped up inside me, acknowledging that I knew enough about the Kin that if they were 'concerned', then it would never be good news for me.

'And... how is it even possible?' I sat up straight. 'I thought DNA is forever. And what does this mean for me, am I going to grow scales or feathers or something?' I was only half joking, for magic can be tricky.

'No.' He allowed himself a small smile as if relieved to hear this very normal response from me, then stretched his arm along the back of the bench again. His dark suit jacket had soaked in the heat of the sun and I could smell the faint scent of cloves and sandalwood from him. 'It's just that... well, we don't know what to expect. The effects appear to come out during the phase of the full moon.'

'Should I be afraid?' I turned my head to squint at him against the sun. It gave me an excuse to lean back into his arm, and I paused like that, feeling the comfort of both the sun and Hugh together.

He shrugged. 'Like I said, no one knows. But that's the reason we're going to Edinburgh, just to make sure. And in Edinburgh...'

But I couldn't let him change the subject like that, for the possibility of having my DNA changed was a huge thing.

'Why doesn't anyone know what's happened?' I insisted. 'How can they tell? Are they able to do genetic testing to see if something's gone wrong?'

I was full of questions and they were all coming out. 'And surely this must have happened to someone else at some time. Isn't there anything in the Chronicles, or even the Sagas from before the time of the Kin?' I brought up my hand to shield my eyes, the better to see him.

At this last question his eyes slid away, and I knew he was avoiding something. I poked him in the chest and demanded he tell me.

Sighing, he brought both arms around me and enveloped me in a hug. The crisp linen of his shirt was smooth against my cheek.

'Yes,' he whispered in my ear, though there was no one else to hear. 'Something did happen once before, many years ago, but I am going to make sure that this time things turn out better. For you, for me, for the Kin as a whole.'

'More to the point,' he continued, dropping his arms and moving slightly away from me. 'Whatever is going on, the Kin want it contained. They want you away from proximity to the Stone and kept close to their resources. That's why we're both going to Edinburgh.'

'But... my studies?' My future? Was I never going to be allowed to learn and practice like a true witch?

'You'll keep up, don't you worry. And this is the exciting bit,' he said, his voice still in a whisper. 'They're arranging private tutoring in fact. With me.' He paused to watch the effect of his words sink into my brain.

Well this was... pretty good news. I couldn't help the smile forming on my face, but I didn't trust myself to speak. I merely pointed at myself, then at him. He nodded.

'Under the careful eye of the Venerable Nachtan,' he added. 'Which is a whole other story. You'll find out.'

Even as I opened my mouth to, I don't know, shout or scream my excitement, he shook his head, cautioning me to stem my flow.

'The only thing is,' he said, his voice pitched low again, and he darted a glance around the empty garden as if ensuring we were still alone. 'Us? We can't be. We need to be strictly professional in all our dealings, or else the Covenanters will put an end to this plan.'

I shut my mouth, then opened it again, then realizing there was no arguing against this, shut it once more and nodded. 'But, we'll still be together?'

'Yes,' he said, and his eyes crinkled up at the edges as they always did when he was pleased. 'But like I said, we have to keep us under wraps. For now.'

He left me then, alone with my thoughts and emotions and the frisson of excitement at this last news. Things were looking up. Hugh was a good teacher, I knew from past experience, remembering how he'd taught me to camouflage and to 'fly' with my mind, and I had no doubt my knowledge would increase in leaps and bounds under his formal tutelage. My future was secure, we just had to be circumspect in our relationship, at least in front of the Kin's eyes.

But the other stuff? It explained why I was feeling so fantastic, sure, but I couldn't help but be disappointed to find out that all this good energy wasn't coming from me. It was the effect of my contact with the Crystal Charm Stone and the moon working together. Not me at all.

Or was it? It came to me that the reverse was true, actually. If the Stone had altered my DNA, then the power was mine, wasn't it? I could claim this power, it was me. Even if it was only during the time of the full moon that my power was magnified, it was still mine to claim.

Which led onto a whole other, inevitable realization. With this incredible moon-enhanced magic power, I surely now had the means to find the Ice Kingdom and rescue my mother, maybe even in a month's time. I didn't know how to do this yet, but I would find a way.

Hugh would frown on this, of course. So now I had two secrets.

CHAPTER 3

Johanna's study was lit only by the soft glows of lamps on her oak desk and the fire in the grate, and her eyes were almost hidden in the shadows.

'These good feelings of yours at the moment? You do realize that they are of a temporary nature and won't last.' Johanna, the First Elder of the Witch Kin and Master of Scarp, spoke in her severest voice as I sat before her. 'We need to remove you from the island before the moon reaches its maximum fullness.'

She pushed a mug full of dark liquid towards me. A sour smell wafted in the steam rising from it. 'Here, drink this. It will make the voyage easier.'

'Voyage? Aren't I going to Edinburgh by helicopter like everyone else does?'

'I believe that Hugh explained you are an unknown quantity?' One eyebrow lifted inquiringly, the rest of her face could have been set in stone.

I nodded, reluctantly.

'Well then, you realize that we can't risk your presence in any mechanical vehicle, especially one which is airborne. Not so close to the full moon. Not until we understand more.'

Her voice turned a tad, taking on an unaccustomed kindness through her brisk manner. 'You'll be travelling by ferry to Edinburgh. The ferryman will be able to handle anything that arises.'

'What, all that distance?' I wasn't too sure of the geography of this new land, but I was pretty sure Edinburgh was a hell of a long way from Scarp, especially by water and in that tiny boat that carried students and supplies back and forth from the main island. 'He's going to row me over the North Sea in that? It's little better than a coracle.'

She smiled at that. 'His boat may look like a flimsy reed vessel, but it is much more than that. Now please, drink up. It will help your journey.'

I scrunched up my face and swallowed two mouthfuls. It was vile, but if it helped prevent seasickness then I was all for it. My family lived in the city back home, not in the outports and bays, and they didn't make their living from the ocean like so many others did, but I'd still travelled on enough dories and other small vessels to know that me and big seas didn't go well together, and I really wasn't looking forward to going all that distance in the tiny open boat. I said that, after I wiped my mouth and winced.

'Oh, this will take care of all that,' Johanna said. 'It's a sedative. You won't notice anything at all of the journey, in fact. We are placing you into what you might call a magical coma. This will help balance your energies which have been so upset by the moon's cycles.'

'What?' I pushed the mug away from me, and searched wildly around the room as if to look for escape. Was I imagining it, or could I already feel a soft, fuzzy comfortable feeling spreading through my limbs? 'You're sedating me?'

'It's only temporary,' she assured me calmly. 'And only for the duration of the trip. This is for your own safety.'

She looked on as my body visibly relaxed, yet my mind was still racing.

'I don't... don't want...' My voice was slurring, and it was damned difficult to move my mouth.

'It will not hurt you. You will be closely monitored each step of the way. Now, just come over to the sofa, and lay down.'

I could feel my body lurching up and in that direction, although my mind screamed at me to run away. But then I descended into a lovely dark warm place where I didn't need to worry about anything anymore.

I have only vague memories and impressions of my journey, like snippets of dreams forgotten upon waking. I remember being warm and rocked, the ferryman's dark hood rising above me with the stars and full moon behind him, and the good feelings of late, my mania if you will, slipping gently away from me, leaving my body and mind feeling nothing, just blankness.

·····•·••····

The first thing I saw when I next opened my eyes was a pale sun trying to push its way past bright yellow curtains, succeeding only in bathing everything in an unnatural neon glow. I was no longer on the ferry. This must be Edinburgh, then and I had managed to comatize my way all the way down to the Firth of Forth; well, that was one way to beat seasickness.

I felt okay. I looked within for after-effects of the vile drink Johanna had fed me, but there was nothing. I wiggled my toes and shifted my legs. All in good working order, so I took a moment to examine my surroundings. The walls of the bedroom were papered with images of soft violet thistle heads, bound together by green traceries of leaves and vines against a cream background. Heavy wooden furniture crouched against the low ceiling and the slanted dormers. I could hardly move for the weight of blankets covering me. As I struggled to push them off me, I saw to my horror that I was no longer in my own clothes of jeans and hoody, but now dressed in a flannel nightgown. I had no memory of doing that myself, so someone must have done it for me. That was too creepy to dwell on.

I placed my feet on the cold linoleum floor and realized that this nightie reached all the way to my ankles. The damp chill in the air caused me to shiver, so I grabbed one of the grey scratchy blankets and huddled into it, using it like a cloak.

'Ye're up then. About time, I'd say, if you asked me, not that anyone would,' a small voice chattered at me from my right. It was nearer to the floor than any voice had a right to be, and I peered down to find the source.

What I had taken to be a large doll in a rocking chair pushed itself up – or I should say herself – and stood before me, all three feet of her. She was a vision in brown – her hair, her long old-fashioned dress, her eyes – except for the once-white apron which covered her front and the mob cap which tried to contain her curls. 'And I can get back to my chores, now, heaven's sake, I've enough to do without having to mind you.'

She paused before turning to the door. 'Well hurry up, then, Mrs. Mac'll be waiting for us both and wondering what's keeping us. It's nigh on half past eleven, and no' a wee'un washed,' She disappeared in a flurry of skirts but before I could hear her light tapping of footsteps descending the stairs, she poked her button nose back inside the room. 'Not that we have wee'uns here, no, not right now, that's just a saying.' And she was gone again.

I stood slowly, looking all about me for my clothes.

'They're in the wardrobe!' The screech came up from a distance. 'And get a move on!'

Sure enough, my usual costume of jeans and hoody and underwear and socks were all neatly folded and hung inside the heavy wooden closet. Every single item had been freshly laundered and, judging by the crisp folds, starched and ironed as well, yes even the socks and underwear. The mysterious Mrs. Mac was waiting, hopefully with a full table because I was starving. My clothes rustled as I moved, and I had to hold my body in perfect posture or the starch in my t-shirt would itch the back of my neck like crazy.

The house I moved through in search of that little person was unremarkable save that none of the furnishings matched, except in their degree of fade and age. The threadbare carpet runner on the narrow stone stairs appeared to have been a tartan pattern in its earlier life, while the hallway walls were papered with faded Victorian roses. All the white painted doors were firmly shut.

After descending two flights, I ended up in the front entrance, coloured glass in the arched transom above the double door and in the wide panels on each side of it. A different carpet runner, one of blue and pale red stripes, led towards the back of the house and thence down a few more stairs, where I could hear a great banging of pots.

I don't know what I had been expecting, but the kitchen was a strangely modern room, in as much as the latter part of the last century could be said to be modern. A white gas stove, a small white refrigerator, white cupboards above and below a wooden countertop. The little female who had been minding me as I slept was now standing up on a step stool, hand washing pots almost as large as herself.

When she caught sight of me she screeched again. 'No' in here! Mrs. Mac is in the parlour!' She flicked a large quantity of suds my way as she pointed out of the kitchen.

There were only two other choices of doors along the dark corridor on the main level of the house, so I chose the front of the house, guessing that should be the parlour. I hesitated before turning the handle. Should I knock first?

I decided to err on the side of caution and politeness, and was answered by an imperious voice bidding me to enter.

The woman, I took her to be Mrs. Mac, was standing by an ornate fireplace when I opened the door, and she gave me the once over as I stepped inside the room. She was a matronly kind of person, middle-aged stout, dressed in a blue day dress with court shoes, and her hair was the same style as the Queen's, a helmet of tightly controlled waves set back from her wide face.

Mrs. Mac nodded as if confirming to herself.

'Welcome, Dara,' she trilled, rolling the 'r'. She sounded sort of like the Queen, but even more regal and Scottish to boot. 'Please have a seat. I'll ring for tea.' With that, she pressed a button by the side of the mantel.

While we waited, I looked around the room. There was only one window in this miniature, overstuffed room, and it was almost hidden behind lace curtains with a canopy of golden velvet drapery surrounding it on three sides. The furniture was finely upholstered in pale blue, and a piano was squeezed into one corner. But what really caught my eye was the overwhelming number of knick-knacks placed on every single surface of the room. Dresden shepherdesses rubbed elbows with Toby mugs, which fought for space with china cats, and all were interspersed with tiny plates stating names of villages I'd never heard of. A brass owl leered out from behind a Victorian porcelain doll and a carved wooden elephant. There was too much more to take notice of.

And the walls, papered in Edwardian stripes of green and white, were likewise covered with photos in frames, ranging from early stiff black and white shots of women in long dresses and men with mutton chop sideburns, to little framed shots of people in bathing suits by the seaside. It was a room overwhelming in its memories, as if the owner could bear to let nothing go.

Meanwhile, Mrs. Mac had taken a seat on the tightly stuffed sofa across from me and sat with her hands in her lap and legs crossed at the ankle, graciously smiling upon me. 'If you wouldn't mind opening the door for Brownie,' she said at last. 'She sometimes finds it difficult to juggle both the tray and the handle.'

The little maid was waiting outside, carrying a silver tray loaded with a teapot, cups and saucers, milk jug, sugar dish and a plate of biscuits. She didn't say anything, merely shot me a dirty look as she pushed past me and laid the tray on a side table with a thump.

'Thank you, Brownie,' Mrs. Mac trilled. 'That will be all. Oh, I believe we'll have that roast for luncheon tomorrow, if you would be so kind to prepare it.'

'Now, Dara,' Mrs. Mac turned her attention on me before Brownie had even left the room. 'As you'll be staying here as my boarding guest, I feel it's important to lay down a few Rules of the House, so as not to cause Unfortunate Misunderstandings during your time here.' She gave me a benevolent smile before continuing.

'There will be no coming and goings at all hours. This is a Respectable Home, and the doors are locked at ten o'clock every night. Brownie has a long day, and we can't have her woken up to let you in whenever you feel inclined, that's far too much of an inconvenience for the poor thing. So if you will respect this, we will all get along famously.'

She poured two cups of tea and handed me one. The china was almost thin enough to see through, and the faded gold leaf around the lip showed it to be of a great age. A fine cup yes, but the tea was weak and watery.

I reached over for a biscuit before they were offered because I was ravenous, having had no breakfast yet and nothing to eat since leaving the island. She frowned slightly at this, but said nothing. I was glad to note that my extreme taste sensitivity had faded, for although the shortbread was slightly stale, the butter in it was delicious. Yet the small shortbread hardly made a dent in my hunger, and I eyed the plate for a second helping as I licked the last crumb off my finger.

'Meals,' she continued. 'Breakfast is served at half-past seven in the dining room, summer and winter. You will not be partaking of luncheon as you will be at the castle with the

Venerable Nachtan.' Here, her eyes fluttered with pleasure, just a little, and she leaned in as if to impart a confidence. 'The fact that you are studying under such a great gentleman is the sole reason I allowed Hugh to convince me to take you on. I don't commonly take paying guests, you realize, only Very Special Cases.'

The Venerable Nachtan again. Who was this person? I interrupted her prepared speech to ask.

Her hand rose to her throat as she gasped. '*Who* is the Venerable Nachtan?'

CHAPTER 4

M rs. Mac frowned at my question, until her mind found an excuse for my ignorance. 'But of course, you're from the Colonies, that might explain your ignorance.' She took her teacup and saucer in hand and leaned closer, speaking in a reverent tone. 'The Venerable Nachtan is the greatest living witch in the world. Naturally, he is Scottish, and the oldest witch, also. He has performed great feats over his lifetime, and through the years he has contributed more to the Common Knowledge of Witchery than any other person.'

'Knowledge?' I stared at her. My heart was beginning to race. 'You mean, spells and things? Magical knowledge?'

She sniffed haughtily. 'Of course, magical knowledge. What other kind of knowledge is there?'

'So, he would know everything there is to know?' My mind was racing to match my heart. The Venerable Nachtan would know how to get to the Ice Kingdom from here. Could it be this easy? Would he share this knowledge?

And how could I ask him without Hugh finding out?

'If he doesn't know it, it's not worth knowing, I assure you,' she said genially, delighted to see that I was suitably awed by the greatness of the Scottish witch.

'And I'll be working with him,' I said, more to myself.

'He will oversee your education,' she reminded me. 'You would never be working *with* him, as if you were an equal.' She trilled at the thought, then returned to her listing of the House Rules. 'The evening meal is served at seven, if you are partaking of it. If not, you will receive no food. I can't have you in the kitchen bothering Brownie. We must have Discipline in these matters.'

Just then the doorbell rang.

'Ah, that will be Hugh now.' Mrs. Mac sounded relieved, but made no movement to go greet him. Instead, we listened as Brownie thumped her way down the stairs and wrestled with the heavy front door.

'They're in the parlour,' Brownie's grudging voice came through to us and then we heard the front door slam and the little maid clumped her way back up the stairs.

Hugh appeared at the sitting room door like a breath of fresh air in this strange, claustrophobic old house, or maybe it was just me grasping for anything familiar. His dark curls glistened with moisture and his dark peacoat showed damp spots, although I could have sworn the sun was shining not half an hour previously when I'd awoken. His presence filled the cluttered space, suddenly making everything a little more bearable. I stood up, a little rudely perhaps but I was quite ready to leave with him, to escape this house. I needed to breathe.

'Mrs. Mac, how are you today?' His voice was warm and he had turned the charm on full throttle, and he didn't sound like he was going anywhere fast. 'Dara's not causing you any trouble, I hope?'

Mrs. Mac's manner visibly melted under the force of Hugh, and she even tittered. 'Och, now Hugh,' she said flirtily. 'I'm just explaining the House Rules. I believe we'll muck along fine, Dara and I.'

'I'm sure she'll give you no issues,' he replied smoothly, arching an eyebrow at me, then he nodded as if he understood exactly how I was feeling. 'Well, I'll take her out of your hair then, Mrs. Mac, and let you get on with your day. I know you're a busy woman. No need to bother Brownie, we'll see ourselves out.'

With that he quickly ushered me out of the parlour and through the double front doors of Mrs. Mac's establishment. I found myself outside in a tiny square or plaza, lined on three sides by tall stone and brick houses and on the fourth directly across from us a concrete wall, with greenery showing over its top. It was gloomy here, with the mist shrouding the uppermost levels of the homes, each three or four stories high. Mrs. Mac's house was the smallest in the square, but her stone walls were freshly painted and the wrought iron fencing immaculate and free of rust, despite the hint of salt sea in the moist air.

Hugh heaved a sigh of relief as the door closed behind us.

'Well then,' he said, and paused as we took each other in. He opened his arms and I fell into them, aching for his strong hug.

'Happy Birthday, by the way,' he whispered. 'I think that got lost in all the excitement.'

I nestled in his arms a moment longer, loving the soft scratch of his wool coat and the strength of his arms. 'A day late, but thank you.'

'Hmm,' he murmured into my hair. 'But I'm guessing you didn't get any cake.'

I shook my head against his shoulder. 'Not a bite. Or a card.'

'How does it feel to be a full adult? You're twenty-one, right,' he said.

'Almost as old as you,' I remarked, at which he laughed and I loved feeling the rumble deep inside him. He gave me an extra squeeze before letting me go.

'So you've met Mrs. Mac. I'm sure you have many questions. Come on, we can talk as we walk.'

'Where're we off to?' I asked as we turned left down a narrow lane leading out of the square.

''Eventually, to Edinburgh Castle, where we'll begin working under the Venerable Nachtan. But not yet. Today, we're going to be tourists. I'll show you around Edinburgh, the old part where we are now.'

He stopped to look at me quizzically, taking in the whole of me from head to foot. 'How are you feeling, by the way? Do you have any leftover effects from the magical coma?'

I sure did. I was a little muzzy and discombobulated, although I couldn't think of that word at the time. 'What do you think?' I shot back at him. 'Being put under and losing a whole day, how should I feel?'

'Three days, actually,' he replied absently as he looked both ways before leading me across the road. 'The Kin felt that was for the best, to get you over the moon effect.'

'Three?'

Hugh jumped at my tone, then a light dawned in his eyes. 'You're probably really hungry, aren't you?'

'Well, yeah,' I said with as much sarcasm as I could muster. 'After three days of not eating because I was sedated against my will.'

'They woke you up enough to get water and broth in you,' he mumbled and had the grace to look a little embarrassed as I glared at him. 'It was for a good reason, believe me. The coma is not something the Kin did lightly, but they were very worried about the power surges you were experiencing. You were also knocking out the Wi Fi on Scarp, and that was frustrating. Johanna had to keep rebooting the system.'

'Well, I'm sorry for inconveniencing her. And they're sure it was me doing that?' I demanded as I turned on him. As soon as the words were out, I remembered how my phone fizzled every time I picked it up on the day before the full moon.

Maybe there was something to what he said, after all. I looked down at my feet and kicked a pebble out of my way.

'So we'll get a late fry-up on the way before we begin our tour.' He took a moment to size me up. 'You do look rather pale.'

I had a million questions for him, but no strength to marshal my thoughts. After a couple of twists and turns, we came out on a wide cobbled boulevard that sloped down to the east. A wave of faintness overcame me and I stumbled a little on the uneven surface. Hugh placed his arm around my shoulders. That felt much better.

'This is the Royal Mile,' he murmured. 'The Castle is up to our right, and Edinburgh Old Town is all around us. You can't really see it with all the buildings in the way, but we're up on top of a very high hill.'

We went down a steep incline to a small diner where I was served, as promised, a good fry-up. With that and the coffee, I was soon feeling put back to rights and ready to demand answers to questions which I would think of just as soon as my head cleared a little more. Satisfied, I sat back in my chair to find Hugh watching me.

'You found Mrs. Mac's comfortable enough, I hope?'

'Apart from the God-awful furnishings, and her million knick-knacks, yes,' I replied. 'But I don't really understand why you chose her place. Is she Kin?'

'Oh, she is, but non-practicing,' he offered. 'She lets rooms to students sometimes. Myself, for example – I stayed with her for my university years.'

'Ah, you must have been a Very Special Case.'

He laughed. 'Indeed, Mrs. Mac and her little snobberies.'

'How much does she know of what happened last month on Scarp?'

'She knows enough to keep an eye on you,' Hugh said wryly. 'You will be quite safe until the next full moon. But the

Venerable Nachtan will have all that sorted out long before we have to worry.'

All that? All that power and good feeling I'd experienced, he meant, all the wonderfulness when the magic tide rose in my blood. The Venerable Nachtan would end this? Small trickles of rain began on the window and the city streets quickly blurred.

I was counting on using that power at the next full moon to reach my mother, and no one was going to 'sort that out' for me, not even this Nachtan witch. I remembered then that I couldn't share these plans with Hugh, so I merely set my lips together and forced an agreeable smile in the face I presented to him.

CHAPTER 5

The coffee and greasy bangers and fries soon had me feeling more to rights and gave me the energy I needed to make the long haul back up the hill to the castle. For the most part, I ignored Hugh's commentary on the places we passed, even the Harry Potter references, as I was too busy getting a feeling for this strange place.

Back home, the Kin had drawn a veil between the normal and the supernatural, a curtain dividing the two realms. For lack of a better term, I'd called it the Alt, short for alternate reality. But here in Edinburgh there was no such division and for those who could see it, the magic was thick in the air right here at the ancient top of the city's hill. Tourists and their herders thronged the pedestrian street, yet beyond all this bustle I could see a whole other world going about its daily business. Next to the kilted modern man playing a bagpipe lament on the corner, there was a shoddy man in old-fashioned garb, battered top hat and all, leering at the crowds hungrily. A grim-faced bonneted woman dourly pushed her way through the crowds, a basket of laundry on her hip, until she turned down through one of the narrow gated alleys on the north side of the street.

It was all very strange to my eyes. I'd never seen so many people all together, both human and super natural, and as I scanned the crowd, I thought my eye caught a familiar figure. I quickly looked back into the heart of the bustle, searching. Could it be? The man's slight body had his back turned to me, but the way he held his narrow shoulders slightly hunched, and his shorn blond hair which was covered by a baseball cap … I could have sworn in that instant it was Willem the sorcerer, but that was impossible. He surely would have gotten himself far away from Edinburgh, the very heart of the Scottish Kin. I looked again, but the man had melted into the crowd if he had in fact been there.

I gave a shiver. Were hallucinations part of the aftereffects of the magical sedative? I turned to ask Hugh, but he was already nattering on.

'You'll want to be careful in Edinburgh, especially here in the Old Town,' he said as he eyed a very shady elf lurking in a doorway. 'There's no veil here like you're used to at home, and it's too easy to let the Alt take over your senses. You especially always need to be vigilant, in your state.'

'What is my state? Pariah? Societal outcast?'

He merely shook his head and increased his stride up the hill past the last of the buildings until we reached the large esplanade leading up to the Castle, a flattish parade ground before the Castle gates. Now that no houses blocked the view, from this vantage point near the top of the hill I could see for miles to the city's spread all around.

'Tell me about this Nachtan fellow,' I said, hanging back a little. If he had plans to remove my incredible monthly powers against my will, I needed to be prepared. 'What should I be expecting here?'

'I'll introduce you today, if he's available, but first let's have a tour of the castle. It has a very interesting history.'

I groaned inside at the thought of a history lesson, but let him take me by the hand. It felt good. He would tell me everything I needed to know in time, right now I would just enjoy being with him.

We bypassed the long line of tourists waiting their turn to go inside the Castle grounds. Instead we veered off to the right to a modern tunnel set in the side of the hill situated below the thick castle walls.

'Is this a secret entrance?' I asked, feeling a small frisson of excitement.

'Not so secret,' he said. 'More like the tradesmen's entrance, the castle's back door. You're to present yourself here at eight o'clock every morning except Sundays, and these good people will escort you to Nachtan's quarters.'

He nodded his head at an army jeep with a soldier in attendance.

'Military?' I whispered mock-furiously as I stopped short and pointed my finger accusingly at Hugh. 'Am I a prisoner?'

I was only half-joking, because his comment about fixing 'all that' still stung.

Hugh only laughed at me as he pushed my hand down. 'No, you're here willingly, you belong here. The Castle is still the headquarters of the Royal Regiment of Scotland, and the Kin and the Ministry of Defense have a long-standing agreement to share the space. It's really only within the past few centuries that the two have been split off into separate bodies. These days, we share it with the tourists, too. You need an escort to enter the grounds because, well, these are the times we live in. You'll have an ID badge made, although we still have to go through security every time we enter the grounds.'

He greeted the soldier with a salute and hopped into the passenger side of the jeep, leaving me no choice but to scramble into the back. The tunnel ride lasted no time at all, and the jeep stopped in front of yet another large stone building. A strong breeze whipped through my hair as I looked straight down in awe over a low rock wall at the expanse of the city before us.

'We're pretty high up here,' I said, wrapping my arms around myself for warmth.

'It's a great city,' he murmured. 'It's my home base these days. And if you end up working with the Kin, which is a distinct possibility, I hope you'll make it your home, too.' He edged in a little, to shield me from the wind.

I liked the sound of that. All of that. Maybe this wasn't such an awful idea, not if it could lead to me and Hugh living here, working together. I nestled in a little closer.

He grabbed my hand. 'Come on, I'll show my favorite part of the stronghold.'

We walked up an inclined road, passing stone and brick buildings and cannons until we reached what must have been the highest part of the whole hill. We waited our turn to enter a small, ancient looking structure and, once inside the wooden door, we entered into the tiniest church I'd ever seen. Such a small space, yet it was full of light and peace.

'St. Margaret's Chapel. Do you feel it?' He looked at me, a light shining in his eye. I nodded, I did feel it. This was a side of Hugh I'd never seen before. 'It's the oldest surviving building in all of Edinburgh. It was built by her son, David, after she was canonized.'

'That's the formal process of being made a saint,' he added, seeing my look of query at the word, and knowing that I'd been brought up by atheists.

The door opened behind us to allow another group in, and we slipped out, hand in hand, staying that way as he led me back down the incline to a covered staircase like an alleyway under the surrounding buildings. Hugh nodded at the soldier on guard, and then we found ourselves in a square, as if we were in any old European city and not in an ancient castle stronghold at the top of a hill. Buildings loomed all around us on four sides, but it was quieter here, away from the endless throngs of tourists.

'This is where the Venerable Nachtan's rooms are,' Hugh nodded, indicating the tallest stone building. 'We can have quick look through so you'll be able to find your way tomorrow morning.'

Given the reverence with which Mrs. Mac had spoken of the Venerable Nachtan, I'd expected that witch to be housed in palatial comfort, but the entrance to this building was a plain, unassuming wooden door with only one step leading up to it. Inside the stone walls, it smelled just like an old office building would, of paper and ink and dust. This was a place of work, not a museum or showcase of history for the tourists. Men and women in uniform passed by, nodding cordially, not questioning our presence.

'The Regiment also works out of this building, the old Hospital,' Hugh said in a sotto voice as we walked along the corridors. 'The washrooms are along here, and I'll show you the small cafeteria where you can pick up lunch.'

We walked down a few stone stairs, and into a small yet high ceilinged room. I paused to look out the huge window to see the city far below, and I shivered as I noted the drop straight down.

He then led me down more steps and through a long hallway. There were no windows here, just the unadorned stone walls of the building's foundation. Something about the roughness of the hewn rock told me we were now in a very ancient part of the castle, and the arched brick ceiling was so low Hugh had to bend his head to avoid scraping it.

'The direct stairs to Nachtan's rooms are just around the corner here,' he noted. 'This is the only route to his quarters, I'm afraid. You'll have a bit of a climb.'

'You said he's in a tower,' I objected. 'It doesn't make sense to have to go down before you go up.'

'There's a special magical force field in this part of the building, the oldest section,' he replied. 'The Kin needs this.'

We turned a corner in the passageway.

'What's in here?' I stopped in front of a thick plank door tucked into a nook. It had huge iron hinges, the really elaborate, medieval kind that meant business, but what caught my interest was the sign on the door. It had the Witch Kin emblem, the intertwined letters W and K, followed by the words 'Uncommon Forces'.

'What's so uncommon about these forces?' I laughed, loving the quaintness of the language.

'Ah.' Hugh was at my side and leading me quickly away. 'That's... don't ever go in that door.' He spoke in a very low voice, right into my ear.

'Why?' I whispered back, infinitely intrigued by this. 'What on earth are the Uncommon Forces of the Kin?'

Hugh looked so uncomfortable, I could have sworn he was squirming, and he bundled me through an arched door and up a spiralling stone staircase without giving an explanation. I filed this door away for later, when I could explore on my own.

'So, as I said, Nachtan's quarters are on the top floor,' he continued in a normal voice, but I could still catch an underlying tenseness in it. 'We'll just poke our noses in to see if he's available for an introduction.'

There was no such luxury as an elevator offered here, so we began to make our way up the stairs. I was huffing and my butt muscles were aching just a little.

'This Nachtan,' I said as I paused to catch my breath. 'Tell me what to expect.'

'I thought we'd been through this.'

'Remind me. My brain hasn't been fully up to speed the past couple of days,' I pointed out. 'Magical coma and all that?'

'To begin with, his full name is the Venerable Nachtan, and he will expect to be addressed as such.'

'Jeez, that's pretty formal. What made him so Venerable?'

Hugh stopped and let me catch up with him, then continued in a hushed tone. 'He is the oldest living Kin in the world. He is a very powerful witch, so powerful that he no longer practices or takes part in the ordinary Kin world. The Venerable Nachtan knows, quite simply, everything there is to know about magic.'

'So he's going to, what? Teach me?'

'No. I'm going to instruct you, he's going to oversee, I told you that,' he said. 'Also, he will be advising.'

'I don't get it. Advising about what?'

We were standing on a landing in this twisting stone staircase. There was dead silence all around us except for the hissing of the torches on the walls. No sounds came into this ancient tower, nothing from the busy Regimental offices or the throngs of tourists outside. We could have been alone in the world.

'The Venerable Nachtan is the only witch with direct experience in your case,' Hugh said solemnly.

"My case? But I've never even met him.'

'Alright then, in cases like yours,' he amended. 'Or I should say, the only other case in the history of the Kin.'

'Then I'm not the first?' This was news to me, I'd been told so very little about what to expect.

Hugh shook his head, his face drawn in a grim expression. 'No. And the Kin, well, they made mistakes last time, but fortunately we learn from these errors. And I'm going to make sure things are done right this time.'

CHAPTER 6

That's all he would say. We climbed, and climbed, up and around with not even an arrow slit of a window to give natural light. The only illumination came from the erratically placed lit sconces on the walls. We finally came to yet another arched wooden door, but the stairs continued past this landing. Hugh knocked three times and entered.

Inside the door, the round tower room was bright with glass windows all around. As I allowed my eyes to adjust to the daylight, I became aware that Hugh was speaking with a woman behind a large oak desk.

'Mrs. Battersea, good afternoon.'

'Well, look at you, young Sabiston,' the woman cooed. She was dressed in an impeccable robin's egg blue suit, and her blonde hair was tidily tucked away in a French twist. She peered over her white cat's-eye glasses at me. 'And this is herself, then. Welcome, Dara.'

I smiled, but didn't get a chance to speak, for she continued without seeming to take a breath. 'He's not taking visitors at the moment, Hugh. You'll have to come back another time, not that he wouldn't be pleased to see you. So you'll need to toddle off then, and we'll see you tomorrow.'

She nodded quickly and turned her attention back to the papers before her. In that short space of time, we had been greeted and dismissed. This woman was very efficient.

'Wow. She always like that?' I asked him after he shut the door behind us.

He shrugged and nodded. 'Always,' he replied. 'But she's a very busy woman. She looks after the Venerable Nachtan and other very delicate matters within the Kin.'

We descended the stairs again, passing the Uncommon Forces door on our way out of the building. Hugh didn't mention it, but I wasn't going to let it go. It was just too intriguing.

'Well, what next?' Hugh asked, looking all around us in the sunshine. The clouds had dispersed again.

'I think you need to tell me what's behind that door.'

'Which door would that be?' Hugh looked all around the square.

'You know the one. Inside. The Uncommon...'

He took my arm in such a way that I couldn't wriggle free, and he hustled me back towards the tunnel entrance. 'Not here,' he hissed. 'I'll tell you, but we need to get out of here first.'

A few steps away from the Esplanade of the Castle entrance, he led me to a building on the south side of the cobbled street.

I looked up at the sign above the entrance. 'The Witchery? Seriously, Hugh?' The Scottish Kin didn't seem to even try to hide amongst the Normals, not like back home.

'I bet you could eat again,' he challenged me. 'How about a spot of High Tea, as you're doing the tourist thing today?'

I wasn't too sure about the sound of 'High Tea'.

'I am hungry again,' I admitted. 'But you're not putting more drugs into me are you?'

He laughed, himself again finally, all tenseness gone. 'You truly are an uneducated urchin,' he said beneath his breath as he took my arm again, but his tone held a note of fondness within it. 'A Scottish High Tea is one of life's most unforgettable events. Consider this a late birthday treat.'

The inside of the restaurant was luxurious, that's the only word I could find to describe the decor, all red velvet and dark wood, fine linens and gleaming silverware. But we didn't linger in there, the waiter brought us out to a glassed-in conservatory kind of room. We were the only customers, and it was totally private here.

'This must cost a fortune,' I mouthed to Hugh behind the server's back.

He cracked a grin and nodded. 'Get used to it. We're on the Kin's tab today, and if all goes well for your future, you'll be living in style all the time. Oh, that reminds me.'

Reaching into his inside coat pocket, he pulled out a small plastic card, a credit card like no other I'd seen before. Some cards are Onyx, some are Gold, some are Platinum, depending on the level of credit given, and all are a visible status symbol of a person's financial worth, but this card sparkled like a chandelier fully lit for a ball, prisms of colour escaping into every corner of the room.

'A credit card for your expenses while studying,' he said as he passed it over to me. 'I don't need to tell you to use it wisely, do I?'

I held the plastic reverently, letting the rainbow of reflected light play over the table. I'd never had my own credit card before, and couldn't even think what I would buy with it. But I also knew that there was nothing free in life, and that bills come due eventually, and I would still have no money to pay for any purchases. I shook my head and began to hand it back to him.

'No,' he said, laying his hand on mine. 'It's yours. Any amounts are automatically paid by the Kin accounts. Don't worry about it, it's for business expenses, you'll get used to this.'

Free credit? I guess I could get used to that, I thought with a grin as I tucked the plastic into my wallet.

Being poor all my life, I'd learned to watch money carefully, but one thing I didn't realize was that costs are not always tallied in finances. Everything comes at a price, especially the free stuff, and I had just unwittingly handed over all my privacy as if I'd voluntarily placed a GPS tracker on myself.

·····•••••···

The high tea was the most sumptuous repast I'd ever had. My previous best experience with fine dining had been the Indian take-out Aunt Edna's boyfriend used to bring us, but this was far, far beyond that.

First of all, they uncorked a bottle of champagne for us, and then the silver platters began to arrive, the tiers loaded with tiny trimmed sandwiches of combinations I would never have thought – beetroot and candied walnut, cucumber and a lemony sauce, crab and honey. The second platter held savouries like quiches and sausage rolls and other pastry wrapped delights, while the third held sweets, puff pastries with cream, tiny petit-fours, individual cheese cakes and chocolate eruption cakes, all of them miniature and individually sized. It was heavenly. The champagne went down quickly, so we ordered another one.

When I couldn't possibly eat another bite, I leaned back with a smile. Now to satisfy another urge.

'So. The Uncommon Forces. Tell me.'

Hugh lifted the bottle and refilled our glasses, then looked down and smoothed a non-existent wrinkle from the table-cloth.

'The name says it all, really, don't you think?' He looked up at me.

I shook my head. 'No, not even remotely. More explanation, please.'

He sighed, puffing his cheeks out, then double-checked to make sure the server had left the enclosed garden space. He played with an unused fork as if to buy time, then took a deep breath.

'These are the special forces of the Kin,' he began. 'More of a... a shadow division, really.'

'What, they can't be seen?'

He gave a small smile at what he saw as a joke, but I was seriously trying to understand what he was saying. 'They're an elite force, specially trained in magic and firearms together. They're called into action when... when there is a serious upset in the magic world.'

'That's a good thing, isn't it? Sort of like a magical U.N. army?'

He shook his head. By the downturn of his mouth I could tell he wasn't happy to share this information. 'No, the U.N. tend to be peace-keepers, whereas the Uncommon Forces are used to quell perceived insubordination. In any jurisdiction of the world.'

'I don't understand. Their existence is approved by the Kin, right?'

'Part of the Kin, yes. The Covenanters put them into place after Auld... after some issues experienced back in the early part of the last century. Not all of us agree with their continued existence, we'd like to see them disbanded. But witches like Cromwell insist on keeping them funded. Well, he would. He's the Commander in Chief of the Uncommons.'

'Are they... bad?' My brain was a little sozzled by the champagne now, and my vocabulary was slipping out of reach.

'They can be,' Hugh said dryly, as he looked up at me. 'They tend to kill first and ask questions later. It doesn't give the rest of the Kin a good rep in the global situation.'

'Wow.' A special team of magical troopers, ready to murder any opposition. Not a good thing if their direction was in the wrong hands. 'Are they ever used against... your own people?'

He set his mouth grimly. 'It has happened.'

'But in what sort of circumstances?' My thoughts were running, in a fuzzy kind of drunken way, along a path that wasn't comfortable. If these shadowy Uncommon Forces could be used against witches, and they were under direct control of Elder Cromwell (who really didn't approve of me), then this begged the question – could they be used against me? Never mind that I was planning an illicit trip to the dimension of the Ice Kingdom, for no one knew about that. Without Hugh's protection in this unknown world, my position might be very tenuous indeed.

He must have seen the expression on my face, for he shook off his memories and tried to lighten the mood. 'Hey, this is supposed to be a celebration! Drink up, birthday girl. We'll go out on the town.'

We raised our glasses. In this subdued light, his eyes reflected the green of the hot house plants all around us, while a stray ray of the lingering sun caught the gold glints deep within.

I had to find out more about these Forces, for forewarned was fore-armed, and I needed all the ammunition I could get.

·····•·····

We didn't end up going out on the town, after all, not in that sense, but I wouldn't have had it any other way. Once out into the warm spring evening, we somehow ended up with our arms around each other as we wandered out onto the Royal Mile, the spine of the mound leading to the Castle.

'Ach,' Hugh said with a rare sigh of impatience. 'Why are there still so many people around?'

'Tourists have no curfews?'

He laughed and tugged me closer, but then his voice grew solemn. 'You know, we really need to find a quiet place to talk, and I think a pub might be too loud.'

'We were just in a private room in an exclusive restaurant,' I said, turning my head to rest against his shoulder. 'How much more secluded do you need?'

'Yes, I see your point,' he said. 'However, The Witchery is a Kin place. I need to discuss... Well, there's things which, I think, you may not yet fully comprehend.'

'I'd say there's a lot I'm not understanding right now. It's been a bit of a whirlwind, and yeah, I'd love to talk.'

By this time, we were near a huge church, closed to visitors for the evening so the throngs were thinner here. There was a stone platform in front of it with a short flight of steps leading up. We tucked ourselves away in the corner furthest from the road, sitting on edge with our feet dangling. Under the guise of settling my satchel on the stone, I shifted a little until our legs were touching. Both of us pretended not to notice.

Hugh was silent for a moment. 'Not sure where to start,' he said as he leaned his arms on his knees and laced his fingers together.

'I'd like to know...'

He shifted his head toward me, sending me a wary glance.

'Okay,' I continued, not quite knowing how to approach this, but deciding to just jump in. The deepening shadows lent a solitude to our perch on the platform, and in the dusk I felt I could approach subjects which I'd been terrified to broach in the harsh light of day. 'The Crystal Charm Stone. The full moon. What does this mean for me? For my future? I know the Kin have me here in Edinburgh to keep a close eye on me, but what happens next? Once they figure out what's happening, where am I?'

'Your future.' He looked up at the crowds still milling around the statue over to our right. They were gathering for an evening tour of haunted historical places, everyone laughing and well-oiled by a liquid supper. 'Your future is in your own hands at this point, for it is entirely possible for you to leap-frog straight into working officially with the Kin.' He slid his eyes down to me, to see how I was taking it, and when I looked up at him he gave a little grin at my obvious shock.

'Me?'

'Yes, you,' he continued. 'What you've done is nothing short of amazing. Yes, the Kin are anxious to keep an eye on you, and to watch for anything, but that's because we want to learn. You didn't go up in a flash of fire when you took the Charm Stone in your arms, it didn't harm you. Instead, there was an obvious transfer of power which has probably burned right into your very genes. Do you realize what this could mean for all of the Kin?'

I thought about it for a moment. 'But... but they could have unlimited power... And how about if this got into the wrong hands?'

'Exactly,' he said, excitement shining in his face. 'For so long, we have not dared to approach the Stone, cowering in the face of legends and historical fact. But you've broken that stale-mate, you're forcing us to investigate further, but it has to be done in a very secure manner. The power of the Crystal Charm Stone is not to be treated lightly.'

This was almost unbearably astounding. Exciting yes, for the promise it held for my future. Unlimited power? Yet on the other hand, given my track record...

'I hate to break your bubble, Hugh, but you might be putting a lot on my shoulders here,' I said sombrely.

His arm snaked over my shoulder and hugged me. 'I have faith in you, Dara,' he whispered. 'You're going to do it, you'll prove me right.'

I sighed, thinking of my mother in the grasp of the Ice King, and my plans to rescue her the first moment I could. I also thought of Cromwell's Uncommon Forces, and shivered.

'I hope this faith isn't misplaced,' I replied slowly, trying to break it to him gently. 'I mean, just look what I've screwed up in my life so far.'

'Like I said to Johanna, the incident on Scarp just showed how you make the right choices when push comes to shove. You chose not to give the Stone to Willem. You helped us search for him, although he did get away. You've proved you are maturing.'

I lay my shoulder against his chest. The wool of his pea coat was warm in the sudden chill now the sun was gone, and I bit my lip, trying to view my past misdeeds from this new angle. 'Wow. You really see it like this?'

He nodded, his chin brushing my hair.

'But Elder Cromwell,' I said, shaking my head. 'Pauline's dad, and all his crowd. They don't hold that opinion.'

'Well, no.' Hugh cleared his throat and loosened his arm a fraction. 'Not exactly. Of course, you're aware of how the Covenanters tend to hold fast to the traditional stance, and it may take a while before we can get them to see this viewpoint.'

'And until they do an about-face? What do I have to expect from them?'

His arm completely dropped from my shoulders and he resumed his position of interlaced fingers. I was realizing he did this when he wanted to think before he spoke, as if his fingers acted as a filter for his words. He let out a deep breath through pursed lips.

'You'll just have to work on proving yourself to them, all of the Elders,' he said slowly. 'You need to soak up everything the Venerable Nachtan gives to you. Obey the rules of Mrs. Mac's house, and they are there for your protection, mind. And don't...'

I reached up to whisper in his ear. 'And don't mess it up.'

He stood up from the low stone wall, and turned to me, lifting me to my feet. His eyes shone with a new light, an uncertain expression, even a shyness. 'Exactly,' he whispered back to me. 'Just think of our future. You and me together, Dara.'

I leaned against his chest to hide the big grin on my face. Finally. Of all my hopes and dreams, this was way up there on the list, and if this could come true, then anything was possible. With Hugh at my side, the world was my oyster.

'Are we a thing now?' I asked into his coat.

The rumble of his laughter bubbled up. 'Yeah, maybe,' he admitted. 'But can you define 'thing'?'

I lifted my head. 'Kiss me. Kiss me like you really mean it. Then we'll know if we're a thing.'

And he did. We did. And yes, we proved beyond a shadow of a doubt that we were a thing.

Chapter 7

In order for this thing between me and Hugh to work, and for us to realize the best possible future together, I had a lot of work to do, especially professionally. I giggled a little when Hugh put it like that in his oh-so-serious voice, because I'd never thought of myself as a professional witch. But I was, or I would be, if I could just sit through the sessions with the Venerable Nachtan and soak up every bit of knowledge he offered.

And then some, because I was determined that this mysterious Nachtan would hold the answer to my most pressing need – how to get to the Ice King's dimension from here.

Early the next morning I climbed the short walk up to the trades entrance tunnel to the castle, showing my new ID badge to the soldier waiting with a jeep. When I found my way back to the old hospital where the Venerable Nachtan's rooms were located, I followed our footsteps from the previous day through the basement corridor, hurrying by the Uncommon Forces door with a shudder. Hugh hadn't specifically spelled it out, but really? I'd come pretty close to being dispensed by these troops. That would never happen again.

Mrs. Battersea sat at her large desk, surrounded with an organized mass of papers. She wore the same cut of suit as before, but today it was a coral version with cat's eye glasses to match. She nodded to me when I poked my nose in, and told me to go on up to the Venerable Nachtan's rooms, last door up the stairs.

No one answered my knock there, it was quite possible I hadn't been heard so I opened the heavy studded portal and timorously walked in, not knowing what to expect.

Like the office below, this was a round room, but unlike Mrs. Battersea's domain it was a haphazard mess, all brightly lit by the dome of glass which comprised the ceiling. Almost all the walls were lined with books and papers, stuffed into the shelves any which way, and around the room was a vast assortment of objects which looked vaguely Renaissance and early scientific in origin, all brass and wood but like the books, everything was covered with a thick layer of dust as if it hadn't been disturbed in many, many years. My eye was caught by what appeared to be a giant snow globe without the snow, a full two feet in diameter, which was dark and empty inside save for a single figure seated at a desk, for all the world like a stone statue except for the quill in her hand which was moving slowly, infinitesimally slowly across a page of a book.

Hugh spoke first. 'Good morning, Dara.'

Our eyes met. His were hooded and almost devoid of recognition, formal like his tone. I opened my mouth to chide him but he continued.

'Venerable Nachtan, may I introduce Dara Martin de Teil-hard.'

That's not my name, I wanted to say, but instead I found myself almost dropping into a curtsey as if I was meeting royalty. For perhaps the first time ever in my life, I became self-conscious of my attire, the childish uniform of hoody and jeans and sneakers, and wished I'd had the forethought to wear something a little more dignified like a skirt. I did have one somewhere, I was almost sure.

For the presence of the Venerable Nachtan was august, there was no other word for it. Tall and thin and just a little stooped, his face was lined with deep furrows as if the sum of his knowledge and years was too painful a burden for that physical body. His hair was long and white, his beard still grey around his thin lips, the black robe he wore was as ancient and dusty as the room around him. He said nothing and did not expect me to reply, he just stood and looked at me like I was a particularly distasteful bug under a scrying glass.

Hugh shot me a warning glance as if to tell me to be on my best behavior, like I needed that. He pointed to a chair a distance away, then sat down himself. The ancient one remained standing.

At last, the Venerable Nachtan began to start to speak, clearing his throat at first with a small ahem. And then another, longer and rumbling ahem, and yet another, until he sounded like a steam engine getting up enough steam. I stared at him, horrified and waiting for a word from him, but he continued to stare right back at me as he cleared a massive amount of detritus from his vocal cords.

Finally, he stopped and, leaning over, spit into a foul looking brass bucket at his feet. He took his eyes from my face only to peer into the bucket.

'Such youth,' he began after he'd lifted his head again. His voice was deep, and authoritative, dry and scored with years spent in the solitude of his tower. It was also surprisingly clear. 'Like the other, when we were both young enough.' With that he shot Hugh a look of fierce intensity, as if to ask why the time of the Venerable Nachtan was being wasted on the likes of me.

'Your boldness astounds me,' he continued, leaving no doubt I was now in the firing line, his eyes like flint fixing me in their glare. 'I have read the reports of your past misdeeds. I fear you must have great powers of persuasion that you have made it this far into my presence, and that is reason enough to act against you, to put a permanent end to this.'

I could feel the blood draining from my face. Was he saying... the Kin needed a permanent and final solution to Dara Martin de Teilhard? No one had warned me that I was on trial again. I risked a glance at Hugh for reassurance that I was hearing wrong, but that coward kept his head resolutely down and would not meet my eye.

'Of course, you are of the female persuasion,' the ancient one thundered on. 'That is not your fault, but I blame your father for not keeping tighter reins on you. Then again, you were born of emotion, and that weighs heavily on your life's path.' Now my cheeks were burning. He meant that my parents weren't married, that I was the result of an extra-marital affair. He shook his head. 'Perhaps you cannot change this direction, for being female, you are run by emotion and cannot control yourself, but if that is true, then you must needs be stopped.'

I really couldn't believe what I was hearing. That anyone, even an ancient witch like him, would express such misogynistic views in this day and age! The man should be shut away and stopped himself, instead of being venerated by the Kin. So what if he knew more magic than anyone else? This was not acceptable, and I refused to be spoken to in such a manner.

I opened my mouth to tell him so when I felt Hugh staring at me, hard. When our eyes met, he gave the tiniest shake of his head. I glared back at him, putting all my feelings into that glare so he would understand, all my hurt and anger and frustration...

All those emotions which were presently running my mind. Just like the old witch had said. I blinked, took a deep breath and steadied my thoughts, lifting them out of the outrage which squawked and twittered inside my head. Once I had regained a semblance of calm, I lifted my eyes to find Nachtan staring at me from his great height. I knew he had seen the turmoil in my mind at his words.

'Well done,' he said with a nod. 'But you will need much work on that. One of your handicaps is, as I said, that you are female and are naturally more easily swayed.'

He let a silence grow in the room before he spoke again. 'Because of your extreme youth and emotionality and your obvious disregard for convention, you have proven you are not to be trusted. The Covenanters would have you cursed and locked underground to contain this insolence, this hubris, and to prevent further serious mishaps.'

He removed a pipe from deep within his robe and took the time to fill it from a leather pouch, tamping the tobacco firmly in, then casually snapped his fingers and it was lit. The old witch thoughtfully drew on it, staring at me the whole while.

'And, once upon a very long time ago, that was my choice of action also,' he continued. Was that a note of regret coloring his voice? Surely not. 'But these are different times, with different ways. Who is to say what is right? Perhaps the Age of Reason has run its course, and the so-called Age of Aquarius is now upon us. If you would believe such flummery.'

The Venerable Nachtan turned to stare at the large crystal ball with the stone figure inside it, and appeared to be lost in thought. I snuck a glance over at Hugh to see how he was taking this very odd monologue, but he had his hands clasped and his elbows on his knees with his head down, almost as if he were in church listening to a sermon.

'What know you of Empedicles of Athens?'

I jumped in my seat, for Nachtan was addressing me again.

'Who? What? Sorry, I'm not sure...' I threw a panicked look at Hugh, but he ignored me.

'Of course you're not, your education has been sadly lacking. Every witch should be familiar with the classics.' The ancient man unerringly reached for a book from the thousands that lay in no order along the shelves, and held it out for me to take.

'Read that, it is an important foundation for you,' he said. 'Now leave us, child, for Sabiston and I have much to discuss. Tomorrow, then.'

With that I was dismissed.

The heavy wooden door slammed shut behind me all on its own, and I stood on the stone landing trying to process what had just happened in that room. The emotions I had so successfully tamped down came rushing to the fore. That misogynistic old bastard! How dare he talk about me like that? No wonder the Kin were so screwed up on all levels when they venerated an old relic like Nachtan. Talk about the Dark Ages, which was probably when he was born, and how old was he anyway? Shouldn't there be mandatory retirement for witches when they reached, what, one hundred and fifty years old?

And Hugh – he'd been no use whatsoever, just kept his mouth shut and his head down as if what had happened was a perfectly normal thing. What a useless arse that man could be! And Hugh was supposed to be the one teaching me, not that shrivelled-up old guy.

I took a deep, steadying breath and admitted, through my anger and betrayal just for a moment, that Hugh had been right when he said we couldn't let any of the Kin know about Us. Not yet, not with the prejudice still rampant in such high up levels as the Venerable Nachtan himself. That ancient relic might no longer be a practicing witch or a part of the government, but he held a lot of sway.

And there was no way the Venerable Nachtan would help me find the way to the Ice Kingdom, I knew that was off the table. It was going to be all up to me, then, the rescuing of my mom. I set off down the stone stairs, stomping my feet until I realized the ancient rock didn't care and I was only hurting myself. But it was better than crying.

CHAPTER 8

The short jeep ride released me to the open air and I slowly made my way down the Royal Mile. After the weird hour spent in that smoky room I hated to go back to Mrs. Mac's claustrophobic house, and I was feeling a little peckish, and a coffee sure wouldn't go astray. The sun still shone weakly on the endless throngs of tourists, so I intended to find a coffee shop for an expensive cappuccino and a big slice of cake. This glittery new Kin credit card needed the exercise.

Like yesterday, a figure caught my attention as my eyes passed over the crowd. Incredulous, I turned my head and really studied the mass of people, searching for that slight body. Yes, that could be Willem. I stared hard, but he had his head bent down in conversation. I couldn't pick out his companion, but in a flash he had disappeared again, the red cap no longer visible in the mass of humanity.

Was I going nuts? I shook my head. Maybe I just needed that caffeine and sugar. There was no way, there was no conceivable reason on earth for Willem to have stayed in Scotland. He might be mad, but he wasn't stupid. I shoved aside every bad memory of him and looked forward to my treats, bringing my tray outside to sit and watch the world go by and to think.

I didn't know where to start with my search on how to get to the Ice Kingdom. No sense asking for Hugh's help, this went without saying, despite his promise on Scarp. One of the things I liked (loved? Best not go there, not yet) about him was that he was so honourable, but this also meant he felt bound by the rulings of the Kin and would not go against them. Me tripping off to another dimension when I was supposed to be studying? This would definitely be considered going against all that.

How to get from here to there? That was the question. I was pretty caught up in my thoughts, so much that I'd forgotten to eat my cake. A slight movement from under the table brought me back to earth, though, and a nasty smell filled the immediate vicinity.

'What the hell?' I said out loud, thinking it must be a large stray cat or dog brushing against my legs.

I sat back to peer under the table but when I saw what it was, I almost jumped out of my seat. The creature looked back at me, aghast at being caught, trapped between the table legs and chairs. Protuberant eyes flashed left then right as it searched for escape, and its filthy stocking cap was knocked askew. There was no way out, so it chose offense as the best defence.

'I only wanted a bit of cake, you mean old greedy-guts! You're not eating it, now, are you? Think you'd spare a crumb.'

'What... Who are you?' I looked around to see if any of the humans nearby had noticed the strange creature, but no one was taking any notice.

'Let me out, you fat slag, don't be such a bully to a helpless wee goblin.'

Well, this all made a lot more sense. My dealings with Goblin folk in the Alt back home were rare, for they tended to hang out in sewers and gutters and other places I'd prefer not to enter, and besides, they had a worse reputation than the fairies for being utter shitheads.

'Fat slag indeed. At least I don't stink like you,' I muttered as I pulled my legs aside to allow him out from under the table.

He unfolded himself and bared his wide mouth at me, his narrow sharp teeth all yellowed with fuzz. 'You're a meanie. Some of us haven't had the same opportunities, y'know, and don't have nice hot baths waiting at home. Some of us got to make do with what we're given. Now, you giving me that cake or not, y'selfish hag?'

'Eat the frigging cake, then,' I retorted. 'And get out of my sight.'

He snatched it off the plate and scoffed it down, not bothering to shut his mouth as he chewed. 'That's all then?' he said after he swallowed. He looked longingly at the plate as he scooped up the last bit of icing with his finger. 'I'm starving, y'know.'

'What, do you think I'm rich? I'm not buying more food just to give to you because you're whining.'

'Ye're American and you got no money?' he sneered. 'Try pulling the other leg.'

"I'm Canadian, you asshat, and besides it's none of your business.'

He slid his eyes around, looking at the empty table. 'How come ye're alone? Ye got no friends?'

'I like my own company, thank you very much. Can you take a hint?'

Apparently not. Uninvited, the goblin jumped up to sit in the chair next to me. 'I could show you around, if you'd feed me, like,' he wheedled. 'Earn a meal. I'm from here, I know this place like the back of my hand. Americans, they always like a guide.'

'Why would I hang out with a smelly goblin?'

He eyed me suspiciously, then sniffed at the air around me tentatively. 'You don't smell so good yourself, you smell like... You're a fecking witch, aren't you?'

'What if I am?'

I could almost hear the thoughts racing in his large goblin head. 'You're a witch, and you're from the Colonies...' He leaned closer and I saw a light dawning in his eyes, then fear obliterated everything else. 'You're that one! You're the new Auld Meg! Frig that, Ah'm not getting involved in this one!'

With that, he tore out from the sidewalk cafe, knocking over chairs in his haste and pushing past people that unwittingly stood in his way.

There's no way I could let him get away with that. How did a goblin know about me? Was I that infamous here in Edinburgh? I'd only just arrived in the city.

What did he know about me that I didn't? And that name had cropped up again – Auld Meg. My body reacted even as these thoughts flashed through my mind and I took off in the path that he'd cleared through the crowds, intent only on getting my hands around his scrawny neck to wring information out of him.

Seriously, I had no intention of setting into motion all the awful, terrible things that happened later. You have to believe me on that one, because Cromwell and the Covenanters sure didn't.

••••••••••

The little greaser was right, he knew his way around the Royal Mile and he dashed this way and that, down alleys and up lanes, until I guess he thought he'd lost me. But I was close on his tail, and I simply followed my nose as we came back out on the main boulevard.

'Seriously, the Cathedral?' I panted as I paused outside St. Giles, the massive Gothic stone church looming up above my head. I didn't look to the right, to the spot where Hugh and I had sat the previous evening. 'Are goblinkind even allowed into holy places?'

There was no line-up at all to get into the Cathedral, which was a good thing because I didn't have time to stand around queuing. I pushed past the blue-haired volunteer at the desk. She wasn't happy with me, but I didn't need the brochure she refused to hand over anyway. My nose was on full alert for the little green critter.

Yet once inside I had to stop, if just for a moment. Even though I was raised with no belief in God, basilicas and cathedrals always get to me the moment I step into the main body and look up. Wa-a-ay up. The air and the space created by the soaring arches, the stained glass like jewels of light, they leave me speechless every time. I can't help it, the beauty overcomes me.

And it gave the goblin time to hide, but I soon sniffed the sneaky little bastard hiding inside the Eagle pulpit. Besides, his dirty stocking hat was visible over the wood.

'I see you!' I hissed. As my steps drew closer he gave a squeak, and like a flash he ran off down to the farthest corner of the huge cathedral. Maybe it had been a few years since he'd been inside, maybe he hadn't reckoned on the glass doors barring his way to the bathrooms in the basement. I could see him hesitate, then turn into the section marked The Thistle Chapel.

At the doorway I stopped. This was a small enclosed space, albeit one with a ceiling just about as high as the cathedral's. I carefully shut the two heavy oak doors to prevent his escape.

'Alright, you malodorous scum goblin,' I said with gritted teeth. 'Show yourself, or I'll... I'll unleash a spell on you.' I lifted my arms and pointed my fingers in a threatening manner. So I didn't actually have any spells in mind, and I was huffing and puffing from the chase, but it was enough to scare him.

This all might sound like I was being a little harsh to the pathetic creature, but he was a goblin, and that's how they expect to be treated. I would never have gained respect by being nice to him.

He was quivering behind a pew. With a victorious cry I reached in and tried to lift him by the scruff of his neck, but he was a solid little bugger and I only managed to thump him against the wooden box enclosure.

'Ow! You're hurtin' me,' he cried.

'Then come out and talk to me.'

By this time he was sniffing and snivelling, the snots running freely out his nose. He stood before me and I could finally get a good look at him. I'd never examined one of his race so closely, which is not surprising as they aren't pretty sights. Short with a potbelly but stick-thin arms and legs, this goblin was greenish in colour, sort of like the pallor that comes to a human suffering sea-sickness, but it was his natural hue. His ears were pointed, and his sparse hair looked greasy to the touch.

Voices echoed behind the doors, tourists wanting to come into this chapel, but I wasn't finished with him yet and didn't want any interruptions. I'd been forbidden to use my powers until the Kin figured out how they could harness or defuse my extreme moonlight magic, but surely no one would notice a tiny holding spell. That's if magic even worked in a Christian church, especially a Presbyterian one. There was only one way to find out.

'*O Portae lignum solidum,*' I said under my breath. My Latin was crap as I'd never learned it properly, but it seemed to do the trick of holding the doors tightly shut. I didn't know how long it would hold though, I probably didn't have much time.

'I want to know what you've heard about me,' I hissed as I towered over him in a menacing manner. 'Out with it. I need to know.'

'You're that witch,' he whispered, his eyes huge as saucers.

'Yeah, tell me about it,' I said. 'Seriously, tell me what you've heard.'

A muffled knocking sounded on the door, and a voice raised in question. We both glanced towards it.

'What will you give me?'

I stared him down, pathetic little bugger that he was. I had nothing to give him except the credit card, and that would be no use to him.

But it could buy things for him. I looked at the shoddy boots on his feet. Scuffed and ripped along the edges, the leather was barely holding together.

'I'll get you new boots.'

He gave a squeak of surprise, not expecting any sort of kindness and certainly not this level of generosity, and his eyes were wary.

Someone was hammering on the door by now – I wouldn't be able to keep this up much longer. One thing I'd learned on Scarp was that at the beginner level, spells can't just be cast and left to go about their business, and it takes an inordinate amount of psychic energy to keep an action going. The closed-door spell had about a minute left on it.

'After you talk to me,' I added.

In Goblin-speak, this meant I might or might not follow through with my promises, and this was more to his comfort level.

'Where can we go to have a quiet parley?' I asked, glancing back at the doors which were being pummeled by many fists now. There was quite a commotion building out there.

'I know a place,' he said.

I lifted the spell, fully confident he wouldn't run away this time, not if he thought he could trick me out of the price of a pair of new boots. I sagged a little, not realizing how much energy it had taken to raise a spell on hallowed grounds.

The doors swung open. Quite an angry crowd had gathered out there in the Ante-Chapel, and a man in a dark suit glared at me, ready to give me a right telling off.

'Oh thank God, eh?' I cried in my most Canadian voice, forestalling any yelling as I ran towards him. 'I thought these doors would never open. Oh, the trauma I've suffered here. I oughtta sue you guys!'

That shut everyone up pretty quick and they let me pass out without a word, my new companion quietly at my heels.

CHAPTER 9

H e led me along the Royal Mile, slipping into a dark covered alley that soon opened up into a narrow lane bordered by tall houses on one side of the incline and an iron fence on the other.

'In through here,' he said, squeezing himself through the bars and into the lush green bushes on the other side.

'I can't get through there,' I scowled at him. The space was no more than eight inches wide, with his squishy pot belly it was a tight fit even for him.

His head popped back out of the greenery and he rolled his eyes. 'Told ye you're a fat slag,' he muttered then disappeared again.

Before I could return the abuse, his long fingers had un-latched the gate from the inside and he beckoned me in.

'This is someone's private garden,' I whispered as I looked all around me. The bushes protected us from view from the laneway, but we were directly in front of a lace covered kitchen window and a glass-fronted door. I peered in. The interior was very, very tidy with the bare minimum of furniture in the room.

'It's alright,' he said in a normal tone of voice. 'This is an Air B&B property. They can't rent it right now because of tax issues. We're safe.'

We settled onto the plastic wicker chairs on the small flag-stone patio and stared at each other across the glass-topped table.

'Hey, Goblin – I can't keep calling you that,' I said. 'What's your name?'

'Trevor.' This was said with such bravado that I knew it wasn't the one given by his goblin mother.

'Seriously? Trevor? That doesn't sound very goblinish. No way is that your real name.'

His narrow lips set obstinately. 'I want to be called Trevor. You couldn't even pronounce my real name, not with your clumsy human tongue.'

I shrugged. 'Have it your way, Trevor,' I said, then got down to business. 'I need to know. How do you know about me, and what do you know?'

'Why is that important? Don't you even know who you are?' He was pretty insolent for a goblin looking for new boots.

'Never mind your questions.' I needed to know because there was so much unknown in my life right at that moment. Hints and bits and pieces and promises from Hugh were just not enough. My life was no longer under my control, and knowledge was the only thing which could help me feel I had a handle on things, and give me an idea of where my future was headed. There was a large faction of the Kin solidly against me, and the more I knew what was rumoured about me, the better equipped I'd be. I'd rather not have gotten my information from this smelly, disregarded creature, but right now I had no other options.

I wasn't going to tell him that though.

'You're the witch that's been touched by the Crystal Charm Stone.'

I nodded solemnly. 'That is true.'

'You have powers beyond belief.'

I inclined my head a little. Eh, maybe not that much. At least not right now while the moon wasn't full. But he also didn't need to know that.

'Yes, I do,' I said firmly. 'How did you, a goblin in Edinburgh, find this out?'

He snorted. 'After what Auld Meg did, you think the supernatural world is not going to keep a close eye on the Kin? We're survivors, not idiots.'

'What did this Meg do?' I was beginning to get genuinely curious about this legendary character. 'I mean, I know the Stone gave her powers, but no one will tell me what happened, or how they overcame her. They only say Ooh, Auld Meg, scary stuff. No actual details.'

He looked askance. 'And how did you grow into adulthood without hearing about her and knowing all the ghastly things she did? Were you brought up in a cave?' Then his face lightened with understanding. 'Oh right, you're not from here.' He sat for a moment in thought, kicking his legs, which didn't reach the ground, then adjusted his stocking cap.

He blinked quickly as if making calculations in his little goblin brain, and a crafty look came across his visage as he thought of a way to profit off me. His greed was stronger than his fear. 'I imagine there's a lot you don't know,' he began, sidling his eyes over to me in speculation. 'I imagine you need the help of a native here in Edinburgh. Someone you could have, maybe, on retainer, like.'

Now it was my turn to think, for he had a point. It would be good to have a supernatural on my side in this place where I knew no one except Hugh and the Venerable Nachtan (I didn't count Mrs. Mac, because she'd renounced magic), as I did have loose plans made which involved the next full moon. Oh, yes, I intended to make full use of my extraordinary powers when they came round again, because who knew how long they would be available? The Kin would stop me the moment they figured out how to, I was sure of that, so I had to work against time. I didn't know then how the goblin could help me, but he wouldn't be expensive. An uncertain ally, perhaps, and one I couldn't trust because of his goblin nature, but an ally nevertheless.

I was damn sure I'd get to my mother, somehow, some way, it was going to happen.

I nodded in agreement. 'Okay, a retainer,' I said.

'Five pound a day.' He jutted out his receding chin

'As if!' I laughed back at him. 'Your kind doesn't see five pounds a year. What good is cash to a goblin?'

'Would be nice,' he said deflating, looking down at his ragged boots. 'Just to have money, see what it feels like...'

'No one who can see you to take your money would let you in their shop.' That came out sort of convoluted, but it was true. There were Alt stores that took modern cash, but no self-respecting shop owner would let a goblin darken their doorstep. Word would get out, and it would turn off the nicer kind of customer, and that was never good for business.

'How about food, or more clothing?' I asked him in a far gentler voice. I'd hurt his feelings, and I found myself feeling kind of sorry for him. After all, it wasn't his fault he'd been born a pathetic goblin.

He lifted his head to look at me, a mixture of cunning and longing in his eyes. 'Anything?'

'Within reason.' I stared him down with a frown on my face to make up for my lapse into niceness.

'A red scarf? Can I have a red scarf?'

Seriously? All he wanted from life was a piece of red fabric?

'Yeah, I guess you can, we'll find you one somewhere,' I said in an offhand manner. There had to be the Scottish equivalent of Dollar Stores here – perhaps not along the touristy Royal Mile, but close at hand. After all, Edinburgh was famous for its university, and where there are students, there are cheap stores.

He narrowed his eyes in disappointment, and I realized I'd given into the bargaining too easily. 'That's only to show you around, mind,' he said sullenly. 'If you wanted more it'll cost.'

'You haven't earned your boots yet,' I pointed out. 'So don't get too full of yourself. Tell me about Auld Meg.'

He shrugged and squirmed and squinted over my shoulder. 'She was a terrible witch who tried to bring down the Kin, and she got cursed and put away in a dungeon for the rest of her life,' he said in a reluctant rush, then shut his mouth firmly.

'Oh, no, no, that's not good enough. I don't want the edited version,' I said. 'Give it all to me, everything.'

All I knew about the witch was that like me, she had touched the Crystal Charm Stone and thus upset the Kin. These were bare bones, I needed the full flesh of the story in order to know about myself.

'I don't know that much more,' he confessed as he kicked the table leg.

'Then why is she scary? When you realized who I was, you said...'

'It's not good to talk about her.' He cut in, restlessly.

'Why? She lived what, more than a hundred years ago. And she was stuck in a dungeon,' I said. 'I'm sure the Kin made sure her powers were dismantled or bound or something. It's not like she can hear you.'

The goblin's eyes were round with fright as he looked up at me. 'But she can,' he whispered. 'She knows everything that's going on. And if we talk about her, that'll attract her attention. And I don't know what could happen after that, but I don't want to find out.'

He made to get down from his chair.

'Wait!' I gingerly held fast to his arm, avoiding the spot on his sleeve where he'd wiped his nose. 'You're saying she's still alive?'

'Auld Meg can't die.' I barely heard the hiss of his voice as he tried to squirm out of my grasp. 'She touched the Stone. The Kin can't kill her, because she's immortal, or close enough.'

My body must have gone slack at the shock of these words, and I allowed him to slip away. I slowly let myself out of the tiny courtyard. Immortality, or something like it. Was this what I had to look forward to?

And why hadn't Hugh warned me?

I dragged my steps as I made my way back to Mrs. Mac's house, trying to digest the news of my possible immortality.

CHAPTER 10

I had no chance to discuss the matter with Hugh the next day, for the Venerable Nachtan was with us for the whole session, glaring and glowering at me whenever I messed up an incantation and, quite frankly, making me worse with nervousness.

'Try saying the spell in Greek,' he said venomously at one point, when I absolutely could not get the stupid candlestick to hover. A meaningless use of magic, as far as I could see, but Hugh insisted it was a basis on which to build further spells. 'Your Latin pronunciation is terrible.'

'I don't know Greek,' I patiently said through gritted teeth, trying my damndest not to speak saucily at him.

'She didn't receive a Classical education,' Hugh admitted to him, trying to smooth things over between us.

'This is a bloody waste of my time,' the old witch grumbled as he turned away. He harrumphed and spit into his brass bucket. 'Do we even know if she has the power?'

Hugh glanced at me before he spoke. 'Almost positive,' he said in a tightly pleasant voice. 'And you know the Kin can't afford to take the chance.'

I stood with my arms crossed and my feet firmly planted, so mad at the old guy's treatment of me that I could spit myself. Or cry. I bit my lip hard. What was wrong with this relic, why did he hate me so much?

'Let's just take it from the top again,' Hugh suggested.

'It's not worth the bother,' Nachtan dismissed him with a scowl and a flick of his hand. 'This will never amount to anything.'

'May I remind you, Venerable Nachtan,' Hugh said in a very diplomatic voice. 'There is no margin for error in this matter. We wouldn't want any mistakes to occur. Again.'

The old witch glared at him, and then both sets of eyes were drawn towards the huge crystal ball glowing in the corner. And then they turned to me.

The lines on the ancient one's face were even deeper, set in anger and bitterness, and possibly even regret.

'Oh, do as you wish,' he muttered as he turned his back. 'The female brain has no aptitude for my teachings, we've proven that before.'

He paused by the door to his rooms and said to the walls rather than to Hugh, 'I wish you the best of luck,' his voice rumbling from the depths. 'Just don't get caught in her web like a lovesick fool.' And then the Venerable Nachtan left us, almost but not quite slamming the door on his way out.

···········

After that rather awkward moment, Hugh and I were left staring at each other. I was pretty certain that we hadn't given any indication to Nachtan that we were a 'thing' – how could that rheumy-eyed ancient have picked up on it?

Hugh's face cracked an uncertain grin, and there was a matching one on mine.

I glanced at the closed door, there was no telling when the old witch would return. 'Can you show me how to do some real magic?' I asked plaintively. 'I learned lots of basics at Scarp, but nothing...'

'Nothing flashy.' The smile hadn't left his face.

'Yeah, nothing fun,' I agreed.

He thought for a moment, then began rummaging through one of the cabinets on the wall. When he came back, he held a single water glass in his hand, which he blew on then gave a quick polish with his shirt sleeve. 'How about this? Crystal would be much better, but this will be good practice.'

With the glass vessel on the table, he told me I was going to learn to break it.

'Like karate?' I mimed the chopping actions with my hands.

'No, not like that,' he replied. 'I want you to break it with your voice.'

'Scream at it.' This was weird, but I opened my mouth and began to take a deep breath.

'Stop!' Hugh was laughing. 'This is a very physical spell – it's going to require your entire body, your Intention, and all the power you can direct towards it.'

'So I need to think it broken?'

'You've heard the stories of opera singers who could crack a glass with their voices? You find the resonant pitch of the crystal, or glass in this case, and sing that note with all the volume you can muster, with all your power pushing your Intent.'

'That's not a spell.'

'No, like I said it's physical magic, you're using your entire body to effect a change without touching the object.'

'And this will be useful because...'

He laughed again. 'Because it will show you what you're capable of!' Then he wet the tip of his finger and rubbed it around the rim of the glass, going faster and faster until it emitted a faint hum.

'Hear that?' he called. 'That's the note. Sing that note.'

Sing? This wasn't going to work, I couldn't carry a note to save my life. Never had, never could. 'Seriously, Hugh?'

'Don't be shy. Match this note.' He stopped the movement then, but matched the sound perfectly with his voice. 'High E, come on, if I can do it, you can.'

I tried, but all that came out was a croak.

'Relax your vocal cords, you have it in you.' He hummed again, loudly, so I didn't have to feel self-conscious.

He stopped to listen to me and winced. 'You're a little flat,' he said. 'A lot flat, but keep at it. Once again.'

I finally reached a note that he deemed passable, and then he told me to increase the volume. I kept it up for about five seconds then it all ended in a groan. 'That hurt,' I complained, rubbing my neck where my vocal cords were.

'It's just muscles you've never used before,' he said. 'Do it again.'

And I did, over and over again. At one point he encouraged me and said I had the glass's pitch, and I could see the glass almost shimmering like the slightest wind on a pond's surface, but I couldn't sustain the effort this required. I shut my mouth and shook my head. 'Not working,' I rasped. 'In fact, I don't think it's possible. You do it.'

Hugh took me up on my challenge, although I think he just wanted to show off.

'Alright.' He cleared his throat a few times, stood straight and tall and opened his mouth. Pitch perfect, the sound vibrated through the room and increased in volume, swirling round and round until it settled within the confines of the water glass. I could see the shimmering, the vibrating of the glass as the molecules within it welcomed the tone and drew it in and danced there until the structure couldn't hold anymore. The glass shattered, but in a very controlled kind of way, it sort of crumbled rather than throwing shards everywhere as I'd expected.

We both looked at the mound of glassy pieces on the table.

'Like I said, it's much more effective with crystal, because the crystalline structure absorbs the note and implodes,' he said modestly. 'You should practice this when you can. It's a great confidence builder.'

I laughed and was about to comment when the sound of an ancient throat clearing cast a chill in the atmosphere.

The Venerable Nachtan was glaring at the crumbs of glass on the table. 'Is that my water glass?' he asked in thunderous tones.

'Oh, so sorry Venerable Nachtan, we got carried away,' Hugh began. I swear he was blushing. 'I'll replace it...'

'This is no behavior for a tutor and his charge,' the old witch interrupted him. He was carrying a thick staff and he thumped it on the floor. The sound echoed in the silence all around us. 'Hugh Sabiston, you have been given an immense responsibility. It does no one any good if you allow her to divert your course, using her female wiles to trick you.'

That was so unfair! I opened my mouth to tell the old man off for his nasty thoughts, venerable or not, when Hugh shook his head at me, telling me to can it.

'You are right, Venerable Nachtan,' Hugh said smoothly. 'We must get back to the lesson at hand.'

Hugh picked up where he'd left off when the ancient left the room, running me through the stupid Greek spells that didn't work for me, and all the time I was just burning up with resentment towards Nachtan and his treatment of us yet unable to say a word.

It was exhausting for us both, and afterwards, we parted ways by mutual consent and without even a kiss, Hugh heading down the Mound to the New Town, and me to the Old.

I was angry at the world by then. Myself, because I'd failed at everything that day, from the Greek spell to the glass shattering. At Nachtan because he obviously hated me for being a woman – the unfairness was burning me up. And I was mad at Hugh, too, when I remembered he hadn't warned me about my imminent immortality. Surely that would be too big a possibility to forget to tell a person, wasn't it? It was a purposeful omission, and I admit to feeling betrayed.

I had to find the goblin again for he was the only being in this town that I could actually trust to tell me the truth. He must know where Auld Meg was kept, and if she was indeed alive then I needed to speak with her. I had to know what my future held.

And she would no doubt have other answers for me, like how to get to the Ice Kingdom from here.

Trevor was making himself scarce, there were no signs of him along the boulevard, not even a sniff of his unwashed sourness. I wandered down the southern face of the hill and turned my steps west. I had no destination in mind, I just wanted to leave the cloying Alt air of the castle's environs, the really old parts of the city where magic and memories were thick.

And I found myself in an area of regular people, not tourists gawking and herding, but real people going about their daily lives in the city inhabited by them. Despite the crowds of students, it was a much more relaxed atmosphere. I took a moment to get myself a take-out coffee, compliments of the Kin's credit card, and sat back on a bench by a green space, just watching the world go by.

The sounds of the traffic, and people chatting and laughing, a dog woofing at a bird in the park, it was lulling me almost into a stupor. I could almost forget that I was possibly immortal, and definitely alone and friendless. I couldn't count on Hugh.

Until I heard that laugh, a cackle rising above the murmur of the crowd, the screeching Glaswegian voice that followed.

I'd recognize her voice a mile away. It was Fergie, here, in Edinburgh! Without even realizing I stood up and searched the people all around me. I could still hear her, but no sighting, so I jumped up on the bench above everyone's head, and then I spotted that mass of red curls blazing in the sunlight.

Unmistakeably Fergie, although now her hair was washed and bouncy, not like the last time I'd seen her.

She was too far away to hear my call, so I leaped off the bench and began to run in her direction. My friend was in the midst of a group of other girls, all with shiny hair and perfectly made-up complexions, all shrieking and talking at the same time. Her new friends? But it had only been a matter of days since we'd parted.

Shy to intrude, I quickly texted her. *Hey F – I'm in Edinburgh! Where R U?*

But it bounced back almost immediately. Undeliverable. She'd changed her phone number, obviously.

So instead I sent a more reliable message through my mind, the way Hugh had shown me all those months ago. It was easy now to send out connecting feelers, my magic going out to hers, but I couldn't find anything to hold on to, as if she was a Normal and not a witch at all. Puzzled, I stared at the back of her head. I couldn't have missed contact, not from this short range. So I tried again, throwing myself hard but this time it was like hitting a brick wall, or as if she had a shield up, deflecting me.

Or as if she had been true to her word and renounced magic so entirely that there was no connection to be had between us.

Saddened, I could only follow her and the shrieking harpies at a distance. The group paused in front of an apartment building, cream colored stucco on the outside and double glass doors leading inside. Fergie made a big display of kisses and hugs good-bye, then entered the building. The others kept on their way.

After they'd all left, I crossed the road to look at the name-plates. There it was, top story by the looks of it. F. McBride and S. Farrow. I lifted my finger to press the bell then thought better of it, and lowered my hand again. After all, Fergie hadn't replied to the two emails I'd sent her and perhaps that was on purpose.

I might not be a welcome visitor.

CHAPTER 11

I wasn't to be alone for too long though, I should have known that the goblin wouldn't forget our bargain.

He materialized at my side after I'd made my way back up the steep hill and turned on to the Royal Mile. It was the corner by The Witchery, where Hugh had taken me for that delightful High Tea, back when he didn't mind being seen with me in public. Things change so quickly.

First, I noticed the stench and only then did I become aware of the short figure walking next to me. The esplanade was still full of tourists waiting in lines even at this late hour.

'Much as I don't want to be around you, there is still the matter of the boots outstanding,' he began in an officious voice. 'You can't welch on our deal.'

I looked down my nose at him. His almost bald head was shiny in the late afternoon sun. 'I don't think you've earned them yet.'

He sniffed haughtily. 'Should have known better than to trust a witch.'

'Dude, all you did was hint at things, you didn't give me any information that I need,' I scolded him. 'I thought you wanted to be kept on retainer. Maybe you should start by being polite.'

'I suggest we discuss the matter over cake.' He stopped before a cafe that displayed baked goodies in the window. He pressed his nose against the glass, smearing it with drool at the sight of a tall chocolate confection.

He had a point, and it wasn't a bad idea. At all. My lunches from the Castle cafeteria consisted of dry sandwiches, and dinner at Mrs. Mac's would be hours yet. Her insistence on the 'genteel' hour of seven o'clock for dinner meant that there was a large hole where my stomach should be by the end of the day. I was quite frankly starving as my body cannibalized itself to provide fuel, my jeans were getting looser, and all this traipsing up and down hills wasn't helping me conserve my energy.

'Alright, stay outside. I'll get it.'

I chose a slice of the walnut cream cake, and picked out the chocolate cake for the goblin. We took it as take-out in small cardboard boxes, and sat at the base of a statue outside the Cathedral as we ate.

'I want to meet Auld Meg.'

He snorted and sprayed chocolate crumbs as he turned to look at me full on. 'You're crazy!'

'You are so gross,' I muttered as I tried to flick the crumbs off my hoody without smearing the wet ones. 'And no, I'm not crazy, I'm determined. You said she's still alive, right?'

He shrugged, and looked over the heads of the crowd milling around us. There was a hint of panic in his eyes. 'In a manner of speaking,' he said. 'Not exactly living...'

'No?'

'But she's not dead, either,' he mumbled. He desperately looked out over the tourists as if searching for an escape. I followed his eyes. It might have been a coincidence, but there was that bright red ball cap, the one worn by Willem, or someone who looked a lot like him. I stood up, my finger pointing to help guide me. 'I know that guy!'

Before I could take off into the crowd to chase the evil wiz-ard, Trevor had grabbed my sweater with both hands and was not letting me budge. I'd never realized how much strength the goblin had in those skinny arms, it was like being weighed down by an anchor.

'Don't!' he shrieked.

'Let go of me,' I said, but it was too late. The figure had disappeared again. 'Don't what?'

'Don't...' reiterated the goblin, a guilty look on his face. 'Don't leave before we talk about the boots you owe me.'

I narrowed my eyes at him. What was going on? I opened my mouth to demand an answer, but he forestalled me.

'Okay,' he said. The top of his head was sweating amidst the straggly hairs. 'Okay, I'll take you to Auld Meg.'

'Oh, well then, alright,' I said. 'Let's go.'

'Not in the daylight, y'idiot.' He looked askance as if I knew nothing. He shoved the last bite of chocolate cake into his mouth and tossed his napkin to the breeze. 'Besides, I want m'new boots first. Never trust a witch.'

He sniffed loudly and added, 'And you might not make it back from the dungeon.'

'Alright,' I said, sitting back down. I had no desire to find Willem anyway, not if it really was him. In fact, I'd prefer to live the rest of my life with not seeing him ever again. But I had to meet Auld Meg. 'Fair enough. Let's do it now. Where does one buy goblin boots?'

His face fell at this, and he thought for a minute. 'You said you haven't got any silver or gold.'

'Correct. No cash. Just a credit card and a bus pass.'

'That's no good.' He looked up at me, and then down at my own Doc Martens. He sidled his foot next to mine.

'You're not getting my boots!' I'd had to beg and plead for those last year from Aunt Edna, and they were just getting broken in now. 'Forget that idea, it's not happening.'

'No, no,' Trevor said in his most wheedling voice. 'I don't want yours, they stink of you. But we're about the same size, so I think...'

'You think?'

'You can buy a pair to fit you with your magic card, and they will be for me.'

He made perfect sense, that little green humanoid, and I couldn't argue with his logic. So we traipsed down off the Royal Mile and along a wide avenue to a less ancient, although not so nice, part of town. The buildings weren't as tall but they were still made from the same dark grey stone, and the shop windows fronted right onto the street. We passed fish and chip shops, a dingy looking mechanics' garage, a curry take-out and finally, a thrift store belonging to some charity. He bounced up and down excitedly outside this shop, peering into the smutty window.

'This is it! Oooh, I can feel them in there, waiting for me. Oh, come, quick, stop dawdling!'

I had to push the door open, for apparently goblins were banned from entering human business places, but he raced inside ahead of me once the way was clear. On the back wall of the shop were racks of dusty used footwear, some of it not looking fit for anything, but he was like a kid in Willy Wonka's candy store.

I smiled over at the woman behind the counter, fairly confident she couldn't see that I was accompanied by a goblin. Non-witches can't, you see, as they're totally not expecting to. Says a lot about people and the state of our minds in that we only see what we expect to see.

There were no other customers inside.

His hand was hovering over a pair of pink sparkly running shoes. The kind with satin bows and electric lights in the sole.

'No, sorry,' I muttered loud enough only for him. 'Those are too small.'

He looked at me indignantly. 'No, they look perfect! You have rotten taste, look at the boring old boots you choose to wear, when you have this wide array open to you.'

I shrugged. 'Try it then. I can tell just by looking that they wouldn't fit me.'

He sat on the floor and peeled off his old boots. They were definitely on their last legs, for even as he removed them from his feet the leather on one side fell apart in his hands. Trevor opened the laces of the pretty sparkly pink shoe as wide as he could, and he squished and he squeezed, but it wasn't going further than his elongated toes.

'Didn't you ever read Cinderella?' I bent down and took it from him before his claws ripped through the thin canvas. 'Try these.'

I held out a pair of sensible yellow leather work boots in my size. They weren't in bad condition really, just a little scuffed, and they had steel toes. Quite a bargain at the price.

He shook his head and scowled like a toddler. 'No, they're ugly.'

'You can't wear sparkly shoes, the other goblins will laugh at you.'

Trevor shook his head and resolutely ignored the heavy footwear in my hands, searching back on the shelves for something else. His eye settled on a handsome pair of red high heel lace-up boots, leftovers from the previous century if the layer of dust on them was anything to go by.

Like a child again, he stared up at me, willing me to let him try them on.

'Fine, go for it.' I sighed as I passed them to him. They didn't look like they would last any amount of time on the cobblestones and gutters of the Old Town. The leather was thin and rubbed, the shiny bits flaking off already.

However, they fit him. He wobbled a little as he stood up, but soon mastered the art of prancing in the heels. He refused to take them off so I brought the tag up to the woman behind the counter.

The goblin really owed me now, and I intended to get the Kin's money's worth from him.

·····•·•····

'So why do you have to meet Auld Meg, anyway?' The goblin's face was glum as we walked back along Leith Walk. He'd been very quiet, and was no longer prancing in his high heel boots. He was probably learning what women have known for centuries – just because the footwear looks fab, doesn't mean you can actually do anything in it. 'It's not normal, wanting to come face to face with the wickedest witch to ever live. You know, I'd rather not...'

I'd been thinking hard too, the whole while, but not about fashion. Thoughts of Hugh and his apparent betrayals – although, okay, I could see where he was coming from, but that didn't make it easier to swallow. And thoughts of Fergie, how she was suddenly so much happier than I'd ever seen her. And thoughts of my mom, and how she was stuck in the Ice Kingdom, and I still couldn't get to her.

But foremost, of course, was Auld Meg and her secrets. She might be evil, as Trevor seemed to think, but we were the only witches to have this huge thing in common. We'd both touched the Crystal Charm Stone and lived to tell the tale. I could only hope I wasn't to share her fate.

'Wicked or not, she might be able to teach me something about interdimensional travel,' I answered him, absently. 'I need to get to the Ice Kingdom.'

He stopped next to me and grabbed at my sweater. 'The Ice Kingdom!' he squawked. 'You're going there?'

I'm trying to.' I tried to brush his hands off me, but he wasn't letting go. 'Where ever it is.'

'The Ice King is a terrible being,' he said, shaking his head. I could almost smell the fear coming off him. 'You don't ever want to go there.'

I stared at him, casting my mind back to the glimpses I'd had of the king, all hairy and roaring and covered with animal skins, sitting on his throne of antlers, and I nodded my head. 'Yeah, I don't want to. But I have to.' I pushed the goblin away from me and started walking again.

He hopped up and down next to me, then bounced to catch up with my pacing. 'He's legendary amongst Goblinhood and others. He is more horrible than the worst troll. He will.... he will eat you!'

'Really? I don't think so.' I was sceptical with the confidence of one who'd lived all her life at the top of the food chain, and after all, Mom had been there for the better part of ten years without being made into a meal yet. I was pretty sure Trevor had listened to too many tall tales. 'Well, if I don't meet your Auld Meg, I'll never get there, I'm afraid. Or at least, not in the next couple of years.'

Trevor continued on by my side, his hands glumly stuck in his ragged pockets. 'No one who ever goes there comes back,' he said, his voice full of doom.

I turned on him. 'Why do you care what I do? I'm not asking you to accompany me. I just want you to lead me to this old witch so I can get information from her. Then your job is finished.'

'I wish it was that easy,' he mumbled. Trevor was quiet for a while, then after a quick glance to his left and his right, he gave a nod. 'I'll do it,' he said bravely. 'I'll bring you to the witch. Tomorrow night at the stroke of midnight, meet me at St. Giles.'

With that, he slipped into a narrow alley, leaving me to plod my own way back up the long road to Mrs. Mac's house.

CHAPTER 12

I couldn't hold it in any longer.

'Why does the Venerable Nachtan hate me so much?' This burst out of me as soon as we had left the castle grounds, I kicked at a discarded popcorn carton and watched as it bounced down the hill a little, but that action wasn't enough to relieve my frustration.

Another day of the ancients' snarky comments while Hugh earnestly tried to teach me all the things I would need to know in my future, like how to construct a shield against defence under fire, and how to disable another magic worker who had evil intents. The important, real, interesting stuff. But Nachtan would interrupt and start jawing on about how I knew nothing of the ancient Greeks, and how they had contributed to this bit of knowledge as if anyone really cared how it had come about, and then the thread of concentration would be broken and Hugh would have to begin all over again when the old guy finally shut up. If we could just be let alone to have our classes, we'd get so much further along, and faster.

Hugh sighed in agreement and quickly squeezed my hand before letting it go again. 'He doesn't hate you,' he began.

'No?' I cut in. 'Then why does he act like he does? He contradicts every single thing I say, his automatic answer is 'No, that's not correct'. He makes me feel like I'm one foot high, and the way he's always staring at me like I'm some sort of nasty bug he found in his dish, and he doesn't let me out of his sight, even when he's ignoring me, as if he thinks I'm going to steal his pen or something.'

He stopped to look at me, registering my frustration and gave a short nod as if he'd made a decision on action.

'Alright,' he said. 'Come on. I'm going to answer your questions.' He turned left down Ramsay Lane towards Mrs. Mac's house. I scurried to keep up with him, his long legs were covering the distance quickly.

But he didn't take another left into the alley where I was staying, we kept on going down Mound Place towards the New Town. I'd never been down this way before. Over the iron railing, I could see the spread of green lawns and trees that was the Prince's Street Gardens and further along on the other side of the road the majestic building of the National Gallery.

'Where're you taking me?' I asked when we stopped to watch a train come out through the tunnel beneath the grand buildings.

'My flat,' he said in a low voice as he placed his arm around me in a quick hug. 'That's the one place we can talk and I know we won't be overheard.'

We went on in silence, side by side, our arms not even touching, yet I could feel the heat of his body like an aura. What with all the excitement of coming to Edinburgh, and the things that happened to me so far, I'd never even wondered where Hugh lived, his home base, where he spent his time when he wasn't with me or on Kin business.

We walked for quite a ways through the streets of grand Georgian homes and ended up cutting through a park, he told me it was the Queen Street Gardens (Edinburgh wasn't very imaginative when it came to naming parks) , until we finally stood outside yet another elegant tall building on Abercrombie Place. It was a terrace of houses, all built at the same time and of the same stone, each with tall Georgian windows and grand front entrances. He led me down stone steps into a tiny terrace.

'You live in a basement apartment?' I was somehow expecting something much more luxurious for Hugh's abode, something grander or at least a little cooler.

'No, I live in the garden flat,' he chided me with a smile as he unlocked the black painted door.

'It's below ground,' I said to him. 'It's still a basement apartment, no matter how you try to pretty up the name.'

All the bottom floor apartments that I'd seen back home were cramped spaces, architectural afterthoughts created with the express purpose of helping to pay inflated mortgages. They inevitably had low ceilings and little natural light, so I was shocked to walk into the very opposite of that. The ceilings were high and light and the whole center hallway had an expansive, airy feel. Large windows made the rooms on either side feel like we weren't in a basement at all, and through the window of the room on my left and above the iron railing on the street level, I could see the greenery of the trees from the park across the road.

Yet the flat was sparsely furnished, holding just the basic furniture needed for living, a single sofa in the living room with a modest sized TV, a bed and nightstand in the bedroom. There were no carpets on the blonde wood floors, no artwork on the walls, and no clutter to speak of, nothing that made it a home.

The kitchen, while it held large stainless steel appliances, had a dusty unused air about it. There weren't even crumbs around the red toaster on the counter, the only object in the place with a bit of colour.

'Cook much?'

He shrugged with a small grin. 'Nah, who has time for that?' He passed by the outside door which led to a tiny green space in the back, then gave a small thump to a spot on the wainscoting. Before I could ask him what he was doing, a portion of the wall swung away to reveal a darkened doorway.

Hugh looked at me and indicated his head. I approached the darkness, and saw an iron staircase spiralling down.

It wasn't the steepness of the steps that made me shiver as I paused in the doorway, it was the aura of magic I could feel like a buffering wall. I stroked it with a single finger, it gave a little but sprung back with the firmness and buoyancy of a wall of water.

'What is this?' I murmured, sticking my finger in more and feeling it gently repulsed like a magnetic force. 'How'd you do it?'

'Please, enter into my cave,' he said, bowing slightly. He grinned with pride and snapped his fingers.

The buffering wall disappeared from my touch and lights appeared in the room below. Once we were at the bottom, he gave yet another click and the doorway closed back over, the wall neatly in place.

'This is the only place we can talk where I know we won't be overheard,' he said. This cellar room, like the apartment above us, was all white walls and light coloured wooden floors. There were no windows down here though, but discreet lighting in the ceiling lit the space, showing a haphazardly furnished room. Two large armchairs faced each other, they looked like leftovers from World War II, the nubbly red jacquard all faded to pink. Several generations of cats may have used these chairs as scratching posts in the last century. A wooden table that looked like it had never been varnished or painted stood against one wall, a plain empty surface. Battered filing cabinets stood in a corner, and by them a large bookcase, half filled with papers and books and various clutter. A small apartment sized fridge was the only modern item down here.

'Beer?' Hugh asked as he reached in and drew out two bottles. He expertly twisted off the caps before handing me one.

'Sure,' I said, still speechless at this surprising room deep underground, so much like an iron-lined bunker in its intention. This was a fortress, I could feel the magical spells of protection thrumming just beyond my consciousness, but the question I had to ask was *Why?*

....

We sat facing each other in the armchairs, which I discovered were much more comfortable than they looked.

'Why, indeed,' Hugh said after he took a good long swallow of his beer. 'I'm not sure where to start.'

'Who are you hiding from?'

'Not hiding from, as much as choosing to have privacy from,' he corrected me.

'The Kin?' I couldn't believe it, for Hugh was an integral part of the ruling Kin. 'This whole set up is really necessary to be private from the Kin?'

'Yes, it is. There's a faction of them,' he admitted, his green eyes frank. 'I told you Cromwell runs the Uncommon Forces. He's the military, the policing arm of the Kin. He's also, as you've found out, the head of the Covenanters, the branch of the witches who still follow the traditional lines of thinking.'

'And the Covenanters were the ones responsible for the witch hunts and burnings, centuries ago,' I said.

'Yes, they attempted to scourge the land of all the Halflings who had magic in their veins. They wanted to purify the blood lines.'

His face was twisted in disgust. I'd never seen him be so open with his inner thoughts before.

'And they still do,' I suggested.

He nodded. 'Fortunately the witch hunts were outlawed.'

'You're a half-blood, like me,' I said slowly. 'What I've never understood is, why is your half-blood status so accepted in the Kin? Remember when we first met, down by the harbour back home. How is it that you were able to rise in the Kin?'

'Oh, that,' he said, shrugging it off. 'My family are the Earls of Brannoch. We're aristocracy, reaching back many centuries. Cromwell and his crowd have no choice but to admit us into the Kin.'

'You're related to royalty?' This was a new one on me – he'd never even hinted it before.

'Not particularly recently, we're not,' he replied in an off-hand manner, then he took another swig of beer. 'Not to the present incumbents, the Windsors, at any rate. But I actually rank higher than Cromwell, who is only a Baron.'

'Wait, rank higher? Does that mean...'

He grinned at me in a very unaristocratic manner. 'Yes, when dear old Dad pops it, I'll be the next Earl.'

'Oh.' I sat back in the armchair. I really hadn't seen that one coming.

'It's nothing, not like we're uber-rich or anything,' he continued as if to reassure me.

'Just... plain old rich, and titled.'

'Depends on your perspective, but I guess you're right.' He nodded, then picked up the thread of his story again. 'So Cromwell uses his privileged position to pretty well do as he likes. He usually stays within the lines of acceptable behavior, but I can't trust him not to have spies everywhere. Hence, this charming little private den.'

'Huh,' I said, trying to process all of this new information. 'Okay. And Nachtan. Why does he hate me?'

Hugh shook his head. 'He doesn't hate you! But, it is... complicated.'

'Really,' I said, skeptically. 'How so?' Whenever people used the C- word to explain a situation, they were usually trying to explain away bad behaviour. At least that was my experience.

'Nachtan is the oldest living witch,' he began. 'And has been through much. He lived through the entire twentieth century with all its wars.'

'When was he born?'

'A century and a half ago.'

Ancient indeed, I thought. But how would one get to live to such a great age?

Hugh continued. 'I sometimes get the feeling that he believes he's lived too long. He was present during the whole Margaret Forsythe episode, around the turn of the last century. In fact, he was the one who had to sentence her.'

'Who was she?'

'Who is she, you mean. Auld Meg, as she's commonly known.'

At this, my heart almost jumped out of my chest.

Auld Meg. I couldn't tell him of my plans for that very night with the goblin. I was going to meet Auld Meg, or Margaret Forsythe, and ask for her help. But I could certainly pump Hugh for information, for the more I knew, the better I would feel about the whole affair. I sat forward.

'People have hinted,' I said, and looked at him expectantly. 'But no one will tell me the story.'

....

Margaret Forsythe was a young woman of the Kin, the daughter of a Duke, and as headstrong as the day was long, Hugh said. Born wealthy and entitled, she also had more than her fair share of magic in her blood and the belief that she should be allowed to use it.

Unfortunately for Lady Margaret, she was born into the wrong time and of the wrong gender. This was before the World Wars and the Edwardians and the emancipation of women, and most of the male Kin believed a woman's place was in her home. Women were allowed to practice silly magic, small glamours and such, but would never have been allowed into the hallowed halls to join in with the truly powerful men.

This was not good enough for young Margaret, and she was determined to enact change in the Kin, singlehandedly if necessary. She begged and pleaded with her father for formal education into magic, with the result that her loving Papa hired a private tutor with the strict instructions to teach her only the basics.

The beautiful woman seduced her tutor into teaching her more than that, however, and after a few years she was a fully educated witch, hungry to take her part in the Kin. But Lady Margaret continued to lay low, further teaching herself and practicing on her father's quiet estate for the next decade.

Finally, the day arrived when she deemed herself to have surpassed the majority of the male Kin in knowledge and power. Approaching thirty years of age, she presented herself to the court at Edinburgh to begin her campaign. Unfortunately for her, the Covenanters still ruled the Kin in those days, and she was laughed out of town.

Being of above average intelligence, along with having enough means to carry out her desires, the furious Margaret plotted and planned, finally coming up with a solution which no one foresaw. While the rest of the Scottish Kin were celebrating the full moon of Samhain one year, she simply travelled up to Inverness, on to the Island of Lewis and Harris, and from there made her way to the island of Scarp.

I suspected I knew what was coming then, but I stayed silent to allow Hugh to tell the story.

Lady Margaret had planned ahead, had even gotten her hands on the blue prints of Scarp Castle. She entered the tunnel beneath the Broch and took the Crystal Charm Stone in hand, intent on bringing it back to Edinburgh to fling it in the faces of the ruling male Kin.

She did not take one thing into account, however, and how was she to know? No one had ever attempted such a thing before. Moving the Stone sent reverberations through all the ley lines of the land, as this crystal was at the center hub of all the magic. The disturbance was soon felt in Edinburgh and the Kin were quick to act.

'Margaret was caught, the lodestone returned, and she was sentenced by curse to remain in a dungeon to write all she knew into the last Chronicle, and only when this book was finished would she be sentenced to death.'

And that's why the Covenanters hate me, I thought. This ancient left-over fear of a powerful woman. I looked up to see Hugh carefully watching me. He nodded when he saw what was in my eyes.

'Yes, and that's why you need to fear Cromwell,' he said softly.

'Just one thing,' I finally spoke up after thinking it all over some more. 'You said the Crystal Charm Stone was returned to the broch. But who did that, who brought it back?'

'The Venerable Nachtan was tasked with that job,' Hugh replied solemnly. 'And that is why he is venerated. Through that brave action, he opened himself up to more power than any of the Kin before or since.'

I waited for him to take the next step in logic, to point out the obvious anomalies in this line of thought, but he remained silent. I searched his face, surely he wasn't going to leave it at that? I'd have to do it myself for it had to be said aloud.

'You mean to tell me,' I began. I tried to rein it in, but my temper was rising. All the more because I had to be the one to point it out. 'You mean, a male witch is venerated for the very same action that, when done by a female, means she gets sentenced to life in a dungeon?'

Hugh had the grace to look uncomfortable. 'Well, their intentions were entirely different,' he said, just a tad too defensively. 'She actively chose the role, while he was forced to clean up behind her.'

'You're frigging serious. You really don't see...' My rage could not find words. I'd known all my life, since I became aware of them, that the Kin were a right band of bastards, but this took the cake. 'And she's still locked up, even today?'

'Yes,' he said. 'There is a movement to rectify the whole situation, to re-look at the judgements but...'

'But it's not going to happen in our lifetimes, right?'

'Nachtan was the one to hand down the sentence! We can't very well have a re-trial until he's dead, now, can we? It would be an insult to his name.'

If I had any doubts left, they had dissipated by now. I was going to Auld Meg that night, and I certainly wasn't going to share this with Hugh.

Chapter 13

Hugh was watching me tensely, preparing for my next attack. But what more was there to say? I'd stated the obvious inequality of justice, and he had excused it with bleating, self-justifying Kin excuses. I couldn't stand this anymore, I needed to get out in the fresh air and walk far away from this magic infused environment. So I jumped out of my seat and ran up the iron staircase before he could stop me.

And banged into the invisible wall of the protective force. Dazed, I grabbed onto the iron railing to stop me from tumbling down. 'Let me out!'

He looked at me from below, calmly now. He hadn't moved an inch. 'I'm sorry you're upset, but we're not finished yet.

'It's no use beating against a magic force field with your fists. You're not getting anywhere with that,' he added.

I stopped the useless action and let my hands drop to my side, then stomped my way back down the stairs, each iron step clanging against my boots.

'While you're up, why not get us both another beer?'

Fresh drinks in hand, I slumped back in my chair. 'So finish,' I said coldly.

'The Venerable Nachtan...' He looked up at me. 'You're really not going to like what I have to say. But you have to listen, and to heed.'

I crossed my arms and said nothing.

'He's not giving favorable reports back to the Kin.'

'Of course not, I have the audacity to be female.'

'According to Cromwell, Nachtan is pressing for more direct action on you.'

'Like locking me in a dungeon for the rest of my life?' I thought about what I'd said for a second. 'How long will that be, anyway? Am I immortal now?'

Hugh shook his head. 'No one lives forever. Margaret and Nachtan, well, their lifespans have been vastly extended through their prolonged contact with the Stone. She managed to bring it all the way to Inverness before she was caught, and he had to take it back the same distance. You had less time with it, so there should be less effect.'

'But I'm really powerful! You said it yourself, you've seen me at the full moon.'

He lifted a finger. 'That's exactly it – at the time of the full moon. Not the rest of the month, though, right?'

I shrugged away his point. He was correct. But that still didn't make things good. He was still part of the unfair misogynistic Kin. 'Are you finished? Can I go now? Or are you planning to leave me in this subterranean cell against my will?'

He sighed. 'Look, I just wanted to warn you. You are very powerful, but only at the time of the full moon. The rest of the time, you're vulnerable. And you are being watched very closely. Cromwell is probably monitoring every move you make, no doubt he's following your phone and every credit card transaction. They'll be watching for any strange outbursts of magical activity in the area. Even Mrs. Mac is expected to give reports on you. He's waiting for you to make a wrong move.'

So much for all his previous talk about what a great opportunity I'd been given, to study under Hugh and the Venerable Nachtan. I was a prisoner in Edinburgh, watched closely day and night.

Which led me to wonder – how would I be able to get away with seeing Auld Meg tonight? If spies were everywhere, then someone would know. Damn it. This would require extreme carefulness.

Although my thoughts were racing, I must have appeared calmer so Hugh switched tact, attempting for a lighter, more conversational tone. 'Have you met anyone yet? Been out socializing?'

My heart was full to bursting and just about at breaking point, and I had no room in my head for this silly chat. Hugh, my darling Hugh, had shown me a side of him that I couldn't accept, and in rejecting that side, I thought I had to reject all of him. I was confused and needed to be alone more than ever right at that moment. So I turned on him.

'Who would I meet here, Hugh? You think I'd be likely to go out for a beer with Nachtan? The guards, perhaps, inviting me to meet at their local pub? Or perhaps Brownie, that weird little maid at Mrs. Mac's, maybe her and I could get together for a hen night, have a little bitch session about my landlady's treatment of her?'

He was taken aback by the force of my outburst and laid his bottle of beer on the flat arm of the chair. 'First of all, her name's Patsy. She's a House Brownie. And secondly, this is a university town, Dara. There are thousands of students around in this square mile alone. It wouldn't take much to join a quiz night, meet people.'

'With my curfew? You have to be kidding me,' I said bitterly. The only being I'd met so far was that nasty little goblin, and I certainly wouldn't call him a friend. I badly mimicked a Scots accent, 'Oh so nice to meet you, but I must run home now. What am I a student of? Oh, magic. My university? The little castle on the hill, yes, it's very exclusive, you'll not have heard of it.'

'Alright, alright,' he said, finally getting annoyed. 'I get it. Look, why not come out to dinner with me tonight? Mrs. Mac won't mind your curfew if you're with me.'

I had a date with a goblin at midnight, but I couldn't tell him that. Two hours with Hugh, and me trying to keep up my guard the whole time? There would be warmth and companionship and wine, and I knew myself well enough that I could never withstand all that. I would let something slip, especially with the alcohol. I shook my head. 'No.'

'Come on,' he coaxed, smiling at me. 'You need fattening up, and it would be great to have a break from Mrs. Mac's food, I know that firsthand.'

Perhaps if I said yes, I could persuade him to tell me why he had been stuck under Nachtan's tutoring... But no. Curiosity killed the cat, as they say, and that would have to wait for another time. And there would be other times.

'No,' I said. 'Not tonight. I have studying to do.'

'Since when does Dara Martin worry about her bookwork?' His eyes began to narrow with suspicion, and I knew that he knew I was up to something. Damn – that was a stupid move. I had to backtrack, and fast.

'Actually, Hugh, this whole full moon thing?' I began, and looked away, pretending to be embarrassed. 'But there is a side effect to the tides thing.'

I winced and held my belly. 'It's brought my menstrual cycle to align with the new moon, and I have awful cramps right now. I really just want a night at home with a hot water bottle.'

He opened his mouth, then shut it again. If I wasn't so desperate, I would have laughed to see the great Hugh Sabiston so flummoxed and out of his element. Guys hate period talk.

'Of course,' he said hurriedly.

'Mmmn,' I replied, wincing again. I really had to get a move on. I had things to prepare.

'I'll walk you home,' he offered. 'And we can have a cup of tea with Mrs. Mac.'

He even stopped into the very expensive news kiosk and bought me a dozen chocolate bars, self-consciously showing off the fact that he was a modern man who understood the needs of women at this time of the month, even if he couldn't bring himself to say the words out loud.

·····•·•····

I went directly to my room when we got home, and left Hugh with the uncomfortable job of explaining to my landlady. My act must have been pretty convincing, because Brownie (or Patsy I mean) was sent up with a tray of soup and bread along with a hot water bottle. I gave her a weak smile of thanks as I reclined back on my bed.

She put her hands on her hips and shook her head. 'Ye might have fooled himself with your pretense, but ye're not fooling me,' she said. 'Ye're not at that time of the month, you had that last week. I know, 'cause I'm the one t'does your laundry. What're you up to?' Her little mouth was set in a grim line.

'Just... I'm not feeling myself,' I told her in a faint voice, turning to face the wall. Dang. What a nosy creature she was. I longed to tell her to mind her own business.

'I'll allow ye're not!' she retorted. 'You're planning something, I can smell deceit a mile off. Ye do know you're being watched something awful, don't ye? You can't get away with anything, not with the Kin on your every move.'

She picked up my hoody from where I'd thrown it on the chair and climbed the small wooden steps to hang it in the wardrobe. 'Course, it's not natural, what they're doing. You should be out enjoying yourself, living your life, a young woman like you.'

I flipped around to stare at her, my mind racing. What were the chances I could brazen it out? She was just a Brownie, after all, a creature of no standing in this house. She didn't even merit a name from her employer. But... her bedroom was directly above mine, a poky little attic space that only she could stand up in. I knew from experience that there were no sound barriers between us, just the plank floor of her room, and we could hear every movement the other made.

My plan was to get up at eleven thirty and sneak out to meet the goblin outside the Cathedral. Mrs Mac went to bed at an early hour, but what were the odds I could do this successfully, especially now that Patsy was on the alert?

'If I told you, you'd tell on me,' I said, trying my best to look menacing.

The brownie laughed unexpectedly, not cowed by me at all. 'What, tell her downstairs?' She shook her head. 'The drama's not worth it. I'll not be getting mixed up in anything. I'm just stupid Brownie, who doesn't know anything.'

For the first time she smiled and looked at me, and I could see the intelligence in the eyes which she had up to this point shrouded. I made a decision right there and then. Hugh had said I needed the support of others right now, and I was prepared to take a chance on this ill-treated maid.

'Your real name is Patsy, right?'

A faint look of surprise came over her face which changed to glee as I told her my plan. Well the part about sneaking out anyway. I didn't mention Auld Meg. 'And there's this... person I promised to meet...'

'Don't ye worry about it,' she said fervently, her small brown eyes glinting with pleasure. 'I'll make sure Herself sleeps soundly tonight with an extra dollop of brandy in her tea. Leave it to me. And I'll leave the door unlocked so's you don't make noise.'

'I may be late coming back,' I told her. I had no idea what would happen with Auld Meg, even if Trevor could get me to her.

'I'll cover for ye,' she said, giggling, her rosy cheeks bunched up and a new lightness to her eye. She no longer looked so mousy when she let her personality shine through. 'Ye're a bold one, you are, putting it over the Kin like that. The little witch slips out of their grasp for a midnight lovers' meeting. The other Brownies'll love to hear this one.'

'Uh, well, Patsy, I don't know if we want to publicize this.' But there was no harm in letting her believe what she wanted to.

I'd made an unexpected new ally in Mrs. Mac's house and I was about to meet the wickedest witch in Kin history. Although I had a suspicion she might not be so evil, at least, not more evil than I was. The clock ticked slowly toward the appointed hour as the moon slowly rose over the roofs and chimneys of the Old Town.

·····•······

Patsy was as good as her word. The house was almost silent, only the soft snores of Mrs. Mac's brandy-induced sleep sounding as I slipped down the carpeted staircase in the dark, and the front door was unlocked.

I walked quietly down Ramsay Lane, picking my way along the cobblestones, helped only by the light of a single street-lamp. The main boulevard still had some life even at this hour, the remnants of a tour group in the pub down the road and a few dark shapes lurking in the shadowed alleys. I didn't stop to look too closely, for I didn't want to know their business, and I didn't want anyone to know mine.

The steps of St. Giles were deserted. Did the goblin stand me up? And me after buying those ridiculous red boots for him. I was just starting to curse my gullibility when I heard the tap-tapping of heels on the pavement.

'You came.' I felt relief. And dread at the same time.

He stood in the shadow of the statue and didn't meet my eye, just stood there worrying a cigarette butt with his toe. 'You sure about this, then?'

He sounded as reluctant as I felt, but I had to go through with it. I had to meet with Auld Meg, and now more than ever. I needed to find the way to the Ice Kingdom for the next full moon, because I couldn't trust that the Kin wouldn't attempt to find a permanent solution to the problem of Dara Martin. There was a good chance that if I was caught, I would be placed in the dungeon alongside her, but I had to risk it.

'Yes.' My voice was much firmer than I felt.

'Y'know, I really don't...'

'Trevor, you promised,' I cut in. 'And those boots.'

He looked down at his feet, and bit his goblin lip.

'Come on, let's go,' I said roughly.

Trevor led me down behind the Cathedral, making a winding tour of the back alleys down the hill. We emerged on a narrow road that was surrounded with tall tenement buildings reaching up four or five stories each, with hardly a light to show our way. The shadows were deep here, and the air was chill and damp as if the sun rarely reached the hidden nooks of the alleys.

Yet there was life here. The throb of a mindless dance beat playing in a night club somewhere pulsed through the air, and small groups of people, students maybe, huddled against the cold as they smoked cigarettes and other combustibles.

We had stopped outside a plain oak door which had been strengthened with rusted iron bolts, and perhaps had even been painted, back when Victoria was on the throne of England. There were no windows in the tall stone wall, nor was there a sign overhead indicating what lay inside, but I could hear discordant music, heavy on the bass, coming through in a muffled way.

'That's the best pub in the city,' he said, pointing his thumb in the direction of the music. 'We could stop for a pint, if ye like. You're buying, of course.'

'No, Trevor, we need to do this,' I said, then lowered my voice to a whisper. 'Now. You can't back out.'

'Well, you're going to need human cash then,' he replied, scowling. 'We've got to grease the gates in order to get where we're going.'

He drew me over to a dirty, ill-lit ATM machine outside a newsagents which was still open, though there wasn't much custom around. 'I'd say fifty should do it.'

'I don't think I can take out cash advances on the credit card,' I told him. 'Hugh and the Kin won't be too happy about it.'

Besides which, Cromwell was monitoring every transaction, or so Hugh believed, and it wasn't so he could watch my spending limit.

Trevor clicked his long narrow fingers impatiently. 'Just do it. If you really want to see her.'

'Bossy little bastard,' I muttered, but went ahead. The transaction was completed, with no alarms or magical sirens going off. I counted the notes in my hand then looked at him. 'Okay, that's done. What now?'

He jerked his head in the direction of the newsagent. 'Go buy the biggest bottle of whisky you can get with that.'

'Fifty pounds should get a magnum,' I retorted. 'Seriously?'

'Do I look like I'm joking?' he asked in his nastiest goblin voice. He was nervous, which made me even more nervous.

The single fluorescent light overhead hissed and buzzed as I bought the largest, cheapest bottle of whiskey the store had, and met him again outside. He made me hide it in my satchel, then led me further down the street, around a corner and we continued in to a darkened passage. It looked like we were going under a bridge of some sort, with a soaring high vaulted archway, but it was too pitch dark in this space to tell. I shivered. I wasn't getting good vibes from this place, as if there'd been bad things happening all around us, for many years, as if the evil had infused itself into the very stone of these passageways. I kept close to his side.

The goblin walked carefully in the darkness, eyes darting every which way into the depths. He felt it too, I knew.

Finally he stopped about halfway through the tunnel and knocked on the stone wall. A crack of light opened up as a hitherto invisible door swung inwards. A single candle burned, and a troll stood in our way.

It grumbled something incomprehensible, and Trevor took it aside, standing on his tiptoes as the creature bent down to listen to the words whispered about where its ear should be. Every hair on my body was standing to attention at this point, and I just wanted to drop the bottle and run back through the door. In fact, I did chicken out and I turned to leave, but the door closed shut even as I thought about it. The metal clank echoed in the room like a harbinger of doom.

Trevor clicked his fingers again and motioned me over. He grabbed the whiskey from my bag and gave it to the troll.

'We'll be back,' he said to him. 'So don't have it all drunk by then.'

The goblin waited until the sentry was deep into the bottle before he snatched a candle end, lit it, and led me up through into a maze of corridors and dark rooms, some with bars on the doors.

'Where the hell are we?' I kept my voice at a whisper, for there were all sorts of weird grunts and snorts and moans coming from the dark cells.

'The Vaults,' he said in a low voice. 'The Edinburgh Vaults. Behold, the gates of hell.'

CHAPTER 14

We crept along the passage for what seemed an inordinate amount of time, our soft footsteps echoing in the caverns, the dark spaces beyond empty doorways. My heart was going a hundred beats a minute, the most terrifying experience of my life although nothing actually came out of the rooms to threaten us, and we saw no other creatures, living or dead. We could hear them, though, and smell them too.

Finally we came to the end, a small twisty stone staircase leading up and down. Trevor led me down, and we paused by a tiny window open to the night air, thick iron bars stopping anything but the breeze from entering or exiting. I took a deep inhale.

'Are we in Alt?' I could think of no other explanation for the pure horror of the place, as if centuries of terror and degradation had occurred without cease in this isolated pocket of hell.

He had relaxed a little too, and leaned against the wall. He took off his dirty stocking cap and rubbed the sparse hair on his head. 'Ha! No, this is your reality, although as you know the veil is nonexistent here,' he said. 'This space was purely created by the hand of man.'

'What a horrible place. They sure knew how to build dungeons for the maximum effect in those days.' I couldn't think of another reason for the creation of such a dismal structure, other than for the torture of fellow beings.

'It didn't start out that way. The bigwigs wanted to build a bridge over the valley, linking the hills, right?' He was almost conversational in tone now as if welcoming an opportunity to avoid what lay ahead, and he settled into his story. 'So they did. And being Scots, they couldn't bear to think of the wasted space, so they created rooms beneath the bridge.'

'For people to live in?' I couldn't believe it. I looked around at the damp glistening on the stone walls and the moss growing in the cracks. 'That's disgusting.'

'Not at first, no. These were used by merchants who had their stores up on the top of the new bridge. Some of them had their workshops down here, others used the spaces for storage.'

An involuntary shiver ran up my spine.

'But when they built the bridge they didn't pay extra for drainage, the cheap bastards. All the water from the road above came down through here, so the business owners moved their gear out, then the... the others moved in.'

'You mean, the super naturals? Like goblins and trolls?'

'No,' he replied, and glanced over to me. 'We find our own homes, none would stay in this godforsaken unnatural spot. There's ghosts and shades and demons here now, true, but they're leftover haunts from the human beings who lived here then. Hundreds of them. Prostitutes, the poor, criminals. Murderers and worse. All the outcasts of Edinburgh society, all the tortured souls who couldn't find their way out of this hell of their lives.'

'Jesus,' I breathed. 'Don't suppose there was any running water or...'

'No,' he agreed. 'No sewers either.' Even he wrinkled up his nose, and goblins are usually inured to the worst of the worst.

'Finally, the Council got embarrassed by the state of the place, so they cleared it all out and closed it down,' he continued with a bitter sneer. 'Well, that's the official reason.' His eyes slid over to mine, narrow slits glinting in the candle's flame.

'Do I want to hear the real reason?'

He laughed, a slippery sound which echoed off the low stone ceiling. 'You're about to meet her,' he said, turning to continue our path down the stairs. He talked as he walked, his reedy voice carrying over his shoulder. 'Auld Meg went and got into that business with the Stone, as you know, scaring the shite out of the Kin. From what I heard, they couldn't kill her, it was too dangerous to try, but they managed to curse her and keep her down here in the deepest level of the Vaults.'

'Here?' The word came out as a strangled gasp, and my feet refused to carry me further. 'All those years?'

I had been angry for Margaret's sake, back at Hugh's, about the inequality of justice meted out to her. But it had been abstract then, I couldn't have imagined the reality of this horror of this subterranean purgatory, with the magic as thick as the dankness in the air.

And then I couldn't help but think that no one living being would do this to another, not without good, solid reason. There were thick protection spells laid all over the place – although I didn't recognize them yet, I could smell them for what they were. Whoever had put these into place had been deeply afraid of the threat. Something huge was being kept back here, something extremely powerful. Or someone. My steps slowed.

Trevor had talked about needing the cursed witch's help for my task, back when we were in the open air of the clean streets of Edinburgh, and it had sounded like a good solution. But now that we were here, in the lowest level of the creepiest place on earth, the full implication of what I was about to do hit me. If these things everyone hinted at were true, I was on my way to meet the most terrible and secretive figure in the history of the Scottish Kin, and try to somehow convince her to help me go to the Ice Kingdom. This was just wrong on so many levels. I didn't know a lot, but I was starting to think it would be a good thing to just let cursed witches lie where ever they were. This was not something I wanted to get involved in.

'I warned you about having second thoughts,' he said as he walked ahead, as if he could read my mind. 'Too late now, so just put on your big girl panties.'

Then he paused and turned to face me, holding the candle stub aloft. The goblin's eyes were unreadable in the flickering light. 'Relax. It's okay, as I said, she's held by a curse. She has to write everything she knows, and can't die until her Chronicle is written. I think that's how the story goes.'

'And you think she'll help me? How can a witch cursed to live underground be of any assistance?' My stomach was starting to turn, and it wasn't just from the awful stench of this place. I didn't have a good feeling about this. Also, where there were curses, there was usually a lot of anger built up over years on the part of the cursed. 'Why would she want to help me?'

'I don't know if she'll help you,' he said, shrugging his narrow shoulders. 'But I bet the answer to your problem is written in her Chronicle. If you can take that, then you'll be laughing all the way to the Ice Kingdom.'

'No. No, no, no.' Take the Chronicle? Was he mad? On so many levels, this was a morally wrong, and probably impossible, task. But he'd already disappeared around the last bend in the stairs, taking the only source of light with him.

I stumbled after him, what else could I do? My sleeve brushed the mildewed wall, squashing something, I didn't bear brush it off because then my skin would have to touch it. I didn't want to be left alone in the dark here, in the Vaults, but I had no intention of going along with his suggestion of stealing the Chronicle.

At the bottom of the stairwell, a long, low passage stretched before us. I could feel shadows flickering all about us, and they weren't all caused by the candle's feeble light. I stuck close to Trevor's back, ready to duck behind him if necessary, short as he was.

Auld Meg's dungeon wasn't hard to find, I could smell malevolence in the air like a sour fart, like the forgotten fish dinner in the back of the fridge.

'Maybe we shouldn't go any further,' I whispered to the goblin, leaning down to his level. My body was poised to leap, every neuron was firing. 'This might be a very, very bad idea.' Yes, I needed to reach my mother in that other dimension, but my reptilian brain was screaming at me to flee at any costs if I wanted to live.

He held the candle stub aloft and turned to face me, an unexpectedly determined look on his face.

'You want to get your mother, don't you?'

'Yes, but I just...'

'If you don't do it now, when will you do it?' he cut in and began to scold me in a hissing voice. 'Your mother languishes. And who knows if you'll still have the power of the Stone next month? Can you guarantee that it won't diminish without you being near it? What if you need to, like, re-charge from it or something?'

He turned back. 'We're here now, you'll take the book, go get your mother. No problem.'

'Wait,' I reached out and grabbed him by the shoulder. Something didn't sit right about this whole situation. By bringing me to Auld Meg, the goblin was leading us both into certain danger, and what I knew of him so far was he was always looking out for number one. 'Why are you pushing for this? Why do you care so much? I thought you barely liked me.'

He held the candle away and slightly behind him, so it was in my eyes but not his. 'Because – because of friendship?' His voice was half-hearted on the last bit, as if he knew I wouldn't believe the obvious lie either.

We didn't have time to explore his definition of friendship for he turned away and began to scurry into the depths of the passage, closer to the source of the evilness emanating from the dark. I had no choice but to follow on his heels.

The last cave, room, or cell, was a simple looking affair with a narrow doorway. If there had ever been a proper door fixed into place, it had long ago rotted or been burned for heat by previous inhabitants of the Vaults. There appeared to be no barriers to the room, nothing keeping curiosity seekers out or a cursed witch in.

He stopped before entering, transfixed, his goblin face all aglow in the light with awe and excitement. And hungry greed. Friendship my arse. He had an ulterior motive, but I just couldn't think what it might be.

'Behold, Auld Meg,' he whispered, his face shining in fascination overlain with a healthy dose of fear.

I drew up behind him and looked within the cavity.

It was not totally dark in there, for a faint light shone from the very rocks themselves, like an underwater phosphorescence in the damp of the stone; it was enough to clearly see the outline of what looked to be not a human witch, but a carved statue of one, seated at a desk, with an amazingly detailed and delicate stone quill in hand over a large open book. The figure, like the stone walls, was covered in that eerie green luminescence, and was amazingly lifelike, yet looked to be created from the very granite itself.

It was familiar, for I'd seen this statue before in the glass bubble in Nachtan's room. It must have been a scrying glass then, keeping an eye on Auld Meg. I gave a quick prayer of thanks that this was the middle of the night, and that Nachtan was unlikely to be in his high tower to see me hovering at the doorway of the dungeon.

The goblin stepped into the room, his eyes riveted on the figure as he circled all around it. I followed close behind, too fascinated to listen to the screaming senses which told me to leave and never return to this hell. There was not a sound in the chamber.

Then, with the whispering rustle of sand washed by waves, the statue's eyes followed Trevor. He put his hand to his mouth as he squealed. 'She moved! She's not supposed to be able to move!'

And then her whole head swivelled round so those terrible haunted eyes, the only thing that looked alive in her, could hold me in their glare. The recognition therein horrified me, chilling me to my very bones.

'Dara Martin.' A grating whisper echoed through the chamber, more sand sloughed off her face as she spoke, the underlying muscles stretching as her mouth grew to a grimace. Then she laughed, her mouth open wide so I could see the rotted teeth and the inflamed red of her gums.

The goblin had ducked behind me at the statue's first unexpected movement and was now in full on cower behind me, I could feel his quaking. Dear God, what had we done? What awful menace had we awoken?

'Come closer, my dear one.' All the while, each time she moved or spoke the rock continued to flake off her body until there was barely enough luminescence left on her to highlight the dust in the crevices of her clothing.

For she was still human, or close enough, I could now see. Fear and dread and an awful foreboding took hold of me, like in the long seconds when the eighteen ton semi is headed directly in your path and there's not a thing you can do to avoid the inevitable.

'How do you know me?' My voice was a bare whisper.

She laughed again, that terrible sound, and with great effort, slowly laid her quill down on the book before her. Her voice was hissing, like a snake, and she paused on pertinent words.

'I have written you in my Chronicle. I write the future and the past, and you have come as foretold. Come forward, and accept your destiny.'

I had no feeling in my body, the impulses of mere seconds ago were now dead, and I had no strength to move my feet no matter what my mind was telling me. But I had to speak.

'I don't understand.'

'So much, my dear one, so much to tell you,' she said, then she stood up. The action sent the dust and light sand into a flurry in the air currents. 'Goblin, come out and be seen,' she commanded.

I felt rather than saw Trevor's reluctant movements. His candle guttered and hissed, almost burnt to the end.

'You have done your work well, and will be rewarded.'

His eyes were open wide with terror and I could see his body was shaking too much for him to speak. A dark stain appeared on his pants as his bladder let go.

'Now, Dara, take the Chronicle.' With a gnarled finger she nudged the book closer to me. I shook my head. Her claw-like nail, begrimed with the dirt of years, tapped on the thick paper of the pages. 'You cannot refuse,' she told me calmly, her voice like a million fingers on chalkboards. 'Through your actions, you have set these events in motion, and there is no turning back.'

'No,' I said bravely, though my heart was thudding in my ears and my body was yearning to run, run straight back through that underground corridor and up the stairs. 'This is a mistake. I have not chosen this, I was led here under false pretences, the goblin...' I was stuttering by now.

'The goblin has played his unwitting role,' she said. Her smile on that ancient face was almost gentle despite the harshness of her voice and words. 'He has led you to me, to your destiny. You and I, Dara, will change the world of the Kin. We are the only souls brave enough to seize the Stone and make its power our destiny.'

'No, you're wrong.' I somehow found the courage deep within me to refute her words. 'I never set out to do this. I didn't do it on purpose.'

She ignored me as she continued. 'You alone can free me from this curse.'

'NO.' This defiance burst out of me unbidden. We stared at each other in shock, the crone and I, and although every nerve in my body was screaming at me to run, right now, I was paralyzed with fear.

CHAPTER 15

I didn't know I'd said the word until it was out of my mouth and hanging in the dust and phosphorescence all around us. First Willem, now this ancient crone wanted to use me for their own ends, and it was not going to happen. Not again. This road could only lead to my own ruination, and thank you very much, but I could cause enough trouble for me by myself. I didn't need her help. 'No. I refuse.'

She didn't appear to be angered by my words, instead, she looked on me as if I were a beloved child throwing a tantrum. 'But think what is at stake,' she said.

'What's at stake?' I burst out. 'What is at stake is my future as a witch. My acceptance into the Kin. My... my not being cursed to live underground for centuries! I am not you. I have no intention of following your path, whatever awful things you did to lead you to being cursed. No way!'

Auld Meg merely laughed. 'So why did you brave the Vaults if not to reach out to me? Why did you follow the goblin?'

'Because,' I bit my lip. 'Because you have the knowledge to help me.'

'Yes. We will work together,' she said in a very patient voice. 'You will learn all I know.'

'No, I can't work with you. But my mother. I need you to help me free Mom from the Ice Kingdom.'

'Then you must first free me from this curse!' A sudden breeze whipped the dust around, a foetid wind from the depths of the charnel house.

'No,' I whispered. Then in a stronger voice, again. She was bound by the curse, she couldn't touch me. And she needed me more than I needed her. 'No.' The price was too great. Perhaps she could help me, but the cost was an uncertain future of being an outlaw from the Kin, forever on the run.

'No,' I said for the third time and found the courage to turn to leave the chamber.

'Think of your mother.' Her voice cut clearly through the dust motes, stirring them up again. She was calm and self-assured.

'I am,' I replied, equally calmly now and standing tall. 'I'm thinking of her, and our future. I will not lift the curse.'

'And who will help you reach your goal? Your precious Hugh Sabiston, he who is so ambitious in the Kin? He'll not lift a hand if it means scuppering his chances. The oh-so Venerable Nachtan? You think he'll lose his prejudices?'

I drew a deep breath. 'I will find my own way.' And stepped through the portal.

'Or perhaps your old friend Willem can assist you,' she said. 'He's not so far away, you know. Ask the goblin.'

Her bitter laugh haunted me as we stumbled back through the foetid hallway, the candle guttering and on its last leg. We ran all the way back, Trevor scarpering ahead of me, even in his red heeled boots covering the distance faster than me.

What did she mean, Trevor knew about Willem? If my heart could sink any lower I'd be leaving it behind.

·····•·····

We reached the portal to the Vaults to find the troll still fast asleep, the empty whisky bottle smashed into shards beside him. We carefully picked our way and slipped out the heavy oak door.

What did she mean about Willem? It must have been him I spotted, after all. What was he doing in Edinburgh?

And what ties did Trevor have to that sorcerer? I turned to him, still breathless from our escape and reached out to grab him as the heavy door slammed behind us.

'What do you know about Willem?'

He squealed with fright, his mouth open wide so I could see the rows of needle like teeth as he slithered through my grasp. 'I don't know any Willem, I never heard of him before! I don't know what you're talking about!'

Trevor was terrified of something, and so terrified that I figured he could only be speaking the truth. I dropped my arms and sighed from the depths of my being. The events of the night were catching up with me, my entire body was aching and my mind whirling. I needed to go to bed and lose myself in sleep, but I knew there was no way I could settle, not yet. 'I need a drink.'

Confused, tired, with the adrenaline still coursing through my veins, I needed to sort things out in my head. I so needed that drink. Or three of them, preferably in a quiet place where I could marshal my thoughts.

'I know a place,' Trevor wheedled at my elbow. He flicked his eyes nervously behind me. 'I know the very place! You're buying, right?'

He'd quickly recovered all his old verve and confidence now that we were safely away from the Vaults and the terror of Auld Meg. I stared down at the shit-eating grin on his face. He had gotten me into all this. It was his doing, his role. If it wasn't for him offering, I'd never have known where to find the witch, would never have descended to those depths of hell to risk everything. I paused and looked at him, trying to gather up the spite in me to find the nastiest tone in which to tell him to get lost.

'Only, they won't usually let me in,' he said, his goblin mouth turning down into a sad frown. 'Even Bert, the barkeep, he's an elf, but he pretends he can't see me. He thinks he's better'n me 'cause I'm just a goblin, like.'

That made me pause. The adrenaline was still firing through my system, and maybe I wasn't thinking straight, but after the conversation with Hugh I was still pissed that there was so much inequality in this world I'd found myself in. Of course, it was everywhere, it wasn't just a Kin / super natural thing, but my eyes had been really opened to it today. I couldn't do much about saving my mother tonight, or undoing Margaret Forsythe's curse (not that I wanted to – I wasn't going to open that can of worms) but the pettiness of an elf turning up his nose at a fellow being?

'Really? An elf thinks he's too good for you?' There were levels of snobbery everywhere, it would appear. It wasn't just the Kin. I set my mouth firmly. 'Well, let's just see what he says when this witch shows up. I bet you he'll serve you then.'

I might be too chicken to free Auld Meg and I was certainly no closer to getting my mother from the clutches of the Ice King, but I was still a pretty powerful witch, even if it wasn't a full moon. I felt like showing someone just how powerful I really was. 'Let's go have a word with this Bert.'

....

It was the place he'd pointed out earlier, the one with loud thumping discordant beat coming through the steel door. It creaked open suddenly, letting out a small amount of light and two drunken students.

'Got a light, then?'

I considered summoning up a flare from my fingers, but decided it was best not to show off. I ignored the drunks and stepped inside, Trevor close at my heels.

Judging by the noise level, I would have said the place was packed to the rafters, but on closer look I saw that there were a few empty tables scattered here and there. The majority of the patrons chose to crowd around the bar to keep it within easy access for the next round, yelling at each other over the music as they sloshed their ale mugs, never minding where the liquid spilt.

A band played in a corner with a single spotlight, three lads wearing kilts and Doc Martins and very little else. Two had their heads shaved to show the tattoos on their skulls, while the other had dreads almost reaching to his waist. Their music was a Celtic punk bluegrass mix, and loud, and while they may not have been in perfect harmony, they more than made up for it with their frenetic energy.

On second thought, maybe this was the perfect place for my mood tonight. Quiet thinking wouldn't help me free my mother, not right at this moment. I knew my options, and they were few. There was little I could do on that front, so I might as well just give up trying. But on the other hand, there weren't many people who braved Auld Meg in her dungeon, now were there? And had the balls to refuse her. I might not be as powerful as her right now, but give it a couple of weeks.

'Watch it,' I scowled as a young redheaded man bumped into me. We made eye contact and, even drunk as he was, he got the message and scurried away out of my path.

I walked up with a bit of a swagger and clicked my fingers, fixing the tall skinny bartender with my eagle eye. With his long straight hair covering his ears, you could hardly tell he was an elf.

When the burning force of my gaze caused him to look up, I nodded, and said 'two.' Despite the noise, he understood, and drew up the glasses of beer. He put them on the bar, then looked down.

Trevor was leering up at him in triumph, his lips drawn back to show his needle-like teeth.

'Oi!' Bert said as he took the glasses off the bar again and held them out of reach. 'You! Get out. I told you the last time you're barred for life.'

He looked at me accusingly. 'Whatcha bringing the likes of him in here for? He's a nasty piece of work, and that's really sayin' something for this place.'

'Give us the beer,' I told him shortly, keeping my eyes steady on him. 'You don't want to mess with me. Not tonight.'

Bert's adam's apple quivered just a little, then he nodded and laid the glasses back on the bar. He waved away my shimmering credit card, but said, 'Just the one. Then get out of here, and take that little gobshite with you.'

We moved through the crowd to a small table tucked away in the corner, away from the loudspeakers and sat, not minding the various spills from the table's previous inhabitants. Trevor sipped using both hands to hold the glass, and looked proudly around, hoping to be seen.

'Nice place,' I said loudly.

He nodded, totally missing the sarcasm. 'It's the only place that super naturals can really come in,' he said. 'The only other patrons are students, and they're too drunk to notice us.'

It was true, I saw as I looked around at the patrons. There were some witches, you could tell by the air of glamour they'd cast about themselves, making their faces softly out of focus and airbrushed. They were trust fund Kin kids slumming it for the evening, I could tell just by looking at them, like my half-sister Sasha and her friends at home. There was even a vampire drinking what I hoped was red wine.

Trevor turned to me and put his beer down, his face excited. 'I can't believe we did that. We went down to Auld Meg's dungeon. She moved and spoke to us, and we lived!'

'Keep a lid on it!' I darted a glance around to make sure he hadn't been overheard. 'We don't want to spread that around. There's Kin kids in here, you know.'

I took a sip and considered our night's work. 'Besides, dude, I don't think it's something you want to boast about, not in this town.'

I glanced up at him, about to continue, when I saw his face change from boastful to guarded all of a sudden, as if he'd seen danger in the air. This wasn't the same fear he'd shown in Auld Meg's underground cell, that had been sheer terror at the unknown. No, this new expression was fear of something known, a real threat to his well-being.

'I've got to go.'

I could barely hear him over the music, but he didn't give me a chance to ask what was up, he grabbed his pint as he slipped down from his seat and slithered off between the tables, leaving me alone in a strange bar.

I didn't have time to express my outrage either, for all of a sudden I wasn't alone.

'Dara, you come here often?'

I recognized that voice, it still haunted my nightmares. His voice in my head, the terror of that night on Scarp when I'd carried the Crystal Charm Stone and changed the course of my life forever. But he wasn't in my mind right now, I looked up, and yes he was here, right beside me. Wearing a trench coat and that red ball-cap which he removed before taking the goblin's seat.

'Willem, it... it was you, both those times,' I sputtered. 'I saw you in the crowds, but I couldn't believe you'd have the balls to still be in Scotland!'

He bowed his head in acknowledgement. His short blond brush cut glistened in the purple and green flashing lights by the dance floor. 'I showed myself to you on purpose, you know,' he said, lifting his head again. His flat grey eyes on mine caused shivers up my spine.

'I'll turn you in to the Kin,' I said, my fists clenching.

He laughed. It wasn't pleasant. 'You say you will, but will you really?' And he leaned closer to me. 'I can get you to the Ice Kingdom, without all the terror of unleashing the horror of Auld Meg. It will be far less messy. My offer still stands, Dara. Imagine the things we could do, together, you and me.'

'Never in a million years, Willem,' I said firmly. 'Simply no.'

His pale grey eyes bored into mine, and perhaps the alcohol I'd imbibed had relaxed my guard, but he knew his way into my head and I could feel him there, the seduction of his cold touch brushing against my innermost thoughts. I'd just pulled myself together enough to expel him when he introduced a new feeling or path, I'm not sure what it was, but he took me along with him, just like that.

And we were standing in the Ice King's throne room again. Of course we weren't really there, it was just a thought visitation or whatever you call it, but it was pretty realistic. I could see my breath before me in the freezing air, and huddled my hands into my hoody pocket for warmth.

And Mom was there. She couldn't see me, of course, for we weren't really present. She looked even older, her hair lank and lustreless, as she stirred a huge cauldron of liquid.

It was over in a flash and suddenly the bar was all around me again, the deep bass vibrations thudding through the floor beneath my feet.

Willem was sitting back in his chair, full of his old confidence, his eyebrow lifted. 'I repeat, I can get you there. No one else is willing to help you but me.'

'How can you span the dimensions?' I was still shaking, but stalling, searching my mind for a plan. I needed to get word to the Kin that the sorcerer had appeared again, and right in their midst. Was it possible that Trevor had disappeared so quickly in order to go to alert the authorities?

No, the goblin would have no idea of the struggles we'd had on Scarp, or Willem's role in it all, the Kin would not have advertised that they let a sorcerer almost get the better of them. It was all up to me.

Willem laughed at my question. 'I'll not tell you my secrets, Dara, at least not yet,' he said. 'There'll be time enough for that later, when we are partners.'

'I've told you before. I will never, ever, work with you,' I said. 'I despise you.'

'Don't be so hasty.' He leaned his elbows on the table, his pale eyes glittering. 'You saw for yourself what the Kin did to Margaret Forsythe, because her power scared them. Don't fool yourself, they'll do the same to you. Of course, it will be in a much more civilized, twenty-first century fashion, but it will be a dungeon all the same.'

'No.'

'You know they're just waiting for an excuse, Cromwell and his band of merry Uncommons,' he continued, ignoring me. 'They are no better than the witches who went before them. Scared shitless of a female witch's power, so much that they'd rather subdue her than have her be useful to the clan.'

'No!' I shouted, standing up with such force that the table rocked, the rest of the beer in my pint glass splashing over the top. 'Get out of my life, Willem de Vriezs.' With that I turned and left the bar, walking the streets of Edinburgh till I found my way home again, thinking hard all the way.

Jesus, what a night. I'd met and refused to free the dreaded Auld Meg, then had a confrontation with my arch enemy Willem. I was no closer to being able to get to the Ice Kingdom.

But during my stumblings in the darkened cobbled streets, I finally had the space to allow the heart clenching memory of my mother to arise in my head and to allow myself to feel the deep sadness it evoked. The years of missing her, and wanting her by my side, and then knowing she was so close and I could work with the sorcerer and free her...

But no. Those thoughts were madness, and I knew the steel reality that lurked behind the rosy false picture Willem painted. We would not be free to live happily ever after, me and my Mom, for I would live on the edges of society, always fleeing, never settling, always on the run from the Kin and their laws.

CHAPTER 16

The next day when I arrived at the Venerable Nachtan's chamber, we were alone, just me and the old witch in the large dusty chamber.

'Sabiston has been called out of town,' he informed me, looking down his long nose at me from his seat behind the oak table as if this inconvenience was my fault.

I slumped onto my stool in disappointment, and truth be told I was more than a little annoyed, too. I'd held off on phoning Hugh late last night with the news of Willem's reappearance, because I didn't want to deal with the details and situation in which I'd found out this news. This morning in the light of a new day, however, I'd girded my loins and had been prepared to confess, because this was more important than me breaking the Kin's silly rules about curfew.

The sound of the Venerable Nachtan clearing his throat made me look up. He was watching me carefully. 'Is there anything you wish to tell me?'

Did he know about my visit to Auld Meg's dungeon last night? My eyes darted over to the crystal sphere in its corner. It was covered now by a large square of black velvet.

Nachtan didn't miss that movement and his steely gaze bore into mine.

'There is,' I said, and I swallowed past a hard lump in my throat. 'Something the Kin needs to know about.'

He nodded. 'Yes,' he agreed.

Okay, the ancient relic was aware of what had happened, but I pushed on. 'Willem de Vriejs is in Edinburgh. I saw him.'

His white and wiry eyebrows rose in surprise. It might be the first emotion I'd ever seen him express, apart of course, from his distaste at my presence. 'Indeed?'

'He was....' I had no choice but to confess, at least to part of the story. 'He followed me into a pub last night, down by the Cowgate. He... he wanted me to join him.'

Nachtan looked at me levelly for a long moment. 'And you refused?'

'Yes!' I burst out. 'I'm not having anything to do with him, ever.' I must have been pretty fervent and convincing because the old witch merely nodded.

'Then we must do something about this,' he said decisively. 'It's too bad you didn't alert someone at the time,' he couldn't help but add.

I told him everything I knew, except for the part of Willem getting into my head, and anything about his offer to get me to the Ice Kingdom for I was pretty sure that if Cromwell knew I wanted to do this, he would use it as an excuse to lock me up. Of course, I didn't mention the visit to the Vaults, and if Nachtan knew about that, he didn't say anything.

He left the room to send on my report. When he returned, there was a new look in his eyes, almost respect when he looked at me.

'Now for today's plan. With Hugh called away on Kin business, I will take this opportunity to coach you in your sadly lacking knowledge of the Greek influence on the development of magic.'

I groaned inside. It was going to be a morning of dusty old lectures. 'Don't you want me to help find Willem?'

'Oh, no,' Nachtan assured me as he sat back in his chair. 'Elder Cromwell's forces are on that. You could not possibly add to their search. Now. Pythagorus and his contribution as the basis of all magic practiced by the Kin.'

He loved the subject, I could tell by the spark in his eyes as he waxed on endlessly about it. However, this wasn't getting me any closer to my goals.

·········

Hugh had been called away for a long time.

'At least a week,' he said on the phone that evening.

I lay on the bed in my little attic room with my legs dangling out over the side. 'What's going on?'

He cleared his throat. 'Sorry, can't give details,' he said, his voice stilted with discomfort, then he changed the subject. 'But how're things in Edinburgh?'

I told him the same bits I told Nachtan. Funny how no one had chastised me for breaking curfew. I was starting to get the impression that this rule wasn't so important.

'No, I agree with the Venerable Nachtan,' he said. 'It's best you don't get involved. The Uncommon Forces will be on Willem's tail, and you don't want to get within firing range of them.'

We nattered on a bit after that, about nothing in particular. He assured me he missed me, and vice versa, and I complained about the VN's boring old lectures about the stupid ancient Greeks, and how I didn't see I could learn much from all this.

Hugh merely laughed at that. 'You'd be surprised what gems can be hidden in Nachtan's teachings,' he said. 'And Pythagorus? That's an odd choice for him. We spent four months on Eurypides alone before we even touched on the later Greeks. He must have a reason for it, and you might want to pay close attention.'

When we'd hung up, I lay back on the bed and sighed, kicking my feet. In a week's time I would be that much closer to the full moon and its effects on my power, the powers I was hoping to use to get me to bridge the dimensions to the Ice Kingdom, yet I still hadn't figured out a way to get there.

And after last night's brush with Willem, it was more important than ever. I'd pretended not to care what he said, but still his message rang home with me. Yes, it was quite possible that at any moment Cromwell could have me seized on a trumped up charge, and I'd lose my chances forever. On the other hand, I could go along with Auld Meg, but freeing that witch would turn me into just as much of an outlaw as if I'd actually taken Willem up on his offer. The only choices I had were bad choices, but I was determined never to go that route again. Despite my unsteady footing with the Kin, I had to at least try to behave according to their rules.

·········

I was expected to study with the old witch now with Hugh gone, as if there was no time to waste in getting my head stuffed full of knowledge about the origins of magic in the Western world. Why this was so important, I couldn't quite comprehend.

And all of this wasn't getting me any closer to my goal of going to the Ice Kingdom to vanquish the King and free my mother. After all, it wasn't as simple a matter as thumbing a lift on a fishing trawler that was headed to the ice fields, nor could I use my (considerable) skill at 'flying' my mind over the area to scout it out. I had to actually be present in the Ice Kingdom in order to effect change, and to do that, I had to move between dimensions. And I didn't have a clue how to do that.

Yes, I had gone there with my mind, I had seen my mom and spoke with her, and seen the Ice King himself in all his terrible glory. I'd seen her again, or a leftover flash in Willem's presence. And I did try again, lying in my dormer room at night, yet nothing happened. I guess I needed the proximity of the Charm Stone to do that, or to hold her talisman which Johanna had confiscated.

Yet, my destination wasn't on the same physical plane as my human body, so none of my present knowledge could serve me in this quest. If I could only find a portal, any door into the Kingdom, I believed that my full-moon power would get me where I wanted to be, no problem.

Hugh's suggestion that Nachtan was trying to tell me something did cause me to pay more attention to his lectures, and this diligence paid off, for it was the Venerable Nachtan himself who gave me the first hint of how to get somewhere else. All week long he'd been jawing on about Pythagorus, who I'd always thought was a mathematician, but apparently that great ancient was one of the first witches to practice magic.

'Excuse me.' I had to interrupt his flow. 'Pythagorus. Did you say he was able to be in two places at once?'

Maybe that was the solution for me. If the Kingdom was not in the same physical dimension, then I could be in two places at once, correct?

'This is the first documented instance of this, yes.' Nachtan peered over his glasses. He looked almost pleased at my interruption.

'And it wasn't simply astral projection? He was able to go there?'

'According to his peers, yes, he interacted with them and physical objects at the same time, in different physical places,' Nachtan replied, then gave a small smile, the sides of his face threatening to crack. 'You seem taken with the idea.'

'I find it fascinating.' I wasn't lying. 'How exactly would you suggest he did this?'

Nachtan gazed up at the high round dome in thought, then shook his head. 'He wrote about it, but we don't know that this was the actual route he used to accomplish it,' he said. 'However, the action is certainly possible from a metaphysical stand point.'

'Come again?'

'One would need to draw on an external point of power, in order to split oneself into two, so to speak, and one must also have prior knowledge of the destination.'

'Like knowing where the destination is?'

'Much more than that. One must know the destination. One must have breathed the air, had some emotional attachment of a kind, that is what I mean by truly knowing. One must be carrying a part of the destination within oneself, in order for one to arrive there. Pythagorus was very familiar with his destination – it was his childhood home, by all accounts.'

Well, I'd never been to the Ice Kingdom, except my mind had. And my mother was there. Was that emotional attachment enough? And surely the external point of power – I would reach that with the full moon. I didn't need to be in the vicinity of the Crystal Charm Stone to draw on its power, not like the last time, for its power was already within me, waiting to be drawn out with the tides and the moon.

'And if,' I cut in before Nachtan had a chance to begin clearing his throat again. 'If, hypothetically speaking that is, one had the emotional connection, and the power, what more would one need to do to be physically in two places at once?'

'Well.' He leaned against the oak table which took up so much space in the room, and he rubbed his nose. 'I've never had that question before. Let me think.'

He began to mutter to himself while pacing the room. I sat quietly, my excitement growing. Could it be this easy?

The Venerable Nachtan gave an exclamation, then pulled a book out off one of the many shelves. 'Of course! This,' he said. 'This may be just what we're looking for.'

He beamed at me. 'Yes, here it is,' he nodded, his finger pointing to the open page. '*Parakinesi gia ti metafora*!'

I jumped up and ran to examine the book, but my hopes were soon dashed. 'It's... I can't read this. It's Greek again, isn't it?'

Yes, success of a sort, although it would be hard won, but I figured I could easily google the translation for the particular text I needed. I had a whole two weeks till the moon was full again. I would be seeing my mother pretty soon, I knew it. I could feel it in my bones.

'It's been many years...' He gazed at the book with something approaching fondness, but then my words must have registered. 'Can't read the Greek,' he muttered under his breath. He frowned and shook his head and drew in a breath as if about to say something else, but shut his mouth quickly and fixed me with his beady glare.

I stayed silent, for anything I said would probably give him reason to abuse me again.

After what seemed a long time, he spoke again, slowly. 'When I was a young man, with the idealism that goes hand in hand with youth, I once had a fancy to translate the greatest works of magical knowledge to make them accessible.'

He tapped his fingers on the table in front of him as he looked off into the distance of that long-gone time. 'I didn't finish it, for it was a foolhardy venture,' he continued. 'However, I did manage to translate up to Pythagoras into the vernacular. I still have this manuscript somewhere.' The glimmer of a small light was growing in his eye.

I hated to disappoint him, but I had to confess. 'I can't read Latin either.'

This caused a withering look from him. 'You are the most ignorant of creatures, are you not? The vernacular means the common language. In simple words, I translated these works into English. A waste of time, obviously, but my excuse was that I was young and infatuated.'

He immediately and loudly cleared his throat to stem any comments I might have the nerve to make after this confession of vulnerability, but I wasn't going to say a word to dissuade him from giving me his work. In fact, I held my breath, not wanting to say or do anything that might interrupt this train of thought.

He glanced over to the wall of his study, and I could have sworn his eyes alit on the large covered orb for a fraction of a second. He harrumphed again, then walked to the most untidy of the book cases. 'It must still be here somewhere.'

It took a bit of rummaging, but he eventually found what he sought. It was a hard covered journal, the outer aspects bound in thick, marbleized cardboard. It only took him a moment to blow the first layer of dust off, then he wiped it down with the sleeve of his black robe. He stood for a moment, regarding it. 'Ah, the follies of youth.'

He handed it to me. 'Take it, for any good it might do you. Now be off for the day, I have much work to complete.'

I almost grabbed the book from his hand, I was so excited to finally, hopefully, have a solution to my problem that didn't involve me becoming Public Enemy Number One to the Kin. Gathering my things, I gave a backward glance as I was leaving the room to see the Venerable Nachtan standing over the crystal orb. His back was turned to me, but I could see his hand gently tapping the black velvet of its cover as if he was pondering a decision.

That action made me almost certain that he'd watched us in Auld Meg's dungeon that night. He didn't ever bring it up though, and that made me a little nervous for I would have preferred a confrontation, a bollocksing, anything but the silence. I remembered Hugh's caution that the Kin were giving me enough rope with which to hang myself.

But now I didn't have to mess with Auld Meg or even Willem. I had the means to get to the Ice Kingdom. I couldn't wait for the weeks to pass till the full moon.

·····•·····

The time went quickly enough, to my surprise. True, the Venerable Nachtan still lectured every day about the terminally boring ancient Greeks, but he left me to my own devices more and more, content to leave me with assigned readings while he did his own thing. There was no word on Willem or if Cromwell's forces had caught him. I hoped they had.

Hugh remained out of the country, or where ever he was that he couldn't tell me. We spoke regularly on the phone usually after Mrs. Mac's supper hour. I had little to tell him in the way of my life, and he couldn't speak of what he was presently doing, but we found things to talk about nevertheless, just idle chit chat and teasing, or telling back stories of our lives. I'd forgiven him his thoughtlessness and apparent misogyny about Auld Meg and her lot. Having met her, I wasn't sure I disagreed with the Kin for opting for the choice they'd made. Of course, it might just have been the years of injustice and stewing in the dungeon that made her so crooked.

I did spend an inordinate amount of time studying Nachtan's journal. True, it was in English, however it was all handwritten, and not done neatly. I had to read through ink blotches and places where he'd scratched out a thought and re-written a tiny amendment in the margins. He may have thought he was writing in the vernacular, but it seemed more like a direct translation to me, for the word order was all weird and I had to really concentrate to get the gist of a sentence. I finally gave up the beginning, and went straight to the Pythagorean concepts to see what he wrote about travel.

And it was there, the spell I looked for. The spell to be in two places at once. I was now on my way, so close I could almost taste it. I just had to wait for the full moon.

CHAPTER 17

I hadn't seen the goblin since that night we went to Auld Meg's and I hadn't missed him either, so when he showed up on my tail again I was inclined to ignore him. But he was having none of it, he stayed glommed to my side like an old piece of gum stuck to a shoe.

It was the day of the full moon, and I still hadn't found the perfect place to enact the spell. Nachtan had told me not to bother coming in that Saturday morning, so rather than hang around Mrs. Mac's house and get in Patsy's way, I wandered the town.

Since Hugh had gone, I'd been lonely with no one for company but Mrs. Mac and Patsy and the Venerable Nachtan. I'd never taken Hugh up on his suggestion to go out and try to make friends at a pub night or anything – that wasn't me. I'm more of a loner, but I was feeling the absence of companionship.

My power had been building for the past few days, I could feel it thrumming in my veins, and I welcomed that absolute sense of well-being that I remembered from the previous month. I was relieved too, for Willem had hinted it might not be reliable. But it was, and I was there and I was loving it.

Practical magic, that was the thing. I'd studied the hell out of the spell I'd found in Nachtan's translated book. I knew the words backwards and inside out. I'd even studied the original Greek pronunciation, just in case that made a difference, though it shouldn't. Intention was everything in magic, right?

I wandered over to Mound Place, along the route Hugh and I had taken to get to his flat. The sky was a brilliant blue with not a cloud in the sky, a warm spring day with little breeze. From this vantage point, I could see the emerging new green of the many trees in the Prince's Street Garden below and beyond. Beautiful, yes, but full of houses and buildings and people. I turned back to the Royal Mile. I needed to find the perfect spot in which to perform the spell and it had to be that night. Preferably somewhere away from people, not too built up on, somewhere...

'You still owe me a red scarf.'

He was trip-tripping alongside me, his red boots a little worse for wear.

'Don't owe you anything.'

'Cheap witch b...' I didn't quite catch his last word, but it wasn't spoken with vehemence so I didn't take offence. We fell into step like old companions.

'Cake?'

I looked at him from the sides of my eyes. He hadn't changed any. Still the filthy stocking cap covering up the greasy bristles on his head, still had the jaunty way of sneering at everyone around him. And I still had some questions for him.

'Okay.' We stopped in front of a cafe with its delights on display in the window. 'What're you having?'

He got up close to peer in and I hauled him back. 'Don't make a mess on the window. Someone has to clean that every day.'

'That one,' he said, a long claw pointing to the tallest, most chocolatey confection. The layers of cake were held together with cocoa butter cream and the sides were covered in white coconut.

I carried the cakes in their napkins till we were sitting on our customary seat at the base of the statue outside of St. Giles'. He reached over to grab his portion but I held it out of his reach. I had to ask him something that had been bothering me since the night I'd met Auld Meg.

'Were you working with Willem?'

He gaped at me, showing all his needlelike teeth. 'No!' he squawked with his hand over his heart for sincerity. 'I'd never...'

Of course I didn't believe him. 'Did the Kin get him afterwards?'

He looked to the ground and nodded.

'He's all locked up?'

Trevor shrugged, still not meeting my eye. 'Or whatever it is they do with law-breaking wizards. Now can I please have that cake?'

'Ha! I didn't think you knew the P word,' I said as I handed the sweet to him. I still suspected him of working with Willem, and he must have been embarrassed about it. But if Willem was safely locked away, there was no reason I couldn't use Trevor too. After all, he needed to get his daily cake from someone.

According to the text Nachtan had translated from Pythagorus, the actual place of the spell was of the utmost importance. It had to be a high area on a ley line preferably, those lines of magical energy which transverse the globe. Usually, the earliest inhabitants of an area had already sussed out these places and declared them holy. They're often marked with standing stones and burial sites, temples and churches. Scotland was full of these places, so it should be fairly easy to find one close to home.

And a local goblin would know the best of these.

'What do you want to see?' He hadn't thanked me for the cake, but at least he was holding back on the insults for a change.

'How about some place that's, I don't know, holy?'

'Like a church?' he asked rudely, again spraying the chocolate crumbs at me. 'There's nothing holy left in this town. The Christians are everywhere, in case you haven't noticed,' he said nastily. 'Oh, look, there's a church. Hey. Another church.' He stood in the middle of the street and pointed each time he said the C word. 'Ooh, what's that huge spire down there in the valley? Could it possibly be... another church?'

I tried to flick the soggy crumbs off my front. 'What do you have against churches? They're sort of harmless. In fact, they teach peace and love and tolerance, instead of telling people to kill nasty super natural creatures like goblins.'

He stuck out his lower lip and might have spit on the ground if his mouth wasn't full of cake.

'Your kind should be happy that there are so many churches,' I added, to make sure the zing found its target.

'I don't like them because they take over the true holy places in the land,' he said after he swallowed. 'They mess up the energies for the rest of us.'

I could sort of see his point, and besides, for my purposes I would need a place that wasn't full of human beings wandering around and gawking. An outside spot would suit me better, one that didn't get locked up at night. 'Well, are there any spots around here that you consider holy that haven't been built over?'

'There are a few. But I don't know if I want to show them to you, being a human and all.'

'I'm a witch,' I reminded him, but that didn't sway him.

'Oh look,' I said suddenly, pointing into the tourist shop window across the road. 'That red scarf – it's the exact same shade as your boots.'

He turned and I could see the longing in his eyes which morphed into calculation, as I thought it might.

'Okay,' he said reluctantly. 'I'll bring you to Arthur's Seat. But you have to buy me the scarf first.'

·········

He was quite the sight as he led me through the Royal Mile, for those who had the eyes to see him. Carefully tap-tapping down the cobbled stones in his red heeled boots with the new scarf flapping in the wind, even his cap was set at a jaunty angle. Trevor was the proudest goblin I'd ever seen. The red looked good on him, I realized, sort of cancelling out the natural greenish pallor of his skin.

'Where're you taking me?'

He pointed further down to the end of the road, to a tall hill off to the right. 'There. That's Arthur's Seat. Though of course Arthur was never here, that's just a load of bollocks made up by stupid humans.'

I stopped to take a good look at the rocky summit. 'No church on the spot? That's odd, isn't it,' I thought aloud. 'It's the perfect place for a monastery, you'd think.'

'The King protected it for us,' he replied with a toss of his cap. 'That's the palace of Holyrood, down below it, see, in amongst all the trees.'

'Oh, it's inside the palace estate,' I said. This was not promising. 'I was really looking for a place that would be accessible after dark.'

'Oh?' His eyes lit up at that bit of information and he was onto it like a dog with a rat. 'Why? What are you doing at night?'

Shit. I should have known better than to speak aloud. I certainly didn't want to be dragging a goblin with me to the Ice Kingdom, no matter how well dressed he was. 'Never mind,' I told him firmly. 'That's not your business.'

'Hmph.' He kicked a chip wrapper out of his way. 'You shouldn't have secrets from me. I'm helping you, in fact I'm your only friend here.'

Never in a million years would I have described our relationship as a friendship, but I let that go and hoped he would too.

We were drawing close to the hill, and I was pleased to note there were no gates or wall surrounding it. The sign at the footpath even stated the park was open twenty-four hours a day. Today was Saturday, so there was no charge for us to enter. I wanted to climb in daylight first before attempting it in the middle of the night, moonlit though it would be, just to make sure this was the right location for my plans. I didn't know exactly what I was looking for – perhaps vibes, perhaps just the general setting.

There was a road which wound around the hill to the summit, but Trevor led me up over the rocky crags, straight as the crow flies. It was alright for a goblin, even one in high heels, but it was not easy on this human.

'So why did you want to come here?' Trevor couldn't let it go. We were now sitting at the summit, the Seat. Edinburgh spread out before us in the valley below.

This was the perfect spot. I closed my eyes and looked for the magic within the hill. There, I could feel it buzzing, the ley lines humming and doing their thing. This would do fine. I began to feel excited as I realized how close my plans were coming to fruition.

'I want to commune with nature, alright?' I replied shortly. 'That's all. I miss the wild from back home.'

I could feel his eyes burning into me. To take his mind off my business, I reached into my satchel for the stash of chocolate Hugh had bought me which I hadn't eaten and brought a Dairy Milk bar out of my satchel, dangling it before him. He refused to be teased, snatching the whole thing from my hand and disappearing it into his mouth, plastic wrapper and all. I could only look on horrified as he slowly spit the purple shiny material out, sucking out every last bit of taste as he did so.

'You are really the most disgusting creature I've ever met.' And that was saying something, for I'd experienced the Alt of the old sailing port in my home town.

'You're just annoyed that I'm cleverer than you,' he told me, then he sat back to enjoy the sugar rush.

I had all the elements I needed. The words to the spell, the perfect location and my intention. And the moon was at its fullest, with the power thrumming in me as I sat here on the high spot. I was quite proud of myself.

And I was content to ignore the old adage that states Pride Cometh Before the Fall. After all, I was invincible, or close enough.

CHAPTER 18

S he was in the kitchen of Mrs. Mac's, finishing off the evening supper dishes, standing on her stepping stool to reach the sink. She turned at the sound of my voice, casting a sharp eye up and down the length of me.

"Patsy. I'm going out tonight,' I told her in a low voice. 'Can you keep Mrs. Mac at bay again?'

She wasn't nearly so happy about it this evening, not like last time.

'What are you up to?'

'I'm just... going out to do something I need to do,' I said. And under her hard stare I added, 'I might be a while. Like a day or two.'

'You're practically glowing,' she said. 'That time is upon you.' She jutted out her chin while she thought.

'I know you're doing something they wouldn't like,' she said finally. 'But what'll I tell Mrs. Mac?'

'I don't know.' I hadn't thought about my landlady's reaction if I didn't show up for breakfast tomorrow morning. 'Tell her I'm not well or something. It's not like she'll bother to check on me, is it?'

The Brownie nodded reluctantly. 'Alright then. But what about if Mister Hugh asks?'

I relaxed at her acquiescence. She'd had me worried there for a moment. 'Oh, don't worry about him, he's still out of the country on Kin business. But if on the off chance you're speaking with him, tell him I've gone to get Mom. He'll understand.'

....

Armed with nothing but my book and my intention, I slipped out of the house while it was still dusk, for I didn't want to waste a moment. The streets I followed were quiet, I could hear snatches of revelry carried on the wind in the clear night coming from the hard core pubs as the students celebrated their weekend off from studies, but they did not cross my path, nor I theirs. Even so, it felt like unseen eyes were behind me, although I could see no one else. I kept to the shadows where I could.

At last I stood at the foot of Arthur's Seat. I could have easily taken the road up to the summit, the moon shone so brightly, but instead I went cross country, taking the route Trevor had shown me. The uphill climb didn't bother me at all this time, the energy was pulsing through me like a strobe and I had plenty to draw on. The more I used, it seemed, the more came to me. I felt like I could have run up the hill that evening and not even breathed hard with the effort.

I had no need of a flashlight to light my way even over the rough rocky land, for my eyes were attuned to the tiniest pebble and blade of grass. I could see my skin glowing silver, even in the parts where the light of the moon didn't reach. At this moment of time, with the pulse of the Stone's power humming through my body, I was invincible.

Once I reached the summit, the sun had fully set. Edinburgh spread out before me at my feet, and off in the distance behind me the moon danced on the choppy waters of the sea like an extension of the city lights. Holyrood Castle was invisible behind the dark trees, and there was no other soul around me – I was alone in the midst of a barren wilderness. I was on top of the world, physically and mentally.

I laughed into the ever present wind and tied my hair back to stop it whipping back and forth. This was it then.

There was no need for me to open the book in which I'd copied the spell that evening while waiting for the time to come, I'd memorized it by heart, in the original Greek. I'd Googled a free site which helped you speak like a native, going over and over the pronunciation. I'd thought this added touch was a stroke of genius.

Some people think that in order for a spell to be effective, you need all sorts of external props like pentagrams and candles and incense, but it's not true, especially when the spell caster has the confidence I carried that night. I had me, the power of the Crystal Charm Stone, and my intention and the thrum of the ley lines in the very rock itself, and I should need nothing more to carry me away off to the northern court of the Ice King.

Even the spell itself shouldn't have been necessary, nor the added power of Arthur's Seat, but as it was my first time attempting this kind of action, I bowed to tradition.

I closed my eyes and began the chant, feeling the meaning of each word as it was spoken, and weaving its place into my intention. The wind continued to whip all around me, bringing with it only the far off cries of gulls. After hard concentration and total absorption in my task, I opened my eyes ready to be dazzled by the wonders of the Ice King's throne room. However, there was nothing but the lights of Edinburgh, unchanged from moments before.

What went wrong? I traced back the steps I'd taken in my mind. Perhaps I shouldn't have tried saying the spell in the original Greek – no matter the wonders of the internet, perhaps I'd gotten something mispronounced. No matter, I knew the words I needed in English, too.

I rested for a moment, facing north towards my destination, and took a deep breath. It was important to remain calm and to be centered and confident in all matters when casting spells. Once again, I closed my eyes and pictured the Ice King's cavernous throne room, and my mother in her plain dress. Another deep breath, and I intoned the words aloud, in English this time, all the while feeling my intention like it was reality.

And again, nothing happened.

Fighting against the panic rising in my mind, I furiously thought through all the steps. Everything had been done perfectly and my intention was pure. Perhaps I needed to rethink my approach.

I sat on the highest rock while I sorted things out in my mind. Firstly, the basis of this whole spell was to be in two places at one time, as Pythagorus had outlined. Perhaps I'd been concentrating my intention solely on being in the Ice Kingdom. After all, the old Greek philosopher magi hadn't really explained about the intention part. That must be where I'd gone wrong, for I could think of no other thing that wasn't perfect in my preparation.

Could I intend to be in two places at once? How did that even feel? If I couldn't imagine it, then there was no way this whole plan would work. I cursed aloud at my stupidity, my ignorance, my lack of knowledge, then pulled myself together.

Back in the early days at home, when I'd just discovered the existence of Alt, I'd learned to be very careful about the time I spent there. I had gotten to the point where I could be in both realities at once – like straddling a fence, I could see my own world, with a shadowy Alt superimposed.

It had been a game back then, but this was for real, with very high stakes involved. Was this what I needed to aim for?

The spell had to work this time. Drawing the deepest breath yet, I stood again and faced north.

In my loudest voice, I intoned the words with force, all the while holding myself, my mind, in the two places at once. I was here in this reality on the summit of Arthur's Seat with the city spread below me at my feet, and yet I was also in the cold kingdom, by the great fireplace and beside my mother. I could almost reach out and touch her.

But it was only almost, and it was only in my imagination.

I opened my physical eyes to great disappointment, yet again. I sat on my rock once more and slumped.

Was it me? Had I been too anxious, tried it too soon? Perhaps I should have waited six hours until the moon had reached its absolute zenith. Stupid, stupid. I could kick myself. All this power running through my veins and I couldn't even smarten up enough to do things properly. I let out a roar which surprised even me. I put my whole self into that long cry which came straight from my heart, all my emotions of anguish, self-doubt and plain old annoyance at being Dara Martin.

Thunder cracked directly overhead, and lightning forked dangerously close to my perch. I looked up, way up, to a dome of roiling clouds. The moon was still off to the west, and the sky was clear all around except directly over my head. The skies lit up again, and then came the rain crashing down in a sheet.

'For the love of...' I brought my jean jacket over my head, not that it would do much good to keep me from being drenched, and I scurried along the slippery path to find shelter of some kind. There was an old ruin, a tiny ancient chapel by the looks of it, just down around the bend in the path nestled into a small dale, and I approached its stone walls, huddling there to avoid the worst of the rain.

'You're a feckin' idiot, like I said,' Trevor slumped against the wall next to me, water dripping off his long nose. He looked at me. 'Just stop this, would ye?'

'What? Where did you come from?' I asked him, my voice raised over the howling wind. 'Were you spying on me?'

'Of course,' he yelled back at me. 'Ye wouldn't tell me what you were at, I had no choice, did I? You're awfy stingy, anyone ever tell you that? Now, stop this storm. It's washing all my protective layer away.'

I looked down at the sodden ground, the puddles growing larger by the moment.

'I don't know how to stop it.'

'Ye don't know crack, if you ask me. Not much of a witch then, and you supposed to be this big, new scary power,' he said, rolling his eyes. 'Don't know why I bother hanging out with you, ye're not very good at it. You're more of an embarrassment if you ask me.'

I didn't know how to stop the storm I'd caused, but the weather did lessen somewhat as I turned my attention away from my anguish and the downpour, and fixated on the nasty little goblin.

'No one's asking you, don't you get it? And if you don't like the rain, then move away from my cloud.'

'That's better.' He stood and peered over the wall. 'It's starting to move down to Leith. That place could do with a cleaning.'

We watched together as the tiny storm moved off, dissipating into the wind, carrying with it my anger and self-loathing.

'You really screwed that up, whatever it was you were trying to do.' He couldn't resist sneering at me.

The goblin's jabs couldn't hurt me, for I was willing to admit the truth. 'I know.'

He shifted uncomfortably beside me, then reached up and removed his cap. I looked at the sparse bristles growing on his bald pate while he wrung out the sopping wool.

'What were you trying to do, anyway?' he asked casually. 'Why would you want to bring a storm down on your own head?'

'That's not what...' I began, then stopped. Why bother explaining? 'It didn't work. I don't know why. The Kin were right, I'm just a screw-up.'

I slumped against the damp stone wall, squatting down on my haunches. 'It's no good, I'll never be able to rescue my mother!' And with that the tears began, building to a torrent to outmatch the storm which had just passed.

Trevor squirmed, uncertain how to handle this new storm, hopping from red boot to red boot. 'Don't do that,' he said finally. 'Stop it, okay? Stop blubbering, I can't insult you when you get like that.'

'I can't help it,' I whined through my tears. 'My life is just so shit right now. I'm stuck here, my power is at its max with the full moon, yet I can't even do a simple thing like go to the Ice Kingdom to save her. I am so useless. I'm no witch at all.'

He stiffened at my side, then grabbed my shoulders with both his hands. 'Ice Kingdom? You're still on about that?' He sounded aghast.

I nodded, the flow of tears already ebbing. 'Yeah. Of all places, right? And apparently you can't get there from here. I tried, but I failed.'

'You've actually found a way to the Ice Kingdom?'

'That's the problem, isn't it? I thought I did, but I haven't. I really thought I could do it – I prepared, I translated spells, my power is surging with the full moon and it should have happened but it didn't. All I got was the storm cloud of my own frustration.'

I opened my eyes to see his round ones staring back at me, not six inches away. A goblin's eyes are foreign, in the way a cat's eyes are with the vertical slit instead of a round pupil, yet I could see his reluctance. His breath was sour.

'The Ice Kingdom,' he repeated glumly. The goblin appeared to be lost in thought for a moment and then he wandered away from the stones of the ruined chapel to gaze at the city below. When he turned his face towards me again, it was touched with darkness and urgency.

'If you want to go to the Ice Kingdom tonight, then we'd better get the feck off this hill,' he said. 'The Uncommon Forces are gathering at the base, and looks like they want to join the party.'

I ran over to join him at the edge, almost slipping in the wet grass in my haste, and looked to where he was pointing.

'I don't see anything but shadows down there.' I squinted and shook my head. 'Those are just the shadows of the trees in the wind.'

'What wind?'

It was true. After my own personal thunder storm had moved on to Leith, the hill had been eerily quiet, not a breeze even though we were up so high. I looked down again. The shadows were moving, spreading out over the base of the hill.

'They must have been alerted by my spell,' I spoke breathlessly. 'Shit. Cromwell will not be pleased.'

The goblin looked at me with horror in his eyes. '*Not be pleased*? That's an understatement. How can you be so blasé? Them down there, they kill first and ask questions later. Don't know about you, but I'm getting the hell out of here.'

He pushed past me over toward the western aspect of the hill, and when he saw I was rooted to the spot, almost screamed at me. 'Come on, damnit! We need to get out of here now!'

I was still watching in horror as the swarming blackness grew and climbed up the base of the hill. 'They wouldn't... touch me,' I said to him. 'The Kin want me, they...'

'It's not the Kin!! Does Cromwell like you? Those shady bastards down there answer only to him, and I'm thinking he'd sooner see you dead than a powerful witch. Am I right?'

He was right. He was so right. I turned on my heel and followed him through the knee high grass and gorse. We were fleeing for our lives.

CHAPTER 19

I had no way of knowing if Cromwell's forces were following us along the hills, for the night was now pitch black. The moon's light was uncertain as it sailed between clouds. He led me through secret paths known only to goblins and rabbits down the other side of Arthur's Seat, through a wooded park until at last, we came to the bottom by a paved road lit by streetlights, but not a single car in sight.

'Quick,' he said as he lifted up a heavy storm drain. 'Down here. They probably can't follow our scent in water.'

I looked down into the pitch dark hole. I couldn't see a thing, but the sound of liquid sluggishly flowing seemed a long way down.

'It's just storm water,' he sneered. 'It's the old system they haven't gotten rid of yet. Don't worry, you won't be running in shit. Now go down fast, I've got to close this behind us.'

So I climbed down the rusted iron rungs at the side of the outlet. I heard the clank as the cover dropped into place and the goblin leapt past me and splashed into the water. It came to about my knees, at exactly the height that made moving through it difficult. Not for Trevor though, he scarpered on ahead of me, moving as if he'd lived in sewers all his life, all the while whispering furiously at me to get my ass in gear.

We ran and ran that night. Fortunately for me, the power of the Stone still coursed through me even underground so I didn't tire or flag, and found I could even keep up with Trevor as we made our way upriver.

My sight adjusted quickly down here, with the help of my moon powers. I could even see the glint of eyes of the subterranean creatures we passed, rats perhaps, or something ungodly. I didn't pause to investigate. At last he stopped by another set of iron rungs leading up. I could feel a slight breeze, and the overhead grate showed the dim light of a streetlamp.

Before I could grasp the first rung to haul myself up, he stopped me. 'So what's your plan now?'

I shrugged in defeat. 'I don't know. Guess I won't be trying for the Ice Kingdom now. I'll just find my way home and dry off, if I don't die of pneumonia first.' The stream had only come to my knees, but running through it had caused splashing and I was soaked from the waist down, and my jeans were chafing my thighs. I was cold and miserable and a failure.

'You think it's safe for you out there?'

'Oh come on! Cromwell's forces were just investigating the unknown flash of magical activity, that's all, especially as it was so close to Holyrood Palace. It's their job,' I told him. 'It was a dumb place to choose anyway, I should have gone outside the city to try it. Just didn't think it through enough.' I shrugged off his hand and turned to the rungs again.

'You really believe that?' The sneer in his voice made me stop. 'You really think Cromwell will let you go so easily now he has an excuse to do away with you?'

I climbed off that first rung and stared at him in the dim glow of the streetlight above.

'How do you know so much about the Kin's doings, any-way?'

'I keep my ears to the ground,' he said bitterly. 'You have to, being a Goblin in this town. I'm a survivor. Had enough of my fellows used as casual target practice by Cromwell's blessing. This is the perfect opportunity for him to get rid of you.'

'He won't know I was involved...' I faltered. Of course he would. My magic imprint was on that thunderstorm, just like I'd signed my signature or left greasy thumbprints all over it. 'Well, you're safe, at any rate.'

'Oh, no. The Uncommon Forces smelled me, you can be sure of that,' he said glumly. 'And they've probably put out an all-points bulletin on both of us, right now.'

My legs were suddenly shaky like they were made of jelly, and if there'd been a seat in that sewer, I would have sat. 'What can we do? Where do we go?'

'Even the Ice Kingdom sounds pretty good right now.'

I gave a half-laugh, what else was there to do? 'Apparently, I can't get there from here,' I said. It was my turn to be bitter now. Here I was, supposedly such a powerful witch, and I couldn't even manage a simple Pythagorean spell during the almost full moon and at a ley line meeting place to boot. 'I've just shown that I'm a spectacular failure at getting there.'

'Yes,' Trevor agreed. 'You can't. But you know who can.'

'Oh, no. No way,' I shook my head. 'It's all bad enough, the trouble I'm in now. Not going to add that one to my list of crimes.'

'Auld Meg is your only chance,' he said, pushing me out of the way as he leaped up to grab the first rung. 'I don't think this is the time to get all moralistic on me, not now.'

··········

As Trevor pushed the iron grate back into place, I straightened up and looked all around me. We were back under the shadow of the bridge again, near the entrance to the Vaults. I shook each leg out to encourage the water to drain off my heavy jeans, but it didn't do too much to help. I stood in my own growing puddle of storm water as the water seeped out of my boots and onto the cobbles.

'We're going to need another bottle of whisky for the troll.'

'I can't do this,' I said. 'I can't... Do you realize what this means for me, for my future? Auld Meg thinks I can free her from this curse, and that's the only way she'll help me.'

'And the alternative is...' He stood there under the street-light with his damp little goblin sneer. 'Look, you've only got to steal the Chronicle. She said all the information is written in it. It's not like you're going to be freeing her – I doubt very much that you could break the curse put on her by the Kin! And if we run fast enough, well, she can't just leave the dungeon, now, can she?'

I sighed, because he was right about everything. He was right about Cromwell, and the Uncommon Forces were going to catch up with us sooner or later this evening. Sure, I was a powerful witch tonight– even with all that was happening I could feel the unnatural energies thrilling through me, but I had no way of defending us against the magical forces at Cromwell's disposal. I didn't have the education to match my powers, and I had no idea how to handle them.

And Cromwell wasn't going to let this sit. It wasn't just tonight, it was the rest of my future. Hugh and Johanna might try to protect me if I could reach their safety, but until then?

Why did Hugh have to be away right now? Surely, he would know I'd need him at this point of the moon's cycle. I needed him right now, but he wasn't here.

And I might never get another chance to reach my mother. Would I even survive till the next full moon, let alone to the point in time where I could defend myself against Cromwell and his forces? There were no guarantees of anything.

And that's when I made my decision. I wasn't running from the Covenanters, I was stepping firmly in the direction of my future. Yes, there would be a good chance I would end up being an outlaw after tonight, but I would have saved my mother, and that was more important to me than anything.

I took a deep breath and moved away from the arch to stand in the full light of the moon and I bathed in it, letting it wash through every pore of me. The magic rose to greet it and felt my power. Make it last, this good feeling, it might be the last time.

'The bottle?' Trevor was getting nervous, and moved out of the lamp's reach. He flicked his head at the news agent's. 'Ye'll have to buy another.'

I reached out the plastic rainbow hued card, then realized what would happen if I used the Kin's own credit card. Might as well phone Cromwell personally to let him know where I was.

'Let's hope we have enough cash here.' I took off my satchel and rooted around in the pocket where I always stuffed loose change. I counted out what I found. 'He'll have to be happy with a smaller bottle.'

After I'd given the guy behind the counter all my cash, Trevor knocked at the troll's door and then I heard a ring tone from deep within my bag. It was Hugh. But I'd made my decision and what was the sense of telling him? He couldn't help me now. I reached down into the bottom of my bag and pressed the side button to turn it off, then followed the goblin into the witch's dungeon.

The corridors were still long and blacker than night, with all the weird noises echoing around the damp stone walls. I followed the goblin, looking neither left nor right. I wished the journey would take longer, but it seemed to take less time the second time round, as journeys are wont to do.

We paused outside Auld Meg's chamber.

'Maybe...' I placed my hand on my companion's shoulder. 'Maybe we shouldn't.'

He turned to give me a searching stare in the light of his candle stub. 'Go on back out there then. Go on.'

I grimaced. He was right. Ridiculous to be having second thoughts now. I took a deep breath and walked boldly into Auld Meg's dungeon.

Her eyes were the only thing that moved, and they glittered in the dim lights.

Trevor poked me, urging me to act. I took a step forward, then when Auld Meg didn't move, took another. I saw the smallest of smiles form on her face as if the stone was almost a fluid medium, dust flaking off as the crevices formed. Yet she still did not attempt to stop me.

Emboldened I crossed the room and stood before her, ready to leap back at the slightest movement from her, yet still she did nothing.

'Take it quick!' Trevor squeaked. And just as I moved my hand to lay it on the Chronicle, she began to laugh.

I withdrew my hand as fast as I could, yet the sound coming from her wasn't malevolent or scary or threatening, none of the things I'd been expecting. It was a clear tinkle, overlain with a century or more of dust to be sure, but an amused laugh nevertheless, for all the world as if we were sitting down for tea in a period drama and I'd just delighted my hostess with a witty remark. Transfixed, I could do nothing but stare at the crone.

'Yes, Dara Martin de Teilhard,' the statue said, moving her neck ever so slightly to follow me with her gaze. 'Take the Chronicle.' As she spoke, fine particles of dust fell from her face and her hair, swirling in unseen currents of air.

I stepped further back, uncertain.

'It has everything a young witch needs to know,' she said. The pure tones of her voice belied her age and appearance. 'All the knowledge I have gained. All the spells I learned. How to travel through the dimensions, even, if one would want to rescue one's mother from the Ice King, for example.'

'How do you know?' I gasped.

'You tell me.' The crone leaned towards me. The sand was trickling away from her whole body, and with it the wrinkles on her face that had seemed etched in the stone. 'I am the only one who can help you. Not the handsome Hugh Sabiston, not the Venerable Nachtan in his ivory tower and his books. I am the one who knows all.'

'How?' I whispered again. 'How can you know all this if you've been stuck in a dungeon for so many years without even seeing so much as the light of day?'

'I have been within myself,' she said. 'You think mere stones and spells can hold my mind? You too, have this power, you can never be held, not truly.'

I stared at her, her eyes burning colorless grey yet there were flickers of violet deep within, lined by the coal of the shadows, and my resolve faltered, melting under her gaze. 'But...'

Still I couldn't, wouldn't. If only there was another way.

'Take the book. Think of your mother, Dara.'

And then I did it. I stepped forward, all the while denying to myself that I was actually doing this, leaping the chasm to my uncertain future. I approached the Chronicle, keeping a wary eye on the witch as I did, alert for her slightest movement. She did nothing, merely watched me the whole time.

It sat there, dusty and foreboding on the table before her. A simple act, to place my hands on it and remove it from the dungeon, to take it with me and to irrevocably change my life.

My hands were on the book and a flash of power like blue lightning ran through my arms. It burned but was delicious too, perhaps like the first rush of heroin in the veins of an addict. And in that touch, I was overcome with impressions of Margaret's life, of old fashioned dresses and finery, of Scottish burns and glens on lazy summer afternoons, of a tiny stone castle shared with an illicit lover. Her eyes flared as I snatched my hands away, leaving the Chronicle on the table.

'Take the book,' she urged. 'It's your only chance of survival now.'

She was right, I was in too deeply to turn back now. As I tried to pick it up and ignore everything that flowed from the book to my head, sparks flew in all directions, and I wrestled with the weight of it as if dislodging a boulder from deep within the ground, or a sword from a stone.

And then I was holding it in my arms, the ancient leather and wood binding cracked and dusty, the foolscap vellum stiff. I had the impression that if I listened very closely, I could hear the song it was singing. I quickly stuffed it into my satchel, to avoid the touch of it on my bare skin, and the impressions died away as fast as they had come. 'But...'

'But how does this help me, you want to know.' She was relaxed now, her voice softer. A silvery light came from her body, much as my own skin shone during the full moon. Like it was doing now.

'I am not cursed to this dungeon, as such,' she said, as she reached her hand to her head and removed her hat. Her movements were slow, as if unused to the movement. 'I am cursed to stay with the book, until the Chronicle is finished.'

She shook out her hair, combing it with her hands. 'Christ, I need to bathe, it's been far too long,' she muttered, then looked back over at me. 'The Kin were not punishing me,' she continued. 'But harnessing my power to foresee the future. Until the Chronicle is finished, they cannot take it from me.'

'So why can I? How am I able to hold the book?' It weighed heavy in my bag, dragging my shoulder down.

'Because it is mine still and I have given you permission.' She drew herself up to her full height. I could hear the bones of her spine cracking as she stretched her arms out and over-head, yawning as she did so. 'Until it is fully written, it belongs to me. When they cursed me, they failed to understand this basic law of nature, of publishing, if you will. The author owns all copyright, controls all that happens within their book, until it is set free into the world.'

'So if you never finish it, you won't die?'

'When I die, it is finished,' she replied enigmatically.

'But why haven't you just simply left with the book, if they can't tie you down?'

'Ah child, there's the rub. The cunning Kin cursed the book, also,' she said bitterly. 'I could set quill to page, but never remove it from this place. That's where they concentrated their defensive spells, weaving such a web that I couldn't break it. Yet, in their own fear, they never dreamt that another would do so. You will break that curse. I, however, am still bound to the book, so must follow where ever it goes.'

She laughed, a deep belly laugh this time and the dust danced in the faint light. 'Oh the unseeing Kin. Hoist by their own petard,' she said. 'They didn't have the genius to imagine another Meg. They teach their own children so well, filling them with the fear of me so that none would follow in my footsteps, yet they ignored this half-blood's education, and brought her right to my own door-step. It is ridiculous, yet fitting.'

CHAPTER 20

Auld Meg had lost her years along with the dust, and the woman now standing before me could have been no more than forty, a witch at the prime of her powers, her hair glinting red under the flakes of rock she couldn't shake out.

'Now, come let us depart this loathsome hole. I long to breathe the night air and to worship at Athena's feet once more. We have much to do, and miles to go.'

She turned to leave the accursed chamber.

'Wait!'

The witch paused and looked back at me over her shoulder. She gave a grimace and stretched her neck muscles on either side, still working out the kinks from a century of sitting still.

'My mother,' I began, then gathered up the nerve. 'How are we going to free my mother?'

'Who said anything about freeing her?'

'You did.'

'Did I? I don't recall that.'

'But that's why I'm here, the only reason I came down to your dungeon.' A rage began to creep over me as I clutched the heavy book to my chest. 'We need to do that. Or else... or else I'm not leaving with your Chronicle.' I put my chin in the air and stood firm.

Trevor's jaw dropped at my boldness, and I was rather taken aback too. Here I was, Dara Martin, despised half-blood, challenging the wickedest, most legendary figure in the Kin, Auld Meg. She was plenty scary, but I was sick of someone else wanting to use my power. No, I was going to get what I came for, or the book would stay in the dungeon and Auld Meg with it. She could rot here, it wasn't my problem.

Meg drew herself up to her fearsome height, the dust and phosphorescence sparkling all around in the whirlwind she'd created. The flakes of stone cracked off, flying in all directions.

'Child.' her voice was terrible and echoed through the chamber. Gone was her nonchalant air. 'You dare to defy me?'

'You need me,' I said. It was true. She couldn't move outside the Vaults without my help. If I didn't carry the book out of the room, then she would be stuck here forever. It hummed by my side. 'And I'm not a child. I'm an adult witch. And blessed with the power of the Stone, you said so yourself. I don't have to help you.'

We were at an impasse and stared at each other through the whirling dust. It was a long moment.

She was the first to crack. 'It is not the time to rescue your mother,' she said slowly.

'Then it is not the time to release you from the curse,' I shot right back at her. I made to return the Chronicle back to the table at which she had sat for the past century or more.

'NO!' This time her voice thundered with enough force to rock the whole structure of the Vaults. Nothing moved in the silence that followed except for the trickle of cement dust from the domed ceiling.

Then she gave a deep sigh. 'Dara, please listen to me. The time is not right. There is so much to do before this,' she waved her hand as if swatting a fly. But she was talking about my dream. My driving force. The whole reason I had ended up in this damn country in the first place. I was not letting go.

I placed my satchel on the table's surface, my fingers lingering against the warmth coming through the canvas fabric. It almost felt alive beneath my touch, and it caused an itching inside me like I wanted to open it and devour the power within.

What I could do with the powerful secrets inside this book. She said herself that the way to the Ice Kingdom was written inside. But no, I couldn't take the book, for that would free Auld Meg, and this was my only weapon I could hold over her. I looked up to see her eyes glittering in the last of the candle light.

'We can do this,' she said, weighing her words carefully. 'If you insist. But I have to warn you, I cannot guarantee the outcome of this action. You place yourself in great danger.'

'Surely with our combined power, no one can touch us. You said that yourself.' What was she playing at? Did she have any intention of helping me? Yet, if she was planning to trick me, why bother warning me of danger, why not simply agree, and laugh in my face once we'd left the dungeon? My hand hovered uncertainly over the satchel's flap.

'True, but we don't need to be causing difficulties for ourselves,' she said waspishly. 'Your mother can wait for a more auspicious time, she's in no hardship at the court of the Ice King.'

I stubbornly shook my head. 'No. Not good enough. If you want me to join forces with you, then you have to prove to me that you mean it. Only once we have my mom back from there. Not before.'

'You don't realize what you are setting in motion by these demands.'

'I don't care,' I repeated. What was the threat? I was blinded only by the overwhelming need to see my mother, hold her in my arms, smell the lemon scent of her soap.

'Fine,' she said in a voice which said it wasn't fine, not at all. 'Fine. We'll do as you demand. You'll take your mother back from the Ice King's court, and then we'll just have to pay the consequences and clean up the mess afterwards.'

I nodded. Her words made me feel just the tiniest bit apprehensive, as they were designed to do, but I was not going to let her manipulate me. I was bargaining with a powerful witch, and I had to use the upper hand while I still had it. 'How do I know I can trust you?'

Auld Meg looked flabbergasted. 'You don't know. None of us know if we can trust another. But if I give you my word, then that should do it,' she said, then her tone softened. 'Dara, we're on the same side, you and me. No need to fight it.'

I had to leave it at that, and hope she wasn't lying to me. For after all, she said she needed me, too, and if she betrayed my trust, I could easily withdraw my assistance. I hefted up my satchel over my shoulder again and nodded. 'Alright, then. Let's go.'

Meg hesitated. 'It really would be a better idea to do the mother rescuing thing at a later date,' she began, but when she saw my vigorous head shaking, she shrugged and gave up the battle. 'Have it your way, then, but don't say I didn't warn you. I have to follow where you go, since you're the one with the Chronicle.'

'We will need a third witch, of course,' she added.

'A third... But why? We've got more than enough power between the two of us, surely.'

'No, we need the triangulation,' she answered decisively. 'Hasn't Nachtan taught you anything about Pythagorus yet?'

I stared in dismay. A third witch, she was surely asking for the impossible. I thought quickly. Hugh was out of town, and I doubted he would help at any rate. Nachtan was out of the question.

There were those Kin kids we'd seen in the bar the other night, perhaps I could go and introduce myself and convince one of those bored trust-fund babies to risk their lives and future... As if. But I didn't know any other witches here in Edinburgh.

Except Fergie. My mind went quickly through the pros and cons of getting my (ex) friend involved. She had foresworn the Kin, but I could tell from the glamour about her that day that she hadn't given up magic practice altogether. And I knew where she lived.

'Alright,' I said, knowing full well I could be dragging Fergie to a ruined future. But there was a lot at stake.

·····•·•····

Margaret strode to the door of the chamber, no longer an ancient crone but a powerful witch in her prime, yet she was unable to move through the portal until I did so. Once through the door, though, I could feel her relax and she easily took the stone stairs up into the open air.

She walked through the endless dark corridors of the Vaults with no fears, treading the stone halls like a queen in her court. She held herself straight and her shoulders back. None of the apparitions or creatures of the dark dared approach her.

We came finally to the entrance portal which the troll was no longer guarding, since he was drunkenly snoozing in the corner again. She looked down her nose with disgust, but passed to the exit without comment. Once outside, she drew a deep breath, her face turned up to the almost full moon. 'I've missed you,' she purred, then shook her full hair again so the air became fraught with dust in the beams of silvery light.

I led them down the Cowgate, over to the part of town where I knew Fergie lived. We kept to the shadows as much as we could, but there were no signs of Cromwell's Uncommon Forces. Had they given up for the night? Perhaps I'd just been too paranoid. Too late, now that I'd gone and freed Auld Meg from her dungeon.

'For the interdimensional travel,' I said to Margaret as we walked. 'Do we need to go back up to Arthur's Seat?'

'What, here in Edinburgh?' She shook her head. 'That will never do, no. There are far too many Kin around these parts, and it's too close to the Covenanters.' We scurried to keep up with her as she strode along, whisking her long skirts out of the way impatiently. 'I really need a change of costume,' she muttered, then stopped and sized me up, drawing up her nose at my jeans and hoody.

'No,' she continued walking. 'We're not the same size. Your clothes simply will not fit. Thank God.'

'So where?' I pressed her, ignoring her implied insult. 'If we can't do it around here, how will we get there?'

She stopped again to think, her finger on her lip, then she nodded. 'I know the perfect place.'

'Where?' I asked urgently, but she brushed me aside.

We were getting close to Fergie's flat, and I found myself hoping she wasn't home. But we heard the party even before we turned the corner. Of course the noise was coming from the top floor, from Fergie's place.

I stared and looked up. 'Our third witch,' I said.

Margaret looked up doubtfully at the source of the racket that bounced off the stone walls of the buildings surrounding us. Shadows thronged at open windows and a steady thump-thump of bass emanated from the top story.

'Needs must,' Margaret muttered. The front door was wide open, so I led the way.

The party spilled out of the flat and down the stairs, perhaps the whole building was getting into the fun. I pushed through the crowd, followed closely by Margaret and Trevor. At the top, I couldn't see anyone for the mass of people. I had no idea if Fergie was even here.

Until I heard the shriek of laughter cutting above even the loudspeakers turned all the way up to eleven on the volume dial. I quickly pushed my way through the throng, for there was only one person I knew who could make laughter sound like the squealing of a cut pig.

There she was in the living room. Fergie, standing amongst a crowd of students, all equally with their sails in full hoist. The guys had the unmistakeable air of hard core future engineers, while the girls appeared to be on a '80's throwback party all of their own, the tarty glitter on their eyes fighting for attention with the massive piles of hair on their heads. Fergie, in her too-tight spangled tube top and red curls puffed out to their fullest, looked a little askew, as if her glamour had slipped a tad. Her bloodshot eyes showed she had been imbibing various substances for hours.

I stopped. It still wasn't too late. Until it was.

'Dara!' She welcomed me with an ear splitting scream. 'O-M-G! Is that really you? Never knew you were here in town too!'

She didn't question my appearance at her party.

'Fergie,' I said, without exclamation marks. 'You don't know how happy I am to see you.'

I really meant it, no matter that she'd hurt me by leaving Scarp so suddenly without even a hug good-bye. We hugged this time, and I drew her aside. 'Come over here,' I said. 'I have... some friends I want you to meet.'

I had passed the point of no return.

Chapter 21

'This is Margaret and Trevor...' I bit my lip.

Fergie first noticed Margaret in her full Edwardian Lady regalia.

'How do you do?' she said with an exaggerated curtsy. "Love the dress. Where'd you get it?' She then turned to the third member of our party and faltered.

'This is Trevor,' I said quickly. I threw a pleading look at Margaret. Surely to God she could see that Fergie was in no state to be our third witch.

She shrugged and said in a sotto voice, 'She'll sober up by the time we get there.'

Meanwhile Fergie had withdrawn the hand she'd held out, staring at Trevor with appalled fascination. 'Dara,' she said in a stage whisper. 'I need to tell you something.'

Trevor drew himself up to his small height with a frown and ignored Fergie as much as he could. I could see his feelings were hurt by her reaction, and there was going to be a lot of smoothing of ruffled bristles in our near future.

I bundled her in through the door marked with her name done in glitter glue.

'Dara,' Fergie slurred, still staring at the door which I'd just slammed behind us. 'I hate to tell you, but your boyfriend is a goblin.' She mouthed the last word, like some people mouth the word 'sex'.

'He's not my guy,' I said firmly. 'Now, I need your help with something.'

She sat on the bed, tucking her short glitter skirt in and finished off the bottle of beer she still clutched in her hand. 'Oops, time for another drink!'

'Never mind that for now,' I said. And sat on the bed beside her. How to begin? 'I never expected to see you here in Edinburgh, Fergie.' I was really pleased. Not just because she was my possible third witch, but she was my friend. 'How did you end up here? I thought you might be going back home to Glasgow.'

She beamed. 'I got into a hairdressing course,' she replied, and with her hand tossed back her helmet of hair, which didn't actually move. 'It's all I've ever really wanted to do, you know, add a bit of glamour to the girls on their special nights. I'm going to open my own, exclusive salon one day.'

She really was much happier away from the Kin snobberies of Scarp, and I was delighted for her.

'Y'know,' she said as she leaned closer. 'I felt bad about leavin' you. But everything was so weird, y'know? After that night? The Kin were weird, you were weird. Scarp was really, really weird.' She snorted with laughter now that the weirdness was so far away in time and distance.

'So Dara, how 'bout you?' Fergie leaned back on her elbows on the unmade bed and tried to focus on my face. 'Whatcha doin' here in town? Thought you'd be stuck on that horrible island.'

I shrugged. 'I'm studying at the castle,' I said. 'Special lessons.'

Her face clouded with incomprehension. 'The castle? There's no school there, just the Venerable Nachtan...' Her eyes bulged in astonishment and she only slurred her words a little. 'No! You're never! O-M-G.'

'Yeah, don't know if it's punishment or special treatment because of, you know, the Stone and all that.'

She looked at me with new, albeit very drunken, respect. 'You're my friend, and you're... Oh my,' she said. 'I know someone who's studying under the VN!' She looked around the bedroom as if searching for someone to share her news with.

I placed my hand on her arm. 'Don't tell anyone! I'm actually not supposed to be out past curfew,' I confessed. 'But, Fergie...

'Wha?' she beamed at me. 'Shit, you're glowing, just like before. It's that time of the month for you, isn't it?' This witticism sent her off into cackles of laughter, until the meaning of what she'd just said washed over her. The laughter trailed away to an uncertain note. I had to act quickly.

'Fergie, I really need your help in something.'

'Me? You need my help?' She leaned back in her chair, pride and wariness battling in her drunken haze, then she must have made an internal decision to dismiss the niggling voice in the back of her mind. 'I'm really sorry 'bout Scarp, but I want to make it up to you. I will do anything for you, Dara, anything. Just tell me, and I'm in.' She drained the bottle once again, in hopes to get the very last drops. 'Anythin' I can.'

The music in the next room turned up a notch, if that was even possible, and leaning over to whisper in Fergie's ear, I began.

'I've managed to free Auld Meg, only she's really not old at all, and she's going to bring me to the Ice Kingdom, but we need three witches to make it work, so will you please help me? Please?'

'Umm,' Fergie said. 'What was that bit about Auld Meg? You mean the legend?'

She shook her head, bleary eyed. 'Whatever it is you need, I'll do it. Like I said. I'm s'proud of you, and ye're m'friend. Come on, let's get a drink. This is a party, y'know.'

Her drunken logic wasn't really making sense, but no matter. I'd convinced her to help me, so I could relax. I skirted past the issue of whether drunken consent was really consent at all.

'Cheers,' I said before I downed the last of my own beer. 'Now, we have to get you kitted out.' I stared at the piles of clothing everywhere before picking out a pair of black jeans and a hoody like mine. She could leave the tube top on, there was no way I'd struggle to get a bra on her in this state. With the sneakers I found at the bottom of the wardrobe and her satchel slung over her shoulder, her ensemble was complete. I put the hood up over her hair so she could leave her party incognito.

The four of us made it past the partiers and outside to the street. I only had to tell Fergie we were leaving for an adventure a couple of times to get her down the stairs.

'Where now?' I asked Margaret.

'We'll need to get to Inverness.' She glanced up at the moon. 'Quickly.'

'Inverness?' Fergie echoed with worry in her voice. 'I've got class Monday morning,' she said. 'We're learning to do highlights. I can't miss that.'

'I don't suppose you have a driver?' Margaret asked me.

'No,' I said. 'I don't have a driver or a private vehicle! And I can't use the credit card either, the Kin would be on us in an instant.'

'Well, fortunately for you, my dearest Papa left me the trust with all its amenities,' she declared. With that she closed her eyes and began to intonate loudly, in a language I'd never heard before. Little sparkles of power flashed around her head, like the tiniest multi-coloured fireflies, dancing and pulsing in the air before dispersing into the ether in all directions.

'What is she doing?' I whispered to Fergie and Trevor.

'It's Gaelic,' the goblin replied, his eyes growing wider by the second until I thought they might pop with terror. 'She's calling on a Bodach. I thought they didn't really exist.'

'A Bodach?' Fergie wailed. 'What the hell have you gotten me into Dara?' She turned away from us. 'That's it. I'm out of here. I've got class, and I've got ideas for highlight spells, and I'm not missing out on that.'

I held her arm. 'Wait,' I said. 'What's a Bodach?'

'The motor carriage will be here shortly,' Margaret informed us. 'Ah, yes! There it is now.'

We all watched as a large vehicle slowly rolled out of a mist that had descended on Prince's Street. In the light of the moon, the body glinted red. It was ancient, one of the earliest motor cars I'd ever seen, looking more like a caricature of a car than a real vehicle. I'd seen pictures of Model T's from the States of that vintage, but it definitely wasn't of the same origin. The body was low on spindly wheels, elegantly curved and the hard top square and long. It snorted and rolled to a stop in front of us. I couldn't pick out the driver well, he or she or it was amorphous, grey of vaguely humanoid shape.

Margaret looked at us impatiently as we goggled at this ancient vehicle.

'Well, open the door for me!'

I rushed over to the car and found the handle and the door smoothly opened as if the car was still brand new, not over a century old. Margaret swept in and ensconced herself in the padded leather seat, spreading her skirts out over a full half of the bench so that only a small amount of room was left for me and Fergie to squish into.

Trevor jumped in at the last moment, although I tried to block him by shutting the door. He was forced to find accommodation on the footstool opposite us where he sat and glowered at me.

'Why are you coming?' I hissed at him. 'I thought you were afraid of the Ice King.'

'Never you mind,' he hissed back, spittle spraying across the expanse of the car at me. He took the opportunity to sneer at me before he resolutely turned his head away.

'We're not taking him with us!' I glanced over at Margaret. 'Just the three witches, that's all we need.'

The older witch laughed and flicked her fingers, brushing away my protests. 'Let him be,' she said. 'He doesn't take up too much room.'

'Ice King?' Fergie was coming out of her drunken haze a little. 'Wha' ye talking about? Where're you taking me, Dara?'

'We must go to Inverness, Bodie,' Margaret called to the driver, and the vehicle set off. The interior smelled of leather and wealth, with fine polished wood detail on the window frames and arm rests. I settled into its plummy cushioned seat.

'What she on about?' Fergie poked my side and hissed in my ear. 'And who is that gorgeous witch anyway?'

'Margaret, meet Fergie again,' I said with a sigh. Fergie had forgotten, if she'd even understood, that this was Auld Meg of the legends, but I wasn't about to explain right now.

She didn't look any the worse for the wear considering her century of being locked up underground. In fact, she was positively glowing, as only a powerful woman in the height of her prime and powers can. Confidence and glamour dripped off her with every move of her perfectly coiffed hair, and her long dress, was now immaculate with no trace of dust.

'Is this really the best you could come up with?' Meg looked at my friend disparagingly. And Fergie was a sight, I had to admit, with her mascara smeared into the remnants of her electric blue eyeshadow. 'Still,' she continued, with a roll of her eyes. 'Needs must. A third witch we need, and a third witch we must have.'

'Wait now,' Fergie interrupted. 'What is this? What have you got me roped into, Dara? And don't say I consented to it, 'cause a 'yes' from a drunk woman doesn't count. I don't remember agreeing to do something weird.'

Meg raised an eyebrow at me, telling me to deal with this, that getting Fergie onboard was my responsibility alone, since it was my quest we were on.

'It's like this,' I sighed as I began to tell Fergie the story, giving it the best spin possible. I left out the bits about the Uncommon Forces for I hoped we'd left them far behind in Edinburgh. I also neglected to mention the whole Auld Meg bit too, for I preferred to keep things simple. Her eyes widened, then widened some more.

'Feck's sake, Dara,' she said, then she shrugged. 'Well, you promised me an adventure, and here we are.'

I sat back in the seat, feeling relieved and just a little guilty at the omissions. 'So you're on board?'

'Yeah,' she said. 'But I'm starving. Got anything to eat?'

I gladly dumped out all Hugh's chocolate from my satchel and stuffed the lot into hers. 'That'll keep you going,' I told her.

We moved quickly through the night, but not gently, for the car may have been invented before springs were and so we bounced with any slight dip in the pavement. I felt Fergie rustle uncomfortably next to me. I just hoped she wouldn't get car sick on top of all the booze she'd imbibed previously. Trevor was off in a world of his own, perhaps this was his first ever car ride, he bounced in his footrest seat like an overexcited child, clutching at the window frame as we moved out of Edinburgh, his nose plastered to the window and leaving smeary drips.

CHAPTER 22

I fell into a fitful slumber, and perhaps the goblin did, too, for soon there was no sound from his huddled form at our feet. The Scottish countryside passed quickly in the dark outside, lit only momentarily from breaks in the trees when I could see the full moon washing over the land.

I wished I could sleep and forget everything, but the more the vehicle bumped us along further from Edinburgh, the more I couldn't avoid the fact that I'd reached the point of no return. That ship had sailed the moment I'd chosen to go back for Auld Meg's help the second time. I could have wormed my way around the Kin, maybe, for my little accident on Arthur's Seat, but removing the witch from her dungeon? No way.

Cromwell and his Uncommon Forces were out looking for me in full fury, of that I had no doubt, ready to slap me into the prison next to Meg. Or worse. I swallowed, but that hard lump was stuck in my throat like a razor blade.

Hugh wouldn't be able to rescue me from this one. I'd been given too many chances already. My only slightest hope was that I could go to the Ice Kingdom, get Mom, return and bring Meg back to her dungeon. With the Chronicle. All in one night.

Right.

Yet my actions were justified. I breathed in and closed my eyes, letting the power of the Stone wash through me. I could feel the tingle in my extremities, the rightness of the burning in the pit of my stomach like a hearth. It was at its height, yes, but surely it had lessened from last month. And where was my certainty of last month? Where was the knowledge that I was invincible and could never fail?

And what did this mean for my future? Perhaps the power would lessen each month, as Hugh said it might, in which case this might be my only ever chance to rescue my mother from the clutches of the Ice King, and so I could justifiably argue with myself that my actions were right.

Yet all those arguments wouldn't make a whit of difference in the eyes of the Kin and Cromwell.

And Hugh... I told myself not to think about him, and this would be the only way to get through the rest of this interminably long night.

I looked at the witch sitting next to me, still amazed at the changes in her from mere hours before when she had been like a statue in that deep dungeon. Although the dust of centuries still clung to her, she held her head high and proud, and she had a glamour about her despite her old fashioned clothes. No one would dare call this woman Auld Meg. No, this was Margaret Forsythe, daughter of a Duke, and she knew her place in society.

After a few moments, Margaret looked over at me and I was pulled into her gaze. She remained quiet, with just a small smile on her face. I couldn't tell if it was an angry smile, or a smile at the thought of the revenge she planned on the Kin.

'You're not dressed for the cold,' I pointed out to her at last. None of us were.

She gave a mock shudder. 'The court of the Ice King?' she said. 'Goddess forbid. No, I won't be accompanying you there. The goblin will help you.'

Panic threatened to fight its way up through my chest again. 'How will Trevor know how to guide us?' I asked. 'We need you there!' At least, I was pretty sure we did, for I didn't have a clue what to expect, or what would be expected of me.

She shook her head decisively. 'No, I need to stay behind,' she answered. 'To ensure you make it back in one piece. Triangulation, remember.'

Well, it was a bit of a relief to hear those words, for I hadn't been able to admit to myself that this was a question looming over the whole strange journey, but it only eased my mind a little. Never mind the terrors of the Ice King, or the challenge of wresting my mother away from him, for if we couldn't actually leave his dimension to return home, then the whole crusade would be for naught. Worse even, than nothing, because I would have myself stuck out there, along with Mom.

And Fergie. I darted a look over to her, but she remained fast asleep, her head leaning against the window glass.

She looked down her nose at me critically. 'I must ask you. Why do you dress as a hoyden?'

'My hoodie and jeans?' I scowled. 'I dress this way because these clothes suit me. I walk a lot. I need to be warm and comfortable. I don't have any use for high heels and skirts or corsets. Nobody wears those now anyway.'

My feet squirmed a little inside the Doc Martins, and I tried to shove them out of sight under the seat as I looked down at my hands in my lap. Even in the dark, I could see that they were a little grubby, and I shifted them into the pockets of my jacket.

'But how do you expect to be taken seriously, when you dress as a child? You don't appear to have pride in yourself.' She sat back in her seat and shook her head decisively. 'This will have to change. No matter, time enough to deal with your self-image later, once we've accomplished the task at hand.'

'Umm.' I hesitated. 'If we succeed...'

'When we succeed.'

'Okay, after we come back, with my mom,' I said. 'Well, I'm going to want to spend a little time with her. You know, catch up on the last ten years or so, as you would. So let's not go making any plans yet.'

Also, I planned on clapping Margaret back into her dungeon the first moment I could.

The air around us suddenly dropped ten degrees. The ice was coming from her violet eyes.

'Time?' she spat, leaning towards me and transfixing me in her stare. 'You speak to me of time? You are missing a decade with your mother. I am missing more than ten decades of revenge.' She closed those fearsome eyes for moment and drew a steadying breath.

'Of course you will spend time with Marian,' she said as she smiled at me when she opened her eyes again, her face now soft and gracious.

A shiver ran down my spine. How did she know Mom's name? I wanted to ask her, but I was afraid to. I had to press on. 'So you're guaranteeing that we will return tonight, all of us?'

She gave a one-shouldered shrug. 'That remains to be seen.'

I couldn't get any more answers from her on this subject, but that wasn't the only thing I wanted to find out. I had a burning desire to know what exactly were her powers, and was I going to be like her?

What was my future to be? I thirsted for this knowledge, but didn't dare ask her for fear she'd turn into some kind of dragon and swallow me on the spot. Figuratively speaking of course. But all that had to wait.

'Are we headed back to Scarp?' It made sense. We were on the road to Inverness. That was the path I'd taken those months ago – a flight to Inverness, then the bus to the port town of Ullapool, then on by ferry to the Outer Hebrides. And Scarp, that little island off the larger island of Harris, that was where the Stone was hidden in the broch. It also made sense that we needed the larger power of the Stone to send me through the dimensions to the Ice King. If that was the route to his kingdom, of course, I was still very hazy on that point.

'Scarp,' she repeated, gazing past Trevor through the window to the shadows of the trees rushing past. She gave a rueful smile and turned back to me across the table. 'No, unfortunately,' she said, then sighed. 'But no matter. We will return some day. Just not this day.'

She seemed deep in thought for a moment before she spoke again. 'We are heading for Tomnahurich.'

'Tomna what?'

'The hill of the fairy,' she clarified. 'It was the last stronghold for the Fae before the Great Reconciliation, when the Kin and the supernatural creatures signed the Accord to enable them to share the land.'

'I haven't heard about that,' I said thoughtfully.

'No doubt Nachtan is still jawing on about the Greeks?' She flipped up an eyebrow, and laughed. 'Yet those ancient men, and the many words they said and their ideas, all that is so unimportant for you to know. You are ignorant of the most relevant things.'

'The Accord... Is this why there doesn't seem to be the same division between Alt and our reality here? Is it why, like, goblins can just walk down the street in full view?'

Her mouth drew into a thin line. 'Alt,' she said with distaste. 'What a cruel concept, banishing all the supernaturals. Like repressing a part of the very soul of the Kin.'

'But is there an Alt over here?'

She shook her head. 'No, we coexist, no need to deny the lives of the others. This Alt of yours is a very Puritanical concept, and only the North Americans could have taken it to the extent they have.'

'Why?'

Margaret shrugged. 'Perhaps the American Kin felt a need to blend in more with the Normals? They needed to deny that the supernaturals were equal beings. As far as I'm concerned, it was like cutting one's nose off to spite one's face.'

She continued with intensity. 'We're all creatures, every one deserving of equal chances to live our best lives. No one has the right to subvert, or imprison, or in any other way harm another.'

This would have been the perfect time to ask her how the Kin and the Venerable Nachtan had managed to curse and imprison her, but she had already changed the subject.

'Tonight, with the moon at its fullest, we will climb Tomnahurich and do the ceremony from there.'

'Are there still fairies there?' I remembered the fairies on the South Side Hills back home, and all the trouble they caused. Nasty, spiteful little bastards they were, and I still wasn't sure if they'd brought back Jane's baby, for she had refused to speak to me after that incident.

'We will enter the premises with the blessing of the Fae.'

'Do you trust them?' I certainly didn't, and never would trust a fairy. That was like sending in a fox to take good care of the hens. Fairies were rotten scoundrels, and that's the way they were.

'I will thank you to drop your prejudices,' she said, suddenly very severe. 'We will be the guests of the Fae, and will act accordingly.'

'But...'

'No buts, thank you. Do I need to repeat myself?' She smiled graciously again once she saw my reluctant nod. 'I'm so happy that's settled. Now, that being said, of course you must be on your guard at all times on the hill. It is, after all, territory belonging to the Fae, and even despite the Accord, they will never change their natural ways. I don't want to see either of you lured down to their caverns. Leave the gold and food alone.'

At least these rules were the same everywhere. I nodded.

'So why this place?'

'Edinburgh just wouldn't work for our purposes. There are too many Kin in that grand city, I'm afraid.'

'And there's not in Inverness?' I was sceptical, yes, for I remembered my sole night there bitterly.

'Some, yes,' she said, considering. 'But none we really have to worry about. And we have the protection of the Fae on Tomnahurich. They are not enamoured of the witches, it is an uneasy Accord, at best.'

'They'll give you permission to enter the fairy hill because...'

She nodded. 'Yes, the enemy of my enemy is my friend. The Fae can be invaluable allies, remember this.'

I sat back for a bit to take all this information in. She watched me the whole while with a fond smile.

'What will we do tonight?' I had to know. I had already failed spectacularly once that night. 'What is the... the ceremony that will enable me to go to the Ice King's court?'

She darted a glance at Fergie sleeping soundly next to me, and then the goblin who by this time had curled up like a cat on the floor with his eyes closed. 'You will see, when the time draws near.'

After another moment, I asked her. 'Why is the goblin coming with us?'

'He offered,' she said. 'And you'll need him. He has the nose to guide you through the maze, and time is of the essence. You only have a very small window of time during the height of the full moon. He'll help you save time.'

She would give me no further information. This talk of the enemies of the Kin was making me uncomfortable, so instead I focused on my position of power in holding the Chronicle. I removed it from my satchel, conscious of Meg sitting next to me in the motor carriage. She didn't move, didn't speak when it was in my lap. Hardly daring to breathe at my boldness, I caressed the leather bonding for a moment, feeling the warm power pulse and hum like a motor idling, waiting to jump into action. It whispered to me, this book, but I couldn't catch the words no matter how hard I listened, they were always just at the end of my perception. So I opened it, feeling Meg's body start at the presumption.

I could hardly believe my eyes. The pages were blank. I quickly flipped the heavy linen sheets, but every single one of them was as pure as when they were first created. Not a scratch, not a scribble, not even a doodle as she whiled away the many years. The sheets glowed white in the dark.

'What is this?' I turned to her.

She sidled her eyes at me and gave a small smile. 'Did you think I would actually allow just anyone to read my words?'

Well, yes, that had been my assumption at the beginning. I would take her book, and read the spell within to get to the Ice Kingdom and back. She must have seen my disappointment.

She laughed. It was a tinkle of genuine amusement, with no tinge of anger or bitterness in it. 'It's not a grimoire,' she pointed out. 'It's a Chronicle, telling all I know and will know, as per the Kin's curse.'

'But there's nothing written in it. Every single page is blank.'

'To your eyes,' she said. 'And to the Kin's eyes, and anyone else who reads it without my permission.'

Her face hardened and the corner of her top lip drew up in bitterness. 'They can sentence me to dwell underground, they can curse me to write all I know into my Chronicle, but I'm still Margaret Forsythe. I am the most powerful of them all.'

We were passing alongside a long lake, flat and glittering and bright in the moonlight. She stared out the window and continued, her voice quietly dripping with venom. 'He thought he could contain me with his silly curses, when it was I who gave him all the power he has. I've waited long years for this moment. At last! You and I will finish what I started so long ago. Before the end of this night, the Kin will know the anger of Margaret Forsythe.'

A thrill of sheer terror ran up my spine and I looked down at the Chronicle in my lap, useless to me now. I'd thought I could control Auld Meg, but I realized I had irrevocably choked off my future. This angry witch could not be contained. I could only close my eyes and pray to the God I didn't believe, in that not too much blood would be shed.

CHAPTER 23

T he automobile turned off the main highway and in through a stone pillared entrance, the iron gates rusted and hanging askew. The lane was overgrown with grass and tree branches scraped along the car's body. This road had not been used for a very long time.

Yet in the near distance I could see rolling fields of lawn.

'A golf course,' Margaret spit. 'They've turned the entire grounds into a playground for commoners.'

Then the driver took a left turn, deeper into the overgrown woods and I felt us passing through an unseen barrier, a force field of some nature. I tasted the air, yes it was a magical portal. We soon drew up before a single turreted tower, the spire reaching barely past the pines and beeches and briars surrounding it like something out of a fairy tale. I recognized it from the flash of Margaret's memories earlier that night, when I'd first touched the Chronicle.

'What is this place?' The pale stones glowed ghostly in the moonlight.

'This,' Margaret said proudly. 'This is my insurance which my dearest Papa left in place, as he promised he would. Now, I must take a moment to change out of this outfit and collect

some items. I can't present myself to Aonghas in this manner, whatever would he think?' With that she made her way
through the bushes and disappeared into the tower.

I poked Fergie with my elbow to wake her up. She stretched
and yawned, then opened her eyes to see the goblin sitting
down at her feet, quickly wolfing down a bag of chips, or as
he called it, a packet of crisps, that he hadn't offered to share.
Crumbs were flying.

'Oh dear God,' she muttered. 'I thought that was a dream.'

From the shadows of the footwell, he grinned sourly at her,
baring all his teeth.

'Gross!' Fergie turned her face away from the sight. She was
bleary eyed and sober now. 'And who is that woman again? I
thought I knew all the Kin, but I've never met her before, and
she's a feckin' powerful witch.'

I climbed out of the car to stretch my legs and stall for
time. Fergie jumped out after me, staring up at the stone tower
which now had lights in three of its windows.

I drew a breath to re-explain the whole events so far, but
Trevor beat me to it.

'Oh stop your gabbling,' Trevor broke in before I could begin to tactfully tell the story. 'That's Auld Meg, that's who she
is, and we freed her from her curse and Dara needs your help
or otherwise, believe me, she would never have dragooned
you into this.' He gave a sniff and climbed out of the vehicle.
'Scraping the bottom of the barrel, if you ask me.'

'I don't believe I did ask you, goblin,' Fergie sneered. Then
his words finally sank in, and she turned to me, a look of horror
written dawning on her face. 'Auld Meg? That was Auld Meg?
Are you kiddin' me? What the feck, Dara? You mean I was just
in a car with...' She turned to look at the old fashioned vehicle
with the driver grey and still behind the wheel.

'Where the hell are we?' She was screeching now. 'What's
going on? You didn't tell me the whole story, did you?'

'Some friend you're turning out to be,' Trevor bit back at her as he pranced ahead of us in his red heeled boots. 'Besides, it's too late to back out now. You've been seen in public with the witch. Once the Kin realize what have happened, they'll know you were involved, and so you might as well play along. In for a penny, in for a pound, as they say.'

I pushed the goblin out of the way and filled Fergie in as we made our way to an old stone bench. But it all may have been information overload for my poor hung-over friend. She seized on one thing, ignoring the whole 'cursed witch' bit for the sake of her own sanity.

'The Ice Kingdom? How are we getting there?' she stopped and asked. Each individual freckle on her face stood out in stark relief. 'And more to the point, how we getting back?'

I shook my head. 'I don't know all the details, but you have to trust me on this one,' I pleaded with her. 'I'm sorry to have involved you, but I don't know any other witches in Edinburgh except I knew you were there, and it's actually serendipitous, don't you think?'

'Seren-feckin-dipitous, my arse! I bet your precious Hugh doesn't know about this, does he? No way you'd get him involved although he's a better witch than me, but he wouldn't want to besmirch his high-up position within the Kin, huh?'

'Like I said, we were scraping the bottom of the barrel,' Trevor muttered.

'How could you mix me up in this?' Fergie screeched as she stood her ground. 'I don't understand you Dara Martin. How could you ever think I'd be okay with this?'

'I didn't. I didn't think. It's just that...'

I had no more words. The surge of energy from the moon's tide was at its height, yet I felt drained. My life was crashing all round me, yet again. New place, new country, but here I was, getting involved in something way over my head that I had no control over. Again. Why hadn't the Kin just bound my magic when they had a chance, back at Christmas time? I would now be happily attending plumbing school, and preparing for Alice's wedding, having a nice normal relationship with Jack perhaps, totally ignorant of curses and witches and Scarp and the Ice Kingdom.... and Mom.

And Hugh. I didn't even want to go there with my thoughts. After this escapade, I think even he might give up on me. Allowing Auld Meg to escape her dungeon could not be a forgivable offense in the eyes of the Kin. They had put her in the Vaults for a reason.

But... what was the reason? What had she done that was so awful? The legends didn't say, just that she had done a terrible thing and so was banished from the Kin. 'Please?' I wasn't used to begging. 'I really need you. This... I can't explain how much this means to me.'

She stared at me with flint-like eyes. 'Your mother, who you thought was dead, is in the Ice Kingdom and can't get out on her own?'

I nodded.

'And in order to rescue her, you and the goblin disrupted a curse laid by the Kin more than a hundred years ago, and freed Auld Meg.'

I nodded again. So far, she was correct. 'Although, I didn't realize at the time...' Fergie cut me off with a sharp shake of her head.

'Don't give me that. I don't want to hear excuses.' She took a deep breath and continued. 'So. Auld Meg is able to help you get to the Ice Kingdom to find your mother.'

'She has the information in her Chronicle. I was just going to take that, but apparently she has to come with it.'

'Auld Meg's Chronicle. Dear Lord.' She gave a low whistle. 'So we've been driven across the country by a Bodach, with Auld Meg, who has been unleashed from the curse it took a dozen Kin to put on her. And which you freed her from. Tell me again, how did you free her?'

'I took the book out of the Vaults,' I said. 'She had to come with it.'

'And it didn't burn you? When you touched it?' She was whispering in awe.

'No, should it have?'

Fergie shrugged. 'I think so, unless the Kin made that part up.'

We walked on a bit further, under the trees and away from Trevor's smelly presence, but he lingered close. Fergie was quiet now. I knew that look on her face. She was thinking hard, weighing the pros and cons of our situations. I began to relax. We sat on the lichen covered bench. Fergie nodded slowly.

'Alright,' she said. 'I don't see that I have much choice, much as I hate to admit the goblin was right.'

Trevor fingered his red scarf and pointedly ignored her.

'But...' she said. 'Where are we again?'

'Somewhere near Inverness,' I said. 'We're going to Tom-nahurich.'

'Jesus.' Fergie continued. 'The Fae. And Auld Meg - I don't understand how she isn't old and wrinkly. She's more than a hundred years old, isn't she? How come she's so gorgeous? It wasn't a glamour she'd put on, I'm pretty good at spotting them. This is her real self.'

'The Stone,' Trevor muttered impatiently. 'It's the effects of the Stone, of course, you dimwit.'

'But Dara touched the Stone, too,' Fergie rounded on him. 'So...'

He turned to face her with a sneer. 'Click, click, see the wheels turning. The brain is a little rusty, but what else would you expect from a Hedge Witch?'

She looked at me with new respect in her eyes, and perhaps a little fear. 'Really? Christ.'

I shrugged uncomfortably. 'Only when the moon is full, or getting there,' I mumbled. 'Other than that, I'm not changed.'

She let out a huge sigh. 'So that's why you were in Edinburgh, so they could keep an eye on you.'

'Yeah. Guess so.'

'How did you manage to give them the slip then? Why didn't they know you were going in to Auld Meg's dungeon?'

I'd been so caught up in the events, I hadn't thought to ask myself that. And there was also that crystal ball in Nachtan's room, like a closed circuit camera aimed at Meg. What of that?

'Well, I'm not so sure we did,' I admitted. 'Cromwell's forces were after me tonight.'

'The Uncommon Forces?' This was whispered. 'So, what? We're on the run, you mean?'

I could only nod.

Margaret came out of the tower looking like a new woman, as if she'd spent hours at a spa or at least a haute couture place. Her fresh outfit had been the height of fashion in the years before the Great War, her ankles saucily displayed beneath her narrow skirt and her hair, too, had been tamed and was newly shined, the auburn waves tidy under her smart hat. She carried an old-fashioned carpet bag at her side.

On her breast was pinned a brooch in the shape of a dragon-fly, the jewels set in copper, twinkling even in the faint lights from the doorway.

More to the point, she was followed by a maid servant of a species much like the driver, the Bodach, who carried a laden silver tray. The aroma of coffee and fresh baked pastries called through the night air like a siren.

'Just a quick bite to restore us all,' Margaret said as she poured the thin silver cups from the tray. 'We're going to need our strength.'

She gave us only the time needed to wolf down the repast before bundling us back into the vehicle. She kept her carpet bag in her lap.

'Bodach, on to Tomnahurich!'

Chapter 24

The old car took us through the streets of Inverness. The castle loomed ahead of us, but before we reached it we turned off and went over a bridge. A huge lump of a hill rose toward the sky on our right. As the car drove around the base of this and turned off the main road and on to a dark gravelled road, I became aware of the pressing need to pee, fueled by the delicious coffee we'd just had.

We rolled to a stop at the end of this lane beneath a wide canopy of trees.

Margaret was the first to exit the vehicle, her eyes shining as she looked up, up at the darkness looming. Bag in hand, she began to stride up a path.

'Wait!' I called out to her, which made her pause as if she'd forgotten she had companions. We all climbed out of the car. 'I really need to...' I nodded towards the bushes to my left.

She sighed impatiently and looked all around us. 'Quick then,' she said. 'We need to get under Aonghas's protection.'

'Do you think the Kin have followed us all the way here?'

She gave a short laugh. 'Oh, yes, that is guaranteed. We'll start, you can catch up.' She turned her back on me and beckoning the others to follow, started at a more sedate pace along the path.

I jumped into a break in the hedge and relieved myself, thankful for the darkness. It wasn't the first time I'd peed in bushes, but that was back home where you sometimes had no choice in the rough barrens and back country. This however, was civilized Scotland, and it felt wrong somehow, even though there were no people around to know. But just as I was refastening my jeans, something rustled at my side. I looked up, and Hugh was standing before me.

'What...?'

He put his finger to his lips.

'What are you doing here?' Damn damn damn. After we'd been so careful, how did he follow us? We had been careful, hadn't we?

And what did his presence here mean? Everything was ruined. We wouldn't be able to save Mom tonight after all, not with Mister Interfering Kin Hugh here. And with that realization came another. My stomach sank further, if that was at all possible.

He must know about Auld Meg.

And he was furious, I could tell by the set of his shoulders and his narrowed eyes, and the way he loomed over me. He'd followed us up here to Inverness just to give me a right bollocking, as Fergie would say.

'Do you know what you've done?' The words were barely making it out of his mouth, his lips were in such a grim line, but he kept his voice low. 'What the hell? I turn my back on you for a moment, and look at you!'

'What?' I decided to brazen it out. 'I just came up here to Inverness, needed a holiday...'

I looked at him carefully, to see if there was a chance he'd believe me, but then he moved. Quickly. I found myself with his hand clapped over my mouth and being dragged physically off to the main path.

'Cut the shit, Dara! You've freed the most dangerous criminal in all of Kin history,' he hissed in my ear. 'Now just come quietly with me.'

Okay, so he knew. But that was no excuse for treating me this way. I struggled yet was no physical match against the strength of his grip. His anger was like a black cloud enveloping us both but my outrage was a flash of lightning striking out blindly yet with accuracy on my target. I still have no idea how I did it, it must have been the power of the Stone and the full moon but without thinking I lashed out at him, throwing him a full ten feet until he landed on the nearest hard surface. In this case, a wooden fence, which was now leaning at an angle after his body smashed into it.

'How dare you!' I stormed over to him, intent on giving him not just a piece of my mind but the whole messy boiling stew of it. Stunned, he attempted to pull himself together but I pointed my finger at him and prepared to tell him off.

His body arched at the same time I became aware of the blue stream of energy coming from my digit, as if I was a human taser. I had to force my finger to curl inwards in order to stop the flow, horrified at what I had just done, yet a bit of me, deep inside, was jubilant and victorious at finding such an effective outlet for my rage. I waited tensely for him to respond in kind. He was a much more practiced witch than me, after all, and he'd had years of training in magical self-defence, but that inner part of me welcomed the blood sport.

'Don't you realize that you are walking into a trap?' he whispered at me from against the fence, wincing as he tried to move his body.

'No, I trust Margaret, I have to, I have no other choice by now. Cromwell was just waiting for an excuse to finish me off, he wouldn't have let me live till the next full moon anyway. I may never have another chance to get my mother.'

'Margaret?' He was struggling to stand. 'It's Margaret, now? Bloody hell, you're on a first name basis with Auld Meg, the most feared witch of all time?'

'Yes, I am.' I had no reason to be ashamed of this connection. I had freed her from the Kin's dungeon. I was her equal, she said. And I told him so as I watched him carefully, following every movement he made, just waiting to block whatever he might send to me.

'Equal? You really think she's going to treat you as an equal? Do you even know why she was cursed to stay underground?'

'Oh, yeah, I do,' I told him. I lifted my finger at him again in warning as he took a step towards me, but the threat of my magic taser didn't stop him. His eyes stayed firmly on mine as he took a second step, and my finger faltered. I let him take me in his iron grip again, but he was gentle as he pulled me toward him. 'The Kin, male dominated, they can't stand to see a woman so strong in power. They felt threatened, their fragile male egos couldn't handle it...'

'What the hell? She's got you blinded by feminist claptrap?' He let go of me suddenly, and I stumbled back. 'Dara, you surely didn't fall for that?'

'So you deny history, Hugh? You deny that the patriarchy did what they could to keep women down and out of power, out of leadership positions?'

'Is Johanna not the Grand Master of Scarp now?' He shook his head helplessly. 'Dara. You have no idea what you've gotten yourself into this time. It's so bad, I ...'

'You what?'

'I can't help you this time. Not if you carry on. If you stop it, right now, this very second, you have a hope of redemption. Possibly. But if you do what I think you're going to do, it's finished. There will be no returning for you, do you understand?'

I was silent. He wasn't aware of my plan to return Margaret to her dungeon. But would I have the opportunity to do this, when all was said and done? Not if the Kin were ready to pounce. Only if I could get him to help.

'Do you understand?' His whisper was practically a yell by now as he grabbed me again by the shoulders.

'You're hurting me!'

He let go of me immediately. 'Ach, I'm sorry. But...' He looked at me and lifted his hand to me again.

I flinched, yet his touch was the gentlest caress, his fingers light on my cheeks.

'Please,' he whispered. His eyes filled my field of vision, the mesmerizing green shot with gold that glowed in the fading light. 'If you do this, you will be banned forever more from the Kin and their world. You might save your mother, but at what cost? She wouldn't want you to do this, Dara. There is plenty of time, later. Your power isn't going to go anywhere, you know this, deep in your heart. You will only grow stronger with time. Please,' he was begging me now, I felt the desperation coming off him. 'Please don't go through with this. For her sake. For mine.'

Were those tears in his eyes? I couldn't tell, because my own eyes were starting to swim, too.

'For us.' His voice was husky. 'Again, please, just wait. We can't have a future if you're banned by the Kin. You will always live on the run. Think of Willem – do you want to be like him?'

I blinked back the tears. I was not going to be like the Dutch failed-sorcerer, never in a million years. Why couldn't he see my side of the story?

And I couldn't believe that what he said was true, that I would always be on the run from the Kin, that we could never be together, Hugh and I. And I would prove it.

'Come with me,' I whispered in his ear. 'You and me, and Margaret, we can show the Kin that there's nothing to be feared from the Crystal Charm Stone power. I'm still me, aren't I? Just a 'me' with more magic.'

His gaze faltered. I pressed on.

'And we can do this,' I insisted. 'With you on our side, they would see, they would listen. I don't want to be on the run, I don't want to subvert anything. I want to be me, and I want to use my power for good, for the benefit of all.'

He closed his eyes. There was pain on his face. I held him in my arms, our bodies warm against the chill of the evening.

'And if you help me, that will let Fergie off the hook,' I said. 'She doesn't want to be mixed up in all this. I need a third witch. Imagine, if you will, what we could do together.'

With those words, he wrenched his eyes back open and stepped away from me as if my touch had scalded.

'Let Fergie go,' he said furiously. 'I repeat, do not carry through with your plans. You don't know what's going to happen.'

'So what, Hugh? What will the Kin do to me? And where are your precious Kin? I don't see them around. If they wanted to stop us, why don't they do it now?'

'Because they're waiting,' he said slowly. 'Cromwell and his faction are waiting for you to act. Don't you understand? They're giving you enough rope to hang yourself.'

We stared at each other in the gloom.

'There will be no return,' he said. 'You understand this?'

I nodded slowly. 'I have to do this.'

'Then, it's good-bye. For us.' He turned then and like a wraith disappeared into the shadows of the hedges, leaving me only with a coldness where he had touched me and a heart torn in two.

······•••····

It was with a heavy heart that I joined the others. Hugh was gone, and I planned to betray Margaret, if I got the chance. But that would be later. First, I needed to use her to get to the Ice Kingdom.

'At the ready, goblin?' Margaret asked.

Trevor nodded. I could feel the excitement growing in his little frame. Was he too touched by the moonlight, or was there something else?

The gate had been locked, but with a word from Margaret the lock clicked and it swung open for us. We crossed under it, and walked into another world, one not visible from the street or with Normal eyes. It was, to all intents, a cemetery with ancient and modern granite stones all lined up in the lush grass and among the old trees at the bottom of the tall hill. Yet, I could tell at once that this was just on the surface of reality, so to speak, in the mundane world. If one delved further in, past the evidence of human life and death, one saw the Alt thrived there, the magic in every tree and bush.

It was this nature that caused humanity to declare places holy. At some level deep within the brain, even mankind could sense the magic within a place, a spot where the ley lines converged and merged, and humans would typically build their churches and temples therein. But the summit of Tomnahurich stood alone, the Christians had not been allowed to claim it, and it remained the last stronghold of the Fae. You could feel the magic of it in the very air, in the oxygen given off by the tree leaves.

We had only walked a few feet within the gate when one of those Fae appeared before us, standing high on a marble tomb and looking down on us. In his hand he held a spear of wood, its point sharp enough to show that it was meant for business. He was dressed in a manner reminiscent of Robin Hood, his clothing made of leaves and petals sewn together, his hose woven of the finest spiders' webs. This Fae warrior was clean shaven, as many of his kind were. He was young, but he was fearless.

'Halt.' This was said quietly, but his voice rang through the space. 'What business have you here? This is the kingdom of the Fae after dark, no humans might enter.'

'I am Margaret Forsythe.' Her voice was strong and confident that she was to be recognized. 'I would speak with Aonghas, Ruler of the Sithechean of Tomnahurich. Bring me to him, lackey.'

The spear did not quiver at her words or her near-insult. 'You are the witch Margaret,' the fairy said. 'The one cursed to dwell beneath the city of Edinburgh. How are you freed?'

'That is a story for Aongas, not you. Bring me to him poste-haste, or you'll feel the lash of my displeasure.'

Watching Margaret holding her own against the fairy, not giving an inch, I felt a thrill, for this was to be my future too. The old Dara, the person I had been before being touched by the Stone and its power, that Dara would have been terrified and ingratiating and pleading for admittance, for the Fae are well-known to be a nasty and conceited folk. Their allegiances turn like quick-silver, they are impetuous in their actions, and never to be trusted, at least the ones I knew were. To boldly walk into their territory and demand an audience with the Fae King, let alone to insult one of them, took more than nerve. It required a full belief in one's own power and an integral knowledge that the Fae would not dare to cross her.

Margaret held her head high, a small smile on her face, for she knew full well this was just a formality. The Fae King Aonghas would grant her an audience, along with anything else she requested, there was no doubt in her mind.

I faltered in my step with the realization that I was hungry to learn all that Margaret had to teach me. Could I really abandon her back to that terrible dungeon?

All of a sudden we were surrounded by the Fae on all sides, every tombstone and monument crowded with their small bodies as they gazed down on the famous witch who dared make demands of their king.

CHAPTER 25

I knew the fairy folk back home, had close dealings with them on more than one occasion, I even broke into their burrow once when the occasion required. Although these specimens surrounding us now were of the same ilk, they were nothing like that sorry lot who lived a hard-scrabble existence on the South Side Barrens in Newfoundland, clinging to the rock and weakened by the salt spray of the cold North Atlantic Ocean in the hopes of being summoned back to their fatherland and Oberon's good graces. Those fairies depended on their sustenance through weeds and road-kill, fighting the gulls and rats for dead carcasses. Rags were their only protection from the harsh winters, and they depended on druggies and drunks and other castoffs of human society to do their work.

But these folk before us – these were the Fae of legend in their full majesty, proud in their heritage and cognizant of their power in the world of supernatural. This was no mere glamour like that worn by the poor fairies back home to hide their true nature, for these Scottish Fae knew their own worth and the power of their King. They owned Tomnahurich.

These beings glowed with their magic, but I knew we did too, Margaret and I, no less than they.

A female Fae stepped up, her silks and gold headpiece declaring she was of royal blood. 'You would speak with my father, Meg of the Vaults?'

'Margaret of the Crystal Charm Stone will speak with Aonghas.'

'And your companions?'

'Dara, also of the Stone's fame.'

The daughter of the king looked hungrily upon me. 'You. The Colonial who dared to break the tradition of the Kin. You are well named, I think,' she said, and nodded to the sentry. 'Let them pass. I will accompany them to the King.'

She turned and walked away, down a long lane way under a canopy of trees, their branches just beginning to leaf. In full summer, no moonlight would have touched us, but now in the spring of the year the Goddess Diana followed us with every step, bathing us in the shadows of the spidery tree limbs. I glanced at Margaret by my side, her head held high, her footsteps unerring even in the dainty boots built for a stroll through Harrods, not a gravelled road. She turned to me and smiled. In that glance I felt the warmth, the solidity of our partnership.

No, I could not even think of bringing her back to the Kin, no matter that I held the Chronicle in my power.

The hill was a huge, unnatural-looking tor set in the otherwise fairly flat landscape. No doubt humans ascribed its existence to the erratic paths of glaciers, but I knew it had to be the work of ancients, of fairies.

The fairy princess led us up a tiny path known only to the Fae. We climbed through the long grasses, coming out again to meet the continuation of the gravelled path.

Here, I paused to let Fergie catch up with me. She was still pale, her hair a solid helmet with not a curl out of place and she wouldn't meet my eye, just trudged up the hill as if she was heading for her doom.

I was still shaken after my encounter with Hugh, where I'd bested him in a magical showdown. I'd never dreamed such a thing would happen, or could happen. The power of the Stone was running high in my blood and I knew, I just knew, I couldn't fail. Yet at the same time, the enormity of what I was doing hit me, for the run in with my lover had brought home to me that my actions were not without effect on others.

'It's not too late to back out,' I said somberly, in a voice pitched that only she could hear.

She didn't reply, just kept putting one foot ahead of the other as we ascended.

I took a deep breath, and admitted what had been bothering me all night. 'It was wrong of me to rope you in. You were drunk, and I forced you to come along, and it was really shitty of me, and I'm sorry. You can leave, I won't stop you. I won't let Margaret stop you.'

'I thought you needed three witches,' she said, staring at the path ahead of us.

I shrugged. 'We'll figure something out.' After all, surely the two most powerful witches in the Kin, on this night of the full moon, surely between the pair of us we could manage to get me to the Ice Kingdom.

She stopped then and turned to me. 'I knew, I just knew there was going to be something big,' she said. 'Being a Hedge Witch, I have precognition. That's why I left Scarp, because I was shit terrified what would happen if I stayed around you. And I was right. But waking Auld Meg! I never dreamed even you would do such a thing.'

Before I could say a word, she plunged in again. 'I always knew I was destined for bigger things than anyone in my family had ever had. Johanna knew this too, that's why she worked to get me to the island. But then I met you and all that shit went down and I didn't want any part of it, so I renounced any ties with the Kin. When I left Scarp, I figured I would settle for Glamouring, and I would excel at it, and I'd still achieve more in my life than my mother, or aunts or sisters, so it would be enough without risking my life, which would happen if I stuck with you.'

'Yet here you are,' I said with a question in my voice.

'Here I am,' she said rather glumly. 'I guess I'm already in trouble with the Kin for just coming this far.'

'You can still leave,' I pressed. 'Tell them the truth, I made you come, you're here unwillingly and you can say you ran away the first chance you could.'

'But how else are you going to bring your mother back?' Fergie asked me softly. I turned to see her smiling at me, and my heart almost burst. Fergie, who pretended to be so hard on the outside yet she melted for any sob story. 'Besides, this is my destiny. You need me. We're in this together, kid.'

'Does your second sight tell how this is going to end?'

'Nah,' she replied. 'Just that it's guaranteed to be messy, because you're involved. But I always knew that, even before I met you.'

Yet another turn, always ascending, and we entered a crater at the top of the hill. Here, away from the trees, we bathed in the full light of the moon rising over the top. And then up again, a stone staircase set in the loam and we entered the throne room of Aonghus.

The Fae of Inverness had no need to hide underground. His throne sat in a long clearing, surrounded by mossy stones with strange carvings on them, not the works of humans. Beyond the stones lived ancient trees, the ancestors of the Fae, their wrinkled faces indulgently watching the proceedings before them.

Aonghas looked upon our approach from his throne of solid rock hewn from the hill.

Margaret gave a small bow in acknowledgement, and the three of us behind her rushed to do the same.

'So then,' he said. His deep voice was soft and almost Scottish, but with foreign Celtic roots showing in his vowels. 'Margaret of Forsythe. Well comest thou to Tomnahurich.'

'I thank thee, mine host.' The old formal language flowed easily from her. 'I come in peace.'

'And peace be with us,' the king acknowledged. He relaxed his stance a mite, leaning back on the stone and immediately dove into the business for the night. 'What bringst thou here to the holy land of the Fae?'

'I wouldst seek the portal to the Ice King.'

'A witch of your stature can accomplish such a task on any mount or meeting of the leys,' he observed. 'I repeat, what bringst thou here to my kingdom?'

The Fae king and Margaret recited these words as if enacting predetermined steps of a familiar dance. They each had small smiles on their faces, and both knew the outcome of this exchange. I realized he wasn't challenging her – this was an age old technique in bargaining. The Fae king was establishing that she needed the use of Tomnahurich, and so would be forced to pay as inflated a price as he could squeeze out of her. It was merely a game amongst equals, with both sides winning.

He indicated a large bench-like stone lying flat, to his side. 'Come, sit here with your protégé, let us talk in comfort.'

Margaret glanced at me and flicked her head. We approached his august presence, Margaret with confidence, and me trying my best to pretend.

'What brings me here?' Margaret laughed, relaxed now and dropping the formal language. 'You know full well. Tomnahurich is the last stronghold of the Free Fae. Every holy spot, any place with magical links in the British Isles, they are Kin-ridden, claimed for their own and controlled by them under the auspice of the Christian churches. This night's business is to undo the curses of the Kin on innocents, and they would never allow me on their properties for that purpose.

The other holy places, the Standing Stones and the like, they simply don't have the protection I need from the Kin.'

She looked at him straight in the eye. 'Aonghas, cast your eye upon me. You knew me when I was a child, growing up not ten miles distant. My story is well-known, what they have told of me anyway. Cursed by the Kin for what? Touching their precious Charm Stone and drinking of the power therein, as if the Stone had only finite power and could not spare a drop for a thirsty witch, as if I had stolen their very life blood from them.

'That's what they said,' she continued bitterly. 'But we all know my real sin was being a female. We were not considered people then, no right to vote on Council, could not hold property, and forbidden to study on Scarp. And because of my boldness, they sentenced me underground to write all I know, all that the Stone gave me.'

She added, 'Which was to enhance their own knowledge, of course. They could not bind my power, not they. Nor would they send one of their own in to wrest the power of the Stone from me. They were fearful then, and are fearful still, jealous of each other like lobsters clawing their escape from a bucket and will not let another soar for fear they will take control over the lot of them. Small minded fools!'

'And where is this Chronicle?' Aonghas asked. He was not avaricious in tone, merely curious. The Fae had no need for Kin knowledge. 'I understand you are bound to it.'

Margaret pointed to the satchel at my feet. 'Dara carries it, for she was the only one able to overcome the spell of Nachtan,' she replied. 'And yes, I am still bound to it, but this is also my choice. I cannot let the knowledge herein be misused or corrupted by those unable to properly wield its power.'

He nodded, stroking his clean shaven chin. 'Yes, so you say.' He then switched his attention to me, a gaze deep and ancient for all he had the appearance of a man in his prime. 'And the young one?'

Margaret's laugh rang out against the last vestiges of sunlight reflected in the few clouds, fiery orange and red in the darkening sky. 'This innocent, cast down and denied her heritage by the very one who brought her into the world. The Kin have been hoist by their own petard in not developing and encouraging her talents from a young age, instead of snubbing her for an accident of birth. The Council have realized too late that they have another Auld Meg on their hands, and in these modern times have no idea how to handle the situation.'

She told him a little of my story, the pertinent parts, painting me not as a rogue witch but a fledgling unable to stay in the nest, one who felt the need to fly in her very soul. A thrill ran up my spine when I heard her words, for it was only at that moment I saw what Margaret had been saying all along. I was fit to be her equal, this awesome, terrible witch of legend. I sat a little straighter on my hard perch.

'They can't stick her underground or in an insane asylum these days,' she continued, casting me a fond glance, as if I were a daughter of her own soul. There was a certain smugness in her tone. 'In these days of equality. And tonight, she will carry out the deed she must accomplish, and then will have shown them all that she is a first class witch and outside of their rules.'

'And so, Meg,' Aonghas replied, his tone very dry. 'You have brought the Kin to my doorstep tonight. Am I to expect trouble?'

Her hesitation in answering was the first sign she'd ever given that she was not infallible. She finally burst out with a laugh. 'They would not dare to break the Covenant between Kin and Fae for such a small matter!'

'Hmm,' he said, not buying her bravado for a moment. 'Just watch them. You are, after all, suggesting that the whole order of the world is to be turned on its head. Small minds do not take kindly to change or to having their positions threatened.'

She drew a deep breath through her nose, her lips clamped tight. 'Then we must make haste to get the deeds done. Have we your permission to proceed?'

'I should just toss you out, Meg, throw you to the wolves who are no doubt baying at my gates,' he laughed. 'But do your business. I don't fear the Kin. Not at Tomnahurich.' Aonghas leaned back into his throne, his manner relaxed. It was only then I remembered with a start how small a being he was. During his conversation I'd forgotten that he wasn't a large creature, his presence was so magnetic and commanding.

'What do you have to sweeten the pot, dear Meg? What do I get out of this, besides a monumental amount of trouble from the Kin?'

She snapped her fingers and Trevor stepped forward, clutching her carpet bag.

Aonghas looked down with amusement. 'A goblin, Meg? You couldn't do better?'

'In this world, we accept our allies where we find them,' she replied crisply. 'And Goblinkind is deserving of as much respect as Fae or Kin. We are all creatures of the One.' She took the bag in her hand.

'I have here not gold, of which you have no need.'

The Fae King nodded.

'Nor jewels or money of any kind,' she added.

He shrugged.

'All I have for you is a promise,' she continued, then opened the carpet bag to bring out a small box, the wood carved and polished to a shine. Even if it wasn't glowing in an almost neon green in the dark, such a box could only hold great treasure.

'My father's ring,' she whispered as she lifted the lid. 'Now mine. Kept in safety by the Bodachs who guard my estate.'

He stared at the box for a long moment, looking at the glowing golden signet ring within. It was her family's personal seal, from the time when letters were sealed with wax and imprinted with the crest from that very ring. It was a Kin ring – I'd seen the same on my father's hand, and Hugh's hand. Imbued by the power of the witch who owned it, it was rarely removed from the finger. Margaret had never had the opportunity to wear it, yet she would willingly let Aonghas hold on to it as a pledge. His face was impassive, and it was impossible to see what thoughts went through his mind.

Then he shook his head slowly and blew his breath out through pursed lips. 'Meg, the forces of the Kin have followed you to my gate because you challenge the very fabric of Kin structure. It is a disruption at the least. And you know I can't take your ring. It is no use to me whatsoever.'

She merely smiled as if she knew all along what his answer would be. 'It is a mere promise, as I indicated,' she said. And then her tone turned acerbic. "I've been sitting in a dungeon for the past century and more, Aonghus, what do you expect? It'll take me a while to sort the Trust. You've known me all my life. You know I'll make it up to you.'

Aonghas sighed in acknowledgement. 'Yes, I well remember you as a child visiting our hallowed ground. You know you are like family, but this? This, Meg, is a step too far.' He then lifted his arm, and pointed us to the edge of the hill whereon lay an altar of stone. 'Go. Be about your witchery, then leave us in peace.'

We gathered our belongings and turned towards the west. The moon was rising to our right, in the north-east.

'And thou willst remember, Witch,' he called out behind us. 'Thy promise. Thee and thy band owest me and mine, and payment shall be when we demand.'

She paused on her way, just for a micro second. His reversion to the formal language indicated to all present that this was not said lightly or in jest. He was doing a favour for Margaret, but there would be a reckoning someday, and woe betide the witch who did not honour her debts. And he'd included me and Fergie on his proclamation, just in case there was any future misunderstanding.

'Aonghas, this is understood, and we three witches are grateful,' she threw over her shoulder, then she sailed off down to the altar, the three of us in her wake.

I glanced over at Fergie, her freckles standing out against the dim light and her face tense. I wish I had words to comfort her, but I had no idea how the night would turn out. I whispered a fervent prayer to the Christian God that Aunt Edna had refused to introduce me to, wishing now that I'd paid more attention in my Religious Studies course. Which was the patron saint who could help me now?

St. Jude. That was it. The Saint of Hopeless Causes.

CHAPTER 26

T he stone altar sat at the end of the grassy aisle, surrounded by the ancient stones and even older trees near the
edge of the clifftop overlooking the small city of Inverness.
Like the miniature town of a model trainset from this height,
the lights at the harbour shone bright and tiny headlights
showed the cars scuttling to their destinations like electronic
ants. I took a good long look at the humanity and civilization
and normality, for there was a strong possibility I'd not see
such a sight for a long time again.

Margaret tied her hair back in readiness and I placed the
Chronicle on the altar. It was a heavy tome, leather and wood
carved, and it appeared to sparkle in the moonlight, the effer-
vescence of tangled magic. She tossed me a look, her smile
dancing with excitement.

'What's going to happen?' I had to ask. So far she had given
me little insight into the evening, or what was expected of us.
I needed to be armed with what knowledge she would throw
my way.

'You shall go to the Ice King's court,' she said, a funny smile
on her face as if puzzled that I didn't understand. 'You will get
your mother, then you will leave and return here.'

'Wait. You said before you're not coming.' Suspicions were growing in my mind, and I smelled a trick.

'Triangulation, remember. I need to stay here to ensure your return.'

'I don't like the sound of that. I'd prefer if you came with me.'

She sighed. 'And is your friend Fergie capable of reading the spell in the Chronicle and bringing us back?'

I only had one answer to that, and she knew full well what it was. I'd seen the seemingly empty pages of that book. The unseen writings could only be read by Margaret.

'Or perhaps you'd prefer to send us both out there and you stay behind?'

'Right, okay I see your point,' I said slowly, still not liking it all. Of course it had to be me that went to get Mom, and it had to be Margaret that was our anchor in this dimension. I wish I knew more about how all this worked, then I would know if she was lying, but I was still too ignorant of all the rules and protocols of magic. 'And the Chronicle?'

'Stays here. It has to stay with you in this dimension only,' she said, then turned that beatific smile on me. 'Don't worry, I won't run away from you. After all, where is there for me to run?'

'But, how will we get back?' Panic was edging at my consciousness again, though I'd managed to keep it down over the evening. 'I don't know the spell.'

'It is not the spell, as such,' she said slowly. 'I thought you understood. It is your Intention that matters. That's all you need. Intention, pure and strong and confident. I will remain here as your anchor, as I said.'

Confidence. I was flush with the full moon's power, I could do anything, I had even bested Hugh in a fight. Yet full confidence required a full belief in my own abilities not to screw things up, and I knew that wasn't one of my strong points.

She must have seen my inner struggle but she merely shrugged. 'Dara. I can't give you confidence, you know this. You have the means to accomplish this within you, or you wouldn't have the desire. Come now, no more of this childish flummery. Accept that you have the power.'

Fergie and I merely looked at each other. I could tell she didn't have the confidence in me either. Meanwhile, Trevor was bouncing around us in excitement, oblivious to our tension, the horrible little toad.

Yes, I was indeed lacking in confidence. To cover my confusion, I took it out on the goblin.

'Why are you so happy?' I muttered at him.

'You mind your own business,' he said smugly. 'You're not the only one getting their dream come true tonight.'

'What, you want to go to the Ice Kingdom?'

'Yes, I want to see the world,' he told me. I could tell he was lying, but there was no time to bicker with him. Besides, if Margaret was right we'd need his nose to lead us through the maze.

I turned my back on him to face Margaret who was patiently waiting.

'Come now, all, gather round.' Her eyes were shining, large like the moon itself. 'Dara are you feeling the power?'

I nodded dumbly. I couldn't ignore it – the longer I stood in the direct beams of the moon, the more the joy infused me. My very nerve ends sang like wires in the wind, and I felt the flow of life through every artery and vein, and my heart pumped loudly. Fergie and I found each other's hands. In this heightened state, I could taste her fear, and I squeezed her to give comfort. 'I won't let you down.'

The goblin danced beside me, grabbing both our free hands to create the circle. He placed Fergie's other hand in mine, and standing in the center, held both our combined fists, lacing his skinny digits in ours so that the bond was inseparable.

His hands in ours were clammy and the thrill in him sizzled static against my skin. He held tightly and would not let us go.

'Dara, you must not linger in the Court of the Ice,' Margaret warned. 'Time is of the essence. The portal which the full moon allows is open only for two hours in our time, and the night is drawing to a close. I have no idea how time passes on the other side. Make haste. Use your time wisely. I can't guarantee that I will be able to hold the door open after the moon goes past its zenith.'

Margaret didn't fuss with pentagrams or candles or incense or any of the usual tools of witchery. She had no need, for she was Margaret Forsythe, touched by the Stone all those years ago, and the power of this crystal still ran through her.

As it ran through me, and would continue to do so for all of my life. Hugh's words of earlier that evening came back to me. The power granted by touching the Crystal Charm Stone was not a limited time deal, it wouldn't run out of juice or ever need recharging. The Stone had changed my very DNA, as Hugh had told me, and was mine forever. I was like Margaret. What a pair we would be.

She was intoning words – should I have been paying attention? Did I need this spell in order to return? No matter – she had said all I would need was Intention. Fergie was still tense beside me.

'Now, Dara, now witches, set your minds to the Ice King. Call him forth and bid you thither.' Her voice rang through the atmosphere, echoing off the ancient stone monuments behind us and forcing itself above the rising wind.

And at that moment I understood why three witches had been necessary, I could see it all. Margaret was our anchor, to keep the connection to home, while Fergie and I were the vessels that rode the magic and the moonbeams, all the way to the Mother Moon and beyond, to the Aurora Borealis twinkling in the skies and on into the Realm of the Ice.

....

We stood on a plain of ice which stretched for miles as far as the eye could see, and ringed on all sides by mountains, the granite of their treacherous cliffs and crags scraping through the blanket cover of frozen snow, too tall to be touched by glaciers.

Yet in this inhospitable landscape, the world was alive with color and we were standing at the very heart of the Northern Lights, the vast curtains of brilliance in technicolor green and purple dancing all around us. I stopped and breathed in the lights, for this was pure electricity, pure magic, the music of the spheres humming in our ears beyond the galing of the wind. This was the very force of life, the leftover exuberance of Creation, the never ending battery of all that animated the world. I stopped in awe at this terrible, raw power.

Directly behind us was the bottom of the huge mountain which rose straight out of the ice and towered far up into the Northern Lights. I could see no footholds to climb, there was no way that wall of ice was scalable. And no entrance was visible.

'What now?' Fergie's voice echoed the despondence I felt.

But Trevor had let go of our hands and was scrabbling away at the base of the glacial mountain, like a dog sniffing a bone. The snow was flying under his efforts, caught up in the wind and blinding us.

'What are you doing?'

'Don't just stand there, come help me,' his voice was muffled. 'The entrance is down here, I can smell it.'

We set to, kicking the mounds of snow away until at last, we had success. The entrance sat in the shadows under a jutting crag, no light showing beyond the pitch black of the cave.

'Sure about this, Trevor?'

It was a small hole in the solid rock underneath all that ice, barely big enough for the goblin to crawl through, let alone Fergie, but it was all we had. He didn't answer – I could already see his butt disappearing into the cave.

'Let me go first,' Fergie said, the reluctance clear on her face. 'That way you can push me if I get stuck.'

She looked at me drearily, then got down on her knees. Half-way through, she only needed a little assistance from me and a pull from Trevor at the other end. The goblin must be stronger than he looked.

'What the feck have you gotten me into?' I could hear her wail from the other side. ''Ah God, get your stinkin' paws off me already!'

Then it was my turn to squish and squeeze, and with both Fergie and Trevor pulling at my arms I was through in no time. I tentatively stood up, but I didn't need to worry, for I could feel through the air currents and echoes that we were in a place taller than my head, but not by much.

'A little light, perhaps?' Trevor was almost jumping on the spot. 'Come on, witches, make yourselves useful.'

I heard the unzipping of Fergie's satchel and rustles as she dug deep inside it, then a small flare of light. She held the smallest oak branch, not more than ten inches long with its end burning brightly. Trevor was already urging us forward.

'Give me the light,' Trevor said. 'I can smell the way. Hurry, slowpoke, ye don't need to put lipstick on.'

'Shut up, goblin,' Fergie muttered as she rooted through her bag till she found what she was looking for. She placed her satchel around her shoulder again, but I noted that she hid her hand from my view, and she met my eyes with an almost guilty glance. 'What?' she asked, around a mouthful of Mars bar.

I shrugged and shook my head. I could not have eaten a morsel, my stomach was in such tight knots. We had actually crossed dimensions into the land of the Ice King – I was still stunned about this and trying to wrap my head around the fact. Hugh had told me this was practically an impossible feat, assumed I could never, ever do this on my own. He'd wanted to wait until the stars were in alignment or the political situation was auspicious or some such. If I'd waited for Hugh, we wouldn't be here right now.

Of course, Hugh's way probably wouldn't put anyone in danger. I closed my eyes against that idea. I was steeling myself for the battle to come, and there would be no Hugh to the rescue this time. He'd made that clear. Just when we had admitted to ourselves, and each other, that the attraction existed, and we were finally in a position to act on it. Just when...

I had to turn my mind away from those thoughts. I had to think of what was happening here and now.

Trevor had already started to leap forward through the rock passage, his long nose quivering as he found the route. It was strewn with boulders and large chunks of ice and very large ancient bones, so it wasn't easy going. Fortunately for us, the oak branch was spelled to Fergie and if he got too far away from her, the light would dim. He was forced to wait for us and keep pace.

The passageway was narrow and low, hewn from the bedrock of the mountain, perhaps by years of water action, or perhaps by living creatures. It was hard to tell in the light of the single flame bobbing with the goblin's impatient dance through the tunnel.

'Slow down a little,' I told him. 'I know we haven't got much time, but I'm going to twist an ankle or worse at this speed. Then we'll be even slower.'

He did slow down again, just a little. I could hear Fergie rustling inside her bag again, and I envied her appetite, I couldn't think of eating.

I was beginning to sweat, as my heart raced and my stomach roiled. Was it a fever coming on?

We weren't alone in the tunnel system, either, judging from the sounds coming ahead, roars of fearsome beasts, and slithering, the rustling sound of scales on rock. Fergie and I held closer together against the rank smell coming from some of these passages.

'What is this place?' I whispered.

'Smells like dragons,' Trevor called back over his shoulder. 'That's what I'd use it for, if I was the Ice King. Sounds like them too.'

There were many twists and turns in the tunnel, even as we steadily climbed up, and soon it began to branch out to the left and to the right. It was a maze, a labyrinth, the entire base of the mountain appeared to be honeycombed right through, but Trevor led us through them without hesitation, muttering under his breath as he did. He was like a beagle on a scent, if he had a tail it would be sticking straight out.

Perhaps it was being underground and in a strange land, or perhaps it was the physical effect of interdimensional travel, but my stomach was roiling and nauseated. Fear was rising in me, and on its heels doubts were coming in fast and furious.

The goblin was far too eager to reach the Court. What was Trevor's game? Had I been a fool to trust him? Yet Margaret did... but maybe I was being naive in trusting her, too. Maybe this was an elaborate way of getting rid of me, leaving the playing field open for her without competition. Maybe all her talk of me being her protégé was just a load of bull, and she really was the evil witch of legend. Perhaps she was even planning to sell us to the Ice King, in return for God knew what favours that she would use to further her power in land of the Kin.

Chapter 27

'Stop right here,' I growled, reaching out and grabbing him by the scruff of his ragged shirt. His scrawny neck was exposed as he dangled in my hand, kicking and squealing, but I held fast. The torch in his hand wavered and flickered, yet he didn't let it fall. 'What are you not telling us?'

'Let me go!' he squeaked. 'I don't know what you're on about.' He tried one last mighty boot to my knee, but I straightened my arm. He couldn't reach me.

'There's something off about this! Have you been here before?' I asked him, looking over at Fergie. 'Why didn't you tell us this? What is going on here? What have you and Margaret got planned?'

'You're mad!' He sputtered, the spit reaching my cheek even from this distance. I shook him hard.

'Tell us,' I commanded. 'Now. You're taking these tunnels like you grew up in them.'

The goblin fought like a frenzied cat but I wasn't letting him go.

'I've never been here! I've got a nose, I can smell the way up. My nose works properly, not like your inferior little buttons.

Margaret let me come because how else were you going to find the way in?'

And he could be speaking the truth. My mind and body were in such turmoil that I couldn't think straight. I shook my head to clear it. My hand let go of him and he landed with a satisfyingly hard thump.

'Ow!' He stood up and rubbed his rump. 'Ye couldn't find the entrance to the mountain,' he began, furious. 'Ye couldn't smell the path in like I could. You need me, that's why I came. If it wasn't for me, you'd still be waddling around at the foot of the mountain. Ye're too stupid...'

'Shut up already!' I cut off his insults and blocked his way up the passage. 'So, yes, you might be right, we needed some assistance. But what are you getting out of it?'

He blinked up at me, his jaw half open.

'You wouldn't be helping if it wasn't worth it to you,' I reiterated. 'So, why? What's in it for you?'

Now I'd said the words, I couldn't believe I hadn't demanded the answer to this before. Even from my short acquaintance with the goblin, I knew he'd never do anything as a favor for another creature. He always had an angle, some way of profiting from anything that smacked of a kind gesture.

What the hell had I been thinking, back in Scotland, as I allowed Margaret to sweep us up in her plans, and had gone along with it without a backwards glance? Even to the point of mixing up Fergie in this, perhaps endangering her life. My friend, who had vowed never to get mixed up with Kin again, forswearing her future.

What had I done? I could almost taste the vomit in the back of my throat.

He glanced up the passage. 'We haven't got much time.' His voice was a thin reed against the stone walls. 'Margaret said you only have a couple of hours before the power starts to wane, and you might be stuck here for a long time.'

'I'm prepared for that,' I replied, calmly now, even though my nerves had been building and the tension was knotting my guts the whole time we'd been in this dimension. At this point, I was even prepared to leave again without my mother, for my stomach was roiling and I had a very bad feeling that something nasty was brewing. Was it foreboding? I didn't know, but I wasn't going to take any chances. All I knew was that something was terribly wrong. 'Answer my question. What is she giving you, what did she promise you?'

He sighed and hung his head. 'It's my chance to travel and see the world.' He rolled his weird goblin eyes, first left to Fergie, and then over to me. 'That's why I'm here with you,' he wheedled. 'Margaret knew you two would never make it through the maze. I'm here to make sure you get to your destination, and I get to travel to a land that I'd never see, elsewise.'

In a strange little goblin way, that made sense. His kind had a rotten place in life, the runts of the supernatural beings. They had no magic, they were forced to dwell at the bottom of the heap in social terms. And with their distinct physical appearance, goblins couldn't even disguise what they were. They were born to be pathetic, to live in poverty and sewers. No one would ever choose the goblin's lot in life, and perhaps their circumstances turned them into the nasty spiteful creatures that they invariably were.

One could almost, if one was a good person, feel sorry for the goblin.

Perhaps he could see all these thoughts on my face, for when he spoke again, his voice was victorious. 'Never you mind what I'm getting out of the deal,' he hissed. 'I'm getting my heart's desire.'

'What, a matching purse for the boots?' Fergie sneered. Having lived alongside his kind all her life, she wasn't sharing my tender sentiments. She was also looking a little green around the gills, too. The transportation between dimensions must have this effect on humans.

'What treachery is in the works?' I hated to ask the question out loud, for then Fergie would know the doubts that were forming in my mind, the fears that I'd led her into danger. Led? No, I'd forced her to come along, she hadn't had a choice. And all for my own selfish desires. We were in a strange land, another dimension, and I had no assurance we were ever going to get out.

'There's no treachery!' He opened his eyes in a parody of amazed innocence. 'None at all. What do you take me for? Now let's get going, time's wasting.'

Trevor set his rubbery lips tightly together and wouldn't say another word as he glared at us.

This wasn't getting us anywhere. And at this point, what choice did we have but to follow through? I would never be able to lead us out of the labyrinth and back to the ice field. I'd tried to remember each of the twists and turns, but couldn't keep them all in my head.

The goblin led us at a slower pace now, turning back every now and then to smile insincerely at us. In the light of the oak branch, it looked more like a sneer.

I could hear Fergie rustling the chocolate wrappers behind me as we made our way. Stress eating, I knew, and my heart went out to her, but I also thought it couldn't be doing her nausea any good.

We went on, always climbing, until suddenly Trevor stopped, and held his arm out. 'We're here,' he whispered. His eyes shone with a secret excitement, as if he'd found the pot of gold at the end of a rainbow he'd been chasing all his life. That's when I knew for certain he was on nobody's side but Trevor's.

'Douse the light,' I advised Fergie, and took the branch out of the goblin's hand. He didn't even notice my action, his fingers letting the branch go. Ahead of us, the tunnel's end glowed with a pale white light.

Now that we had arrived, I scrabbled in my mind for a plan of attack. Despite having had lots of notice, I hadn't thought this far ahead, being too caught in the worries of getting us all back. Remembering the glimpses I'd seen of the throne room back those months ago by the broch where the Stone had lain hidden, I knew the Ice King would probably be sitting on the dais, surrounded by his henchmen, the trollish looking creatures armored in bones and leather. We would not be able to fight them, not the two of us, and I couldn't count on the goblin's assistance. No, it would have to be a battle of wits.

I could picture the Great Hall from my previous 'visits', when I'd held Mom's talisman and stood by the broch and could travel there through my mind. My mother had been down in a corner of the large room, in a sort of kitchen area, bent over a basin or the fireplace. The hall itself was a room of glittering ice, yet colourful, the walls and ceiling reflecting the burning torches through prisms of rainbow colours all around, with the Ice King himself sitting on the throne of ancient bones. Frost covered his beard and the pelts he wore – or were those his own body fur? It had been hard to make out. I'd even been able to smell the burning pine sap, everything about the space had been so vivid. I had spoken to my mother, although she hadn't been able to see me. We must be so close to her now.

Despite the increasingly sick feelings in my stomach, I couldn't help but allow my excitement to grow. I was going to see my mother again after ten long years apart, really see her this time, I was going to hold her in my arms and be held by her. Marian, my Normal mother, who'd had no business being mixed up in the Kin's politics, being a pawn in Dad's wife's little games, or so I believed. Cate. It had to be her who caused all this, born of an unspeakable jealousy for my Dad's love, and I hated Cate more than I could say at that moment.

But Mom. So close that I could cry, yet I couldn't allow myself the luxury for there would be time for all that later. I hoped.

'We need to sneak in,' I whispered to the other two as I led us to the entrance, keeping to the sides of the hewn rock walls. It was noticeably colder up here, away from the dragon dens.

'Ah God, I think I'm going to be sick,' Fergie said and indeed, she looked even greener than before in the shadows in the tunnel.

'Not long now,' I said for encouragement, more bravely than I felt. 'We'll be back home before we know it.'

'Oh yes? You think you're going 'home' after this escapade?' The words burst out of the goblin's mouth as if he could no longer contain them, and he didn't bother to keep his sneering voice down. 'I overheard what your Kin boyfriend said to you, in the bushes. Ye're totally screwed, you and the ginger slag. There is no going home for you after this!'

'What is all this, then, is it true, Dara? Is he telling the truth?' Her face was pale, each freckle standing out in the dim light from the hall.

I darted a glance at Fergie, then back at Trevor. 'Don't be silly, he's just a stupid goblin. He's only trying to make trouble.'

To avoid having to answer any more questions from her, questions that I didn't want to answer honestly, I sidled up to the edge of the tunnel's rock wall to peer around the corner, and there it was, just as it had been in my visions or whatever they had been on Scarp, but in the reality, the chamber's grandeur was even more terrible and beautiful. The firelight glinted off the sharp edges of the ice crystals hanging from the high ceiling, the razor thin sheets casting their arcs of colour high above my head and I could hear at the very edge of my senses the vibrations of the crystalline structures, the music of the frozen spheres. Being here in the very room, I could now see the cruelty and greed etched into the face of the Ice King, the not quite human and not quite beast of his nature, this awesome visage as raw as winter and as cold as the Arctic seas. He guffawed roughly at a word from his companions, the trollish figures dressed in animal skins and filthy felt, obsidian knives flashing at their belts.

I poked my head out further to see into the corner, and there was my mother, still slaving over the cooking fire. From here, I could now see why she'd always been in the same spot, every time I had the visions of her. A thin silver chain was wrapped around her middle, attached to a large thin bone, perhaps a whale rib, hanging from the wall. She was captive, as she must have been for all those years.

And then my heart dropped, for one of the beasts moved to reach across the table and I spotted Willem seated at the right hand side of the king himself. Willem, the failed sorcerer who'd been the cause of my downfall. He was watching me quietly amid the rough jocularity of the troop, his pale eyes touched with amusement at my shock, and he lifted a horn drinking vessel and had the gall to wink at me.

CHAPTER 28

That was what it meant to see red, I realized afterwards. All coherent thought left my mind at the moment I saw Willem, all memory of the reason we were here in this Godforsaken land, all thoughts of rescuing my mother gone at the sight of the weasel-like face of the sorcerer.

I was about to leap out of my hiding place, my fingers curled ready to scratch his eyes out, to wipe that horrid grin off his face. He was the cause of my downfall, after all, the sorcerer who had tried to use me, to ruin my life. I was set to jump at him when Trevor strode out into full view of the hall's occupants. He pranced into the hall, like a debutante going to the season's first ball.

'Trevor, no!' I must have spoken loudly for the conversation paused and everyone stopped their merriment. A hundred pairs of eyes were now on us. So much for a surprise attack.

For a moment, the only sound was Fergie retching in the corner.

He held his head high, then swept off his cap and bowed low in the presence of the Ice King.

'Your Majesty,' he said almost breathless. His hands played with the dusty fabric of his hat, quivering with anticipation.

'Willem,' he added, and beamed to them both. 'As promised, I have brought the witch. You may settle up.' He glanced back at me, his eyes bright with greed.

'Trevor?' I could not believe what I was hearing, the depth of his betrayal. I had suspected something from him, known he had some ulterior motive, not to this extent. I had given him cake, and those fine red boots, and companionship, and yet, he'd had only one aim in mind. He'd led me here, I could see it now, while working with Willem.

'What is this then?' The Ice King roared from his throne of antlers as he stood. The chamber rang with his anger, his voice was deep and menacing and thundered through the hall, causing the very rock walls to tremble. 'This is not Auld Meg, just a stripling, a whelp! Sorcerer, you have reneged on your promise. You try to cheat me!'

The beast on his left glowered down at us, the tusks at the side of his face gleamed fearsomely in the torchlight.

'Dara?' Amidst it all I heard the whisper from the corner.

'No, sire, this witch is a much better fit for you,' Willem smirked confidently and patted the king on his arm. 'This one has touched the Crystal Charm Stone also, and is still young enough to be formed to your purposes. A half-ling, she will not be missed from the Kin – indeed, you do them a favour by keeping her here. This is an unwanted one, no wealth or connections, nothing to cause the Kin to get up in arms against you. And yet the power flows in her veins, can you not smell the sweetness of her fresh blood?'

'No, never unwanted,' my mother's soft voice came.

'Show him your power!' Willem demanded of me, impatience growing in his voice. 'I tell you, Majesty, I know her magic, have availed of it myself, and then I gave her the gift of the Crystal Charm Stone.'

Trevor coughed politely but insistently. I could tell by the way that he held his back that he was terrified by the Ice King's anger, but his greed drove him on. 'My reward, Majesty? First things first. I was not told to bring Auld Meg, just the fat one. The witch is here, now you must pay the carrier. As promised.'

'Silence, you creature of the night!' The Ice King turned to him and, furious that he had been played for a fool, took his rage out on him. 'This is not Margaret Forsythe! You'll receive what is due you, you treacherous thief.' He banged his fist on the table before him.

'Off with his head!'

At this, the left-hand troll stepped ponderously towards the goblin. Like a slow motion movie, I saw Trevor turn, disbelievingly first to the guard and then to Willem, looking for assistance which would not be forthcoming. Before the goblin could even squeak with surprise, the troll grabbed the few hairs on his head with one hand and with the other, sliced through the goblin's skinny neck with his obsidian blade. The bodiless head gaped in his hand, outrage still on its lips before it was tossed aside. Goblin blood oozed onto the ground, thick and the darkest green, almost black. A pack of four-legged beasts woke up from their slumber by the fireplace and rushed to lick it up, then fought amongst themselves for the remains of Trevor's body.

My world stood still for a moment in time and I could only stare at the spot where seconds before, Trevor had been living and breathing his horrible little goblin self. It had been a nasty and treacherous kind of life, yes, but the quickness of his death was horrific, and I realized how little value life held here in the terrifying court of the Ice King.

Willem had moved away from the king, and was almost upon me.

'Show him your powers, Dara!' Willem was almost screaming with fear by now, his voice high pitched and terrified. He turned to the Ice King. 'Bind her up. She'll soon dance for you!'

The troll wiped his blade on his filthy leather kilt then stepped over and had me in his grasp in a trice. His body was rock hard and unmoving, no matter how hard I squirmed.

I had no time to mourn my false friend, for the pain was immense.

'Bind her with the silver chain, then,' the Ice King agreed, his eyes narrowed. Another troll slipped off the chain surrounding my mother's waist, and fixed it tightly around me till it almost cut off my middle, and still the first held one arm around my neck and with his other had my hand up behind my back almost to the point of breaking.

My body was helpless, but I still had my voice and I rained down curses on Willem for his treachery and on the King for his cruelty. Useless, unmagical curses, never mind my intent.

The sorcerer laughed now, relieved that the Ice King had decided to keep me. His own pathetic head was safe from the troll's blade for now.

'Come on then, my poppet,' Willem said, confident of his position again. 'Show the good King what a treasure you are. He'll only let you live if you're valuable, you know. Don't let me down.' He mock-pouted at me.

'You promised the other one, the first one,' the king growled.

'But Majesty, that one is old and hardened,' Willem cajoled, speaking quickly. 'This one is young, still with many years ahead of her. We can mold her to your wishes, we can siphon off all that lovely fresh magic for your war schemes. A renewable resource, and she'll be willing enough when faced with the alternative.'

He looked at me, so close to me I could see every pore on his face, and he shook his head. 'Just think, Dara, we could have been equals in this venture, had you simply listened to me that night on Scarp. See what happens when you make the wrong choices?'

The pain was wracking my arm so much that I couldn't even think, let alone give a display of my strength. I couldn't use arm gestures, and I had no flashy talents. Nachtan had made sure of that with his insistence on my learning the boring old basics of the Greek philosophers.

I stopped struggling, what was the use? The troll was taking pleasure in my desperate fear and panic. I stood still to await my fate. I would not show any power to the king or Willem, let them kill me if they choose. And I glanced up to the heavens to say a quick prayer to the God I was never introduced to, to save my soul. The crystals in the ice sheets still twinkled serenely, washing the colours of the rainbow around the room, and the faintest sound of their music still floated above.

Willem was desperate now. I could see the sweat on his brow even in the freezing atmosphere of the cavern. 'Just do it,' he hissed as he delivered a ringing slap to my face. 'Show His Majesty that I haven't done him wrong. Or your fate will be worse than the goblin's.'

I heard my mother's stifled sob. 'Dara, is that really you? Please just do whatever they ask,' she whispered. 'If not, they'll not hesitate to kill both of us if we're no use to them.'

I realized she'd made her way over near me. I glanced over at her and drank in the sight of her. She hadn't changed over the years, not that much, except the lines around her eyes and the look of despair drawn on her face. The king frowned and looked threateningly toward Willem, who in turn scowled at me.

I had to do something to save my mother's life, anything to prove my power to the Ice King, but what could impress him in his terrible majesty? Bound as I was by the troll, I couldn't move my body to help my spells or direct my magic to save my life. All I could do was to curse uselessly.

And then it struck me that I did have a weapon, perhaps. I had my voice. I cleared my throat. The king and the sorcerer snapped their heads toward me expectantly. I opened my mouth, and the barest croak emerged, hesitant like the first frog in the morning marsh.

I closed my eyes and drew in a deep breath, and listened closely to that faint echo coming from far above my head. I'd never been able to hold a tune, how could I match that pure tone? I opened my mouth and hesitantly, tremulous, I sought the single note that sounded the song of the crystal structure. Desperation drove me, and my voice quavered, but I poured all my concentration on listening to the ice. And then I found it. I opened my mouth loud and sang the song of the ice crystals, that single ringing note.

CHAPTER 29

It took every ounce of my concentration and power yet I kept the note true, and the very crystal structure within the ice took up the ringing tone, echoing and reverberating throughout the huge chamber that was the Ice King's throne room.

'Stop!' The king roared, his hands covering his ears to stop the pain of the terrible noise. The troll who bound me loosened his grip and dropped to the floor in agony, for his eardrums could not withstand the intensity. The doglike creatures whimpered and ran away.

Still I kept it up, and the note echoed through the round chamber, pulsing and growing till the very matrix of the ice lost its tension and could not hold. I sang for my mom and me, for my future and for that pathetic goblin, disregarded in life and death, and within that music I saw that he'd done the best he could with the choices he had, and I found forgiveness for Trevor, the goblin who'd dared to dream his way out of the gutters. Magnified by the power of the full moon at its zenith, the crystal note like the song of the spheres itself throbbed until the sheets of ice loosened, just a smattering of shards at first falling on our heads like the finest glass dust, then whole sheets began to fall off, slowly crashing to the ground all around us, drowning out the screams of those caught within the range of their terrible smashing.

'Dara!' I felt my hand grasped tightly. 'Come quickly, there is little time!'

'Stop them all!' The Ice King's thundering voice rang through the echoed crashing and tinkling and smashing of the ice walls. 'I'll drink that wizard's blood for breakfast!'

And I found myself at the tunnel entrance with Mom. I risked a glance behind me, and knew I could stop the note now, for the damage was done, and was still happening, with the very ice shearing off the walls of the chamber, and I watched as if in slow motion as the sharpest shard released from the far off ceiling and sailed down through the air, stopping only when it smashed against the king's chest, crumbling into a million shards of crystal. When he toppled under the impact, I felt the ground shudder with the weight of this awesome creature.

Fergie was waiting for us within the tunnel entrance, her face green in the reflected light from the disintegrating chamber. 'This way!' she shouted, and led us down into the darkness.

We followed Fergie's echoed stumblings through the dark, only catching up to her when she paused to light a flare.

'How the hell do we get out of here?' My voice was hoarse and it hurt to speak. The shadows jumped as tunnels forked off in all directions. I couldn't remember the route through the twists and the turns. All I knew was that there were dragons down here, and we needed to avoid them. 'We don't have Trevor.'

'Are they following us?' Fergie's voice was fearful, and her face was still pale in the light of the flare.

'I think - I think they're all dead.' I whispered because it was less painful that way.

'Good. Then follow me.' Fergie set off like she knew what she was doing, stumbling though she was, confidently choosing a corridor at each fork in the paths. I clutched Mom close to my side.

But I was being followed, I could hear a jangle like sleigh bells with every step I took. I looked behind and saw it was only the silver chain still attached to my waist. I grabbed it and tugged, but it was too long to fully take in my hand so I left it to dangle behind me like a tail.

'You sure about this?' I asked her at one point. I thought I recognized a particular rock jut, but she rushed right by it. 'I think we were supposed to turn left here.'

'No, trust me,' she replied, breathing heavily. She held the torch up a little so we could see behind us. 'I left a trail.'

In the flickering light, I saw what she meant. There just at our feet at the entrance to this tunnel, shone half a Milky Way bar wrapper, glinting metallic blue. I was totally awed at her foresight.

'And I thought you were stress eating,' I murmured.

'I didn't have any breadcrumbs, and I really didn't want to be stuck here. There was no way in hell I was going to trust the goblin to get us out again,' she said. 'I was right, wasn't I?'

I nodded in agreement, although she had already turned back to the path and couldn't see me. We climbed steadily downward at a quick pace. Mom had been silent so far, but that wasn't going to last long. Although we hadn't seen each other for ten years, I knew her well enough to know that she had to take time to process things before she knew what she was feeling. But when she was ready, watch out.

And sure enough, she soon started her Mom thing.

'I can't believe you came here,' she began.

'I had to rescue you, Mom,' I said.

'Of all the foolhardy, foolish...'

'Mom, I had no choice.' I turned to her as I hurried her along. 'Would you have left me there?'

'I told Jon not to let you get mixed up with the Kin and magic and all that,' she continued bitterly. 'I knew it would never come to any good. And look at you. What did Willem mean when he said you had burned your boats with the Kin? What have you been doing?'

'Oh, so you tell me off for coming to get you,' I replied as I stomped through the tunnel, hating how truculent my voice sounded. Hell, I was a full-fledged witch now, the terror of the Kin apparently if you listened to the rumours. I'd just rescued her from a life of slavery, or at least, a very cold place where she had to work hard, and I deserved a bit more respect, even if she was my mother. I was no longer ten years old. 'But you were also messing in magic,' I pointed out to her.

'Oh Dara,' she said, her voice turned all tearful and loving now. 'You really are so much like me.' And she took me in her arms and squashed me, trying to put ten years' worth of hugs into a single moment.

The warm touch of her almost made me cry. I leaned into her, as much as I could as we walked fast down past the rocks and boulders in our path. I didn't even mind the stink of sheep's wool or the roughness of the cloth coming from her clothing.

She was silent for a moment after she let me go. 'Ah, the king mentioned Auld Meg... Wasn't she a legend?'

'Yeah, but not just that. She exists,' I admitted.

'Well, we'll have lots of time to catch up once we get back,' she said. 'We'll get back, and go home, and begin to live our lives again. How is Edna, anyway?'

'She's fine. She has a boyfriend, Mark. He's nice. But - ' I babbled as I wracked my brain to think of a way to tell her that there was no going back for me. I wouldn't be returning to our ramshackle home on the hill, or go back to university. I would never again fight with Dad's daughter Sasha, or do any of the thousand normal things. I was on the run, but I could see no escape, for I had nowhere to run to. I had to change the subject. 'How did you get here, anyway?'

'That's a long story, for another time,' she said as she squeezed my hand. 'I thought I was protecting you, but it turned out to be a trap to lure you here. I was so angry at your father and his wife, Cate, that when Willem offered me the chance to do magic, I...' She broke off.

She was silent for a few steps before she answered. 'I got mixed up with things,' she said. It sounded like a confession. 'I was overcome with jealousy and spite when Cate laid down the law, and I ... I messed with things I shouldn't have.'

She sighed. 'You know, I blamed Cate, back then, but it was my own fault. Like I said, that's a story for another day.'

'We don't actually have another day, Mom,' I said. 'When... If we get back, well, I'm afraid there's going to be a reckoning. I may have to ... go away for a while.' Like into a dungeon for a hundred years.

'Nonsense,' she replied, her voice brisk as we followed Fergie through the tunnel. 'Jon will fix everything up, I'm sure. What have you done that's so bad, after all?'

'Dad's back home. We're going to Scotland, where the Kin don't much like me. He's not going to be able to save me even if he wanted to.'

For I'd made up my mind in that short span of time. If we could reach Scotland again, I had to present myself to the Kin and let them do their worst. In doing so, hopefully I would get Fergie off the hook for anything she'd done. This was the only way that Mom would be able to return home to Canada. Margaret? Well, I'd get her back in that dungeon as fast as I could, and she could rot there with her Chronicle.

Fergie made a left turn, her light held high. 'We're here,' she said. Finally, we'd arrived at the exit from the mountain. The small hole glowed with the reflected lights of the Aurora Borealis, marking the way back to reality.

Fergie had no problem squeezing herself through this time, driven by panic as she was, she simply tackled it at a run and dived through. Mom followed her, and then me. We stood outside, blinking at the brightness of the lights dancing in the sky, the air crisp on our faces.

'This is it,' I said. I prayed beyond prayer that Margaret was true to her word and would get us back to Scotland, if only for Mom and Fergie's sake.

Mom gave a shiver and looked all about her at the flat plain of ice. 'Where do we go from here?'

I swallowed. Now was the test. We'd gotten here with Margaret's help, but she was still over on Tomnahurich. At least I hoped she was. After all the treachery I'd experienced with Trevor, I had no idea who to trust anymore. But how could she help us return, if she was over there?

And then I did the math. We'd needed three witches to bring us here, but now we were only two.

I closed my eyes and drew a deep breath. She was right, I had to trust we'd get there, or we never would and then we really would be stuck out here. I cleared my mind, fought against the rising fear of what awaited me in Inverness, and desired to be back. At least for Mom's sake, if not my own.

If Margaret was true and meant what she had said about me and her working together for the good of all, then she would somehow help us back. If not, then... I stopped myself. I didn't need to go back over all that in my thoughts, for that road led nowhere. Literally.

As before, there was no moon shining here, and no way to tell how much time had passed, just the endless prisms of colour dancing in the sky.

'Okay, let's hold hands,' Fergie directed as we stood in the footprints we'd left when landing. Fergie grabbed my hands, and we placed Mom in the center of us, but as I moved, the silver chain around my waist pulled as if it had snagged on something. I tugged on it, but we were in a hurry, and I had to trust it would come with me on the transition to the reality dimension. It had no magic, after all, there were no spells binding it to the Ice Kingdom, it was just a simple chain of forged silver metal.

The Northern Lights danced all around us, their purples and greens and whites bathing us in colours of this strange, otherworldly rainbow. I had no idea how to get back, but the other two were looking at me expectantly.

Fergie nodded sharply. 'Let's do it, then. Get a move on. I'm freezing m'arse off here.'

I shut my eyes and reached out through time and space for her, but could get nothing, only ice and the uncaring caress of the Aurora Borealis. Oh, treacherous Margaret, had she abandoned us?

'What're you waiting for?'

As we stood there uselessly, anger flared at the witch who had started all this. That she would abandon me, she who had been so tender at times, and had prated on about how we were a team and no one could stop us two, not when we worked together. How our joined forces would enable us to escape the Kin, and force them to change, and how she had so much to teach me.

The ice was seeping under my skin, my fingers were numb by now and I could almost feel my internal organs frosting over, yet that flame of anger burned steady within me. I was not prepared to perish here on the ice.

'Meg!' I cried, despairing. 'Margaret! You said you would bring us back, then do it!' As I shouted, my eyes flew open, but I saw only a flash of the Northern Lights before everything flickered and the snows swept up in a whirlwind that blocked out all sight and sound and feeling. And then in that split second, I saw Willem, his hand holding firmly to my chain of silver.

As we left that dimension, I felt the last tug on the silver chain like an anchor.

CHAPTER 30

Everything was quiet now, and dark, and I could smell the balmy air of Tomnahurich, like walking into a greenhouse. I'd done it. I'd brought my mother home as I had set out to do. Without even opening my eyes, I allowed myself to fall into Mom's embrace, and I soaked up the essence of her in my arms. She was bonier than I remembered, and I of course had grown in the past ten years, but I buried my face into her shoulder and breathed deeply, and there, deep beneath the overlying animal smells and the peat smoke of the Ice King's court I found her. The full moon's power still thrummed in me and it was pure joy. I'd done it.

We'd done it. I opened my eyes to find Margaret's violet eyes not two feet from me.

She stepped back. 'Well, that's a relief,' she said. 'You really had me worried, I thought you weren't going to make it in time. Do you know how long you were over there?'

I glanced at the moon to my left. It had travelled far in the space of time we'd been gone. Perhaps two hours had passed. It hadn't felt that long. Or had it?

'You barely made it in through the window of time,' Margaret observed tensely. 'You cut it pretty close. But you achieved your goal.'

Mom hadn't moved from my arms, and she was staring all about her in wonder, at the trees and the life and the stars, then she closed her eyes and took a deep breath, smelling the world she hadn't seen for so long.

Fergie's reaction to her return was more visceral, she was literally lying on the ground and kissing it, trying to hug the shrubs and grasses.

'You did it, Dara,' Mom said with wonder in her voice. 'You brought me back to the world. I think, you brought me to *a* world anyway, but at least it's not there and I'm with you."

'We did it,' I said, squeezing her even more tightly. 'I can't believe you're here. Really here with me.'

'And where exactly is here?' she whispered.

'Scotland,' I told her, and felt her start.

'What? How in God's name have you...'

She was cut off by Margaret. 'We haven't much time,' she urged. 'Look down there, Dara, what do you see?'

I broke Mom's embrace, drawn by the urgency in Margaret's voice and looked far below us to the bottom of Tomnahurich. I saw the lights of Inverness still twinkling in the first light of early dawn, and police and army vehicles, all flashing red and blue and yellow lights.

'It's the Kin,' I said slowly. 'They know we're here.'

'Come!' Margaret barked.

I turned to gather up Mom and Fergie when I felt a tug at my waist again. That damn silver chain! I would be so happy to have that cut from my body. I pulled it with my hand, intending to wrap it around my waist in order to flee when I saw what held it. Willem stood not five feet from me, the chain securely around his own wrist and a frightened look on his face. That had been him grabbing the chain and he'd hitched a ride with us.

'You!' My fury hissed through my clenched teeth, and I dropped my mother's embrace to reach out for his throat. It was an instinctive reaction, this desire to cut off the air he breathed, to finish him off, for that was the only way my anger could be sated. Margaret stayed my hand, so instead I grabbed the silver chain around my waist and whipped it from him, not caring for his scream of pain as the silver tore itself free from his wrist.

'We are on the Hill of the Fairies,' he said bitterly as he nursed his wrist. The blood was oozing out between his fingers. 'Of all the places you could bring me, you chose this land.'

'If you don't like it, you can leave.' I gritted my teeth. 'I didn't ask you to come here. Fly off, or whatever it is that sorcerers do.'

He shook his head. 'Dara,' he said. 'I am not a witch. My magic is physical, chemical. It wouldn't matter anyway. Not here.'

'What are you talking about?' Willem had failed his sorcerer's exams only because he was caught cheating, not through lack of ability. He had powerful magic at his disposal and had planned for more through harnessing the Crystal Charm Stone with my assistance. He was wily and cunning, how could I trust anything he said?

'This is Tomnahurich,' he replied. His gaze travelled out to the horizon, to the water beyond Inverness. And then back down at the flashing lights far below. 'I cannot perform my magic here, on the hill of the Fae.'

'Leave him,' Margaret commanded in a too-quiet voice. 'There are more pressing matters to attend to.' Her face was strained and drawn.

'What now?' I dreaded to hear her answer, despite my previous resolve to turn myself in. Perhaps she had a way out for us.

'It's your choice,' the other witch answered calmly. 'What do you want to happen next?'

'Margaret, this isn't some fiction, some write-your-own-ending book,' I told her. 'This is reality. The Kin aren't going to let us leave. What do we do next?'

She gave a rueful half smile, only one side of her long mouth drawn up. 'And the answer is still – what do you want to happen?'

I wanted to return home with Mom, back to the run-down home on the hill where Edna waited. I wanted to return to a Normal life, maybe settle down with Jack, who I hadn't given a thought to for many weeks, months even. I wanted to put magic and danger and excitement behind me forever, and live the boringest life I could. I had what I wanted now, I had Mom back from the land of Ice, and that's all I had ever wanted.

Margaret laughed after I expressed my desires, a light tin-kling sound rising over the sirens and shouts far below us, but her mockery cut like a blade. 'That time has passed, you have already made choices that negate the desire for Normalcy, for a non-magic life. You made these choices through your actions, every step you took on the journey to lead you to this place.'

'No!' My fists curled by themselves. 'You are wrong! So wrong.'

All those things that happened to me? From the fairies back home, to my half-sister's treachery, from Willem and the Crystal Charm Stone, these had all been outside of my control. I had merely been reacting, trying to salvage the shards of my life as it disintegrated all around me, trying to make sense of everything and myself. None of it had been my choice.

'But this is the time for honesty, Dara. Deep truth. Yes, you needed to solve the puzzle of your mother's disappearance, and bring her back,' she said. 'But what do you really want?' She challenged me with those eyes. 'What have you really wanted all along?'

Margaret lifted her hand to the waning moon overhead. Her face followed, glowing silver, eyes alight as she drank in the power. 'This,' she murmured. 'This is what your heart truly desires. I know you, like I know myself, and I have had many years to contemplate this. You can no longer deny it.' She drew her hand in an arc until her long elegant finger pointed at me.

I couldn't hold it back. The magic inside of me surged again now I was standing in the waning moonlight, like quicksilver snaking through my veins, and I closed my eyes against the deliciousness of the feeling, and I relaxed my hold against it. She was right, of course Margaret was right.

I could feel Mom start. She let go of me as if she'd been scorched. 'Dara,' she whispered. 'What is happening here?'

'This is what I want, Mom.' I turned to her, the mother I'd missed so much over so many years, the person who I'd risked everything for. Yes, my search had been for her, but it had also been a search for myself, and in finding my mother, I had found myself.

Unfortunately, that self was now an outlaw in the eyes of the Kin. I hadn't killed or drawn blood; I hadn't stolen anything from them. Yet, I had trespassed against their rules, their unnatural rules, in discovering my own power. And for this I would pay the consequences. Margaret was right, I did want my power, and I wanted to use it and excel.

But at what cost? A life with no purpose but survival, always on the run. And it would be a long life, thanks to the Crystal Charm Stone, a life without family or a home or meaning.

I could turn myself in, and trust that all would turn out well after the inevitable long spell of imprisonment. But I had few allies in the Kin, I'd burned all my bridges there, having forced Hugh to finally turn his back on me. It would be the honorable action, perhaps, but where I went, Margaret had no choice but to go, so I would be sending her back to her dungeon.

Yes, I'd rescued my mother, but with either choice I made, I'd lose her again. It was a decision that couldn't be made lightly, so to delay the inevitable, I decided to minimize the collateral damage of my actions and escort Mom and Fergie down to the Kin waiting far below. I'd had no business dragging my friend into all this, I needed to make that right, at least.

'You need to leave, Mom,' I said. 'You and Fergie.'

Mom grabbed me in her arms again. 'Oh, no, not without my daughter. I've found you now, I'm never letting go.' The muscles on her wiry arms stood out, and I could feel her heartbeat rising. She was in fight or flight mode, the smell of fear rose from her pores. Fear for me, not for herself.

'The Kin are not going to give me a free pass out of this one.'

'I'll explain to Jon,' Mom said, her eyes growing a little wild. 'You can't have done anything so awful. He'll listen to me, he'll protect you. Come with me, you'll see.'

I shook my head. 'There's nothing Dad can do about this,' I said, but I turned to go down the hill with her. 'We're not back home now.'

There was a rustle in the air, and a sparkle, and Aonghas was with us, his mighty anger palpable as he stood on the granite altar, his jewelled scepter planted like a declaration of war.

'Enough of this, Meg,' he thundered. 'The Kin are getting restless. You lied to me. You must leave, before the Kin break the Pact and enter into the grounds of my land. I have done more than enough for you, and I will not risk my kingdom for this. You must leave, now.'

Mom grew still as soon as he appeared. 'Dear Jesus,' she mouthed into my ear. 'Dara, is that a fairy? Don't you know better than to get involved with the Fae?'

'And I thank you, Aonghas, for all you have risked,' Margaret replied, holding her head high. To me, she said, 'Your mother must go down to the gates. The Kin will not harm her. It is time to say your good-byes.'

'And me?' Fergie finally spoke up. 'What's going to happen to me?'

CHAPTER 31

I swallowed. Fergie had risked so much for me.

'You have served your friend well tonight, Fergianna,' Margaret said. 'What do you choose?'

'I just want to get the hell off this fairy hill and go back home. I'm going to miss classes because of this,' she said. Her face was a picture of misery. 'I just want my normal life back.'

'Mom will plead your case,' I said. 'You'll need to tell them everything that has happened to you. Everything I did.' I shot a glance to Margaret, who nodded.

'They will demand this, and if you're fortunate, you will not be punished,' she said.

I looked from my mother, to Fergie, and back again. They were both staring back at me, one with accusation, the other with a tender love so great it shone. By coercing Fergie to aid me, I had scuppered all of her dreams and plans. Being a witch, even though she was just a Hedge Witch and had renounced all Kin, she was going to have to pay a heavy price for my actions. And Mom – I needed her. There was so much time to make up between us, so much to sort out. Yet, the Kin would not allow me that luxury.

I had to make a choice. Right now.

'Come on, then.' My voice was strangled. I prayed I would have a chance to plead Fergie's innocence before they cursed me and bound my magic and shut me underground. 'It's time to go to the Kin.'

And then I acted without even thinking. I reached down and grasped Margaret's Chronicle. The book was heavy in my hands, the leather warm as I clutched it to my chest. This time, the Chronicle did not give me flashes of Margaret's life, or the rush of power. It just felt right, so good, I could cry to be giving it up. Which is what I would do, along with Margaret and myself.

I put the heavy tome into my satchel as I led the way down the meadowed aisle of the ancient trees. I could feel their wrinkled eyes follow me, their gazes impassive, immune to the petty dramas of more mortal creatures such as us. As we reached the bowl, Mom grasped my hand.

'It will turn out alright,' she said, 'I'll make it so.'

I squeezed her hand and held it close to my body, drinking in her warmth and love while I could.

Fergie lagged behind us, her footsteps slow. I paused till she caught up with us, then I took her hand too. She didn't pull away from me, but she also didn't grasp mine back. When I let her hand go again, it flopped to her side.

'I'm sorry. You know, I'm really sorry about... about every-thing.'

She shrugged. 'Who cares whose fault it is? I chose to join you. Didn't have to come up the hill with you.'

We walked a bit further in silence. A soft rustle followed us, like a rogue wind lost from its fellows. Without turning to look, I knew it was Margaret and her long skirts. She was bound to follow the book where ever it went, powerful as she was she was still bound to the Chronicle which was her creation. It carried her soul, her life's blood. She had no choice but to go where I went, and I was turning us all in to the Kin.

She had the power of flight, I knew, yet she could not use it for I was keeping her earthbound. I cried a little inside, because I was losing a potential life of power. I could have been learning to fly bodily with her, she had been willing to teach me everything she knew. The witch and her student, changing the world of the Kin.

'I'm... I guess I'm glad, though,' Fergie offered. 'You got your mom back, for all the good it's done you.'

'What will happen now?' Mom sounded like she was covering up her fear. 'What will go down now?'

I thought about it. Really thought, before speaking. There was no way to sugar coat it.

'The Kin are angry,' I began. Through a break in the trees, I could see to the bottom of the hill, this time on the south side. The sirens had stopped blaring, but the police and army vehicles had their lights flashing still. A crowd of people stood across the road watching to see the excitement, although not much action was happening down there. The armed figures were just waiting. 'And, well, our time together is pretty short.'

'No!' Mom cried, and she stopped and took me in her arms again. 'I won't let them do this. I won't let them take you away from me. They'll have to peel me off you.'

I smiled into her hair, the thick waves of natural blondish brown shot through with grey. So much like my own, except I'd messed mine up with bleaching and colouring beyond recognition. I tried not to draw the parallel to my life, now was not the time.

We didn't take the fairy paths, the short-cuts down the hillside known only to the smaller creatures. Instead, we followed the gravelled road which spiralled an inexorable route down the hill. Willem was following us the whole way, and I made a point of ignoring him.

But half-way down the hill, I felt something in the air, something terribly wrong and un-fairylike, something that smelled of musty castle rooms and darkness. Something that didn't belong here. I peered into the trees. I could almost see something, but the shadows were blacker than black in the predawn light.

Suddenly, the fae were among us, rushing past in a horde, cutting by us as they fled down the hill on their paths. Aonghas led the horde, his face was grim, his spear held high.

I caught the Fae princess as she rushed past. 'What's happening?'

She paused only long enough to spit at my feet. 'See what you have brought to Tomnahurich? The Uncommon Forces have been unleashed and have invaded our land! Any death of fae will be your fault, and yours alone. Aonghas goes to spill his fury onto the Kin. I told him to allow the Forces to take you witches and they would leave us in peace but he would speak with Johanna himself.'

Cromwell's Uncommon Forces, those beings of shadow and undead, let loose onto Tomnahurich.

'Can this be possible?' I asked Margaret. She nodded slowly, searching the trees all around us.

'We too must run,' she said in a low voice. 'At least until the dawn. All of us, quickly, to the bottom of the hill. It's better to have the safety of the Kin.'

'But Mom will be safe, surely,' I said as I grasped my mother and Fergie by the arms and prepared to take the fairy paths down the slope.

'The Uncommon Forces have no reasoning, they have a task and will fulfill it,' she said. 'Whomsoever is in their way will be mowed down. Come!'

We ran, and slipped and slid down the barely seen paths, in pure fear for our lives. I pushed my mother down the steep rock faces and pulled Fergie as I could. We arrived at the bottom of the hill scratched and bruised and out of breath, but still alive. The sky was lightening slowly, enough that we could now see the gate, but we weren't out of danger yet for I could feel the presence of the unseen shadows close behind us.

Just at the bottom in the moment before the dawn, I stumbled over an ancient gravestone, fallen and slippery with moss. Margaret paused to help me up.

'Run!' I screamed at Mom and Fergie. 'Never mind me, just get to the gates!'

The dawn was inching towards us, but the increased light only better contrasted the shadows behind us.

The Kin stood a ways back, their black robes darker shadows against the flashing lights of the vehicles behind them. Aonghas was shouting and shaking his spear at them, in a terrible fury. There was Pauline's father at the forefront, his hood thrown back to better allow his long nose to sniff us out. He raised his finger in spiteful victory, shouting and pointing as he sighted the movement from under the protection of the trees.

And there, standing right next to him, was the slight figure of Johanna. Her hood too was down, her blonde hair catching the blue and red of the police lights. She stood absolutely still, and even from where I stood I could see the anger on her face. Whether it was directed at me or Margaret or Cromwell for unleashing his forces onto Fae land, I couldn't tell.

Even the Venerable Nachtan had roused himself for the occasion, leaving his tower for the first time in decades to make the journey, to witness my downfall. He stood straighter than I'd ever seen, his staff held out like a scepter rather than a crutch. There was a fire in his eyes, the years and the dust had fallen from him.

And then Hugh. Our eyes met through the flashing lights and the crowd. I could almost feel the burn from those green eyes flecked with gold, but his eyes were unreadable from this distance. I searched anyway, trying to find the love, or at least anger, anything but the inevitable sad disappointment I knew would be there. I saw only horror and fear there, and looking behind me, saw the shadows almost upon us. He made as if to run to my side to save me, protect me from the forces of his own Kin, but Cromwell held him firmly in place. They were struggling, yet there's no way Hugh could have made it to me in time.

So close to the Kin yet we weren't safe.

Mom had stopped, and reached back to me from where I was trying to stand again.

'Just run, Mom!' I screamed. 'Fergie, grab her! They're almost on us!'

Without hesitation Fergie did the sensible thing and took my mother by the arm and forced her the last few steps to the gate where the Kin were arguing with Aonghas and themselves. I saw them to safety and, unable to run, waited for the cold touch of the shadow forces. I couldn't see Willem, but Margaret was waiting with me. This was it, the end of the road for us.

······

But then, just as the uncommon forces had almost reached our little band of outlaws, the sun broke over the horizon, the beams still cold yet bright enough to dissipate the shadows. Before my very eyes, they melted away, leaving no trace of the terror they'd wrought, the sun burning them away like a mist in a glen, banishing the darkness back to where it had been summoned by Cromwell.

I was still clutching Margaret's Chronicle to my chest so all could see it. I took a deep breath and prepared to give myself up, but then Willem appeared at my side. A stir of excitement and outrage passed through the Kin contingent. They hadn't known he was with us. I could almost hear the hounds baying for blood.

It all happened in slow motion – the movement from Pauline's dad as he let go of Hugh and wrenched a rifle from the soldier nearest him, the loud snick of the rifle as he set it, the look of surprise on Johanna's face as she realized what he was doing and her belated attempt to stop him. He was standing away from the other Kin and facing us at an angle.

Perhaps Cromwell was aiming at Willem and was simply a rotten shot, or perhaps he was a marksman and could shoot true. Whichever it was, he aimed and fired and I immediately felt the blow, then found myself flying backwards through the air then lying on my back in the tall grasses, Margaret's screech of pain ringing in my ears, Aonghas' roar of anger at the second desecration of the sanctity of Tomnahurich and the irrevocable breaking of the Pact between Fae and Kin with that shot over the gate.

I looked up, dazed, unable to breathe, my chest a band of pain. I could barely see through the tops of the uncut grass, but could make out the Kin in their black robes at the gates of the hill, unable to come further but their arms reaching out to envelope my mother and my friend. They had reached the gate, though Mom had fought Fergie all the way. I could see the shock and horror on Johanna's face.

The force of the blow which had flattened me had sent Willem off to the side, yet he was still standing upright. The Fae drew closer to him in a ring, there was no turning back for him. Willem hesitated when he saw their movement, spared a glance for me, yet at the same time, Cromwell had unleashed a volley from his rifle as if he didn't care who got hurt or what collateral damage might occur. By the time he'd finished shooting, there was red on the grass next to me where Willem had been just a second before.

I had no time to see where Willem went, for Margaret was wailing like a banshee from the bushes behind me, voicing her own anger and sorrow and rage. It was the last cry of the cornered lioness, knowing its dominion and freedom were soon to be over, and mourning such a short life. I twisted my head to look at her, dislodging my satchel from my chest as I did so.

'Hey,' I could scarcely talk, and coughed up a load of phlegm loosened by the blow. Where I didn't hurt, I was numb. 'Hey,' I said, hoarse. 'Margaret.'

The wailing stopped, and I could hear the rustle of the large pine branches behind me. Cromwell was crazed, mad with frustration. I could not go back there to risk certain death.

'Dara?' It was a hopeful whisper, as if she almost daren't hope.

'Come help me,' I gasped. I lay back again because I didn't have the strength to keep my head up, but I knew that Margaret and the Chronicle had to be saved. 'Quick, before Aonghas and his troops remove us from the hill.'

I had to give her the last chance of freedom. If Cromwell got hold of her, he wouldn't even give her the grace of a quick death. No, he would torture her, just for his own satisfaction. I shuddered to think of it.

'Can you move a little further back in the grasses?' Margaret was hissing at me. 'I can't risk exposing myself to the Covenanter.'

I groaned, but tried. It was painful to shift my back, so I had to turn over to my stomach and crawl one-handed through the weeds, the other hand holding on tight to my bag which held the heavy leather book.

'A little further, that's it,' she coaxed me.

A flash of irritation rose through me. 'Margaret, I'm literally dying here,' I said. 'Can't you shift yourself out of cover and come get the book?' There was a horrific pain in my chest as if all my ribs were broken and spearing my lungs, I felt like all the good had flowed out of me by this time, and I didn't have strength to lift a page, let alone the whole thing. I couldn't shift it another inch.

'Push yourself! I can't let them see me. Come on now, we don't have much time!'

So I did, I found the last reserves of strength in my body and pulled myself over the last six feet till I was good and hidden in the bushes. I opened the flap of my satchel to expose the book.

'Margaret,' I said, feeling like I was at the edge of consciousness.

She bent down to hear me.

'Thank you,' I said. 'Thanks for helping me get Mom back.'

'You can thank me later,' she said roughly. 'Get up, quickly.'

'I've been shot, Margaret. Cromwell shot me.'

'No, he didn't,' she replied and she pointed to the heavy book. 'The Chronicle got the bullet, not you.'

And damned if she wasn't right. There it was, a neat hole, up near the top left of the leather cover. I reached down and felt my chest. It hurt to do so, but there wasn't a drop of blood anywhere. 'Shit. But why does it hurt so much?'

'The bullet has quite an impact,' she said. 'Come, it is time for us to fly.'

CHAPTER 32

I looked up at her face. Beautiful, wise Margaret. How had I ever doubted her? She could have grabbed the Chronicle and left while I was in the Ice Kingdom, taken off for a new found freedom and left me in the Northern dimension with no way to return. But she had chosen to stay and help me, to prove to me that she meant her promises, and in doing so, she had lost any hope. Yes, I had freed her from her dungeon, but at least she had been safe there. Now, all was lost.

'Margaret,' I said. 'I'm sorry. I never meant for all this to happen.'

She ignored me. 'The Kin have broken the Pact,' she hissed. 'Aonghas is almost upon us. It's time to fly off the hill.'

On the other side of the gate below, the Kin argued amongst themselves. Cromwell had crossed the line and was out of control, and he had the guns on his side. No amount of pleading would save me from another bullet.

'Is there any way you can save yourself?' I felt so wretched. She had offered to apprentice me, to teach me all her wisdom from the years, to show me how to manage my magic powers. Not for evil like Willem had wanted. Not for anger and revenge, but to make the world of the Kin a better place.

I managed to crawl to standing, but I had to walk sort of bent over for the first few yards. I looked at the hill before me, there was no way I could make it in this condition, yet I had no choice but to try. Margaret of course wanted to take the rabbit paths straight up the steep slope, and she had to pull and tug me up the way.

'Just let me go,' I panted, pain wracking my chest. There had to be a dozen broken ribs there, the raw edges were rubbing against the muscle. I could almost hear it, and the pain was excruciating. 'Just let me go, and save yourself.'

'Not... happening!' She grunted as she braced her elegant black boots against the rock and tugged me up the stone face on to the real path, the gravelled surface. I lay there, wondering how I could stand so much pain, when I noticed she had stopped. I followed her eyes to the scene below.

Aonghas now strode to the gate, unmindful of the rifles and scopes trained upon him. The bullets, of course, were not made of iron or steel, but copper and lead, yet he looked as if he had no fear. From this distance, I couldn't hear what he said to Johanna, just the rumble of his deep voice, but it looked like he was throwing down an ultimatum, daring Johanna to unleash the troops onto the Fae's sacred ground.

'They wouldn't dare,' Margaret breathed beside me.

And then my eyes met Hugh's. He was looking directly at me, his face showing his mix of emotions – his anger, his grief, and his love. Was this the end, then? The end of a beginning that had hardly started, a flower cut down before it could fully bud. I bit my lip, and then of all things, he smiled. Right at me. And lifted his hands to his lips and blew a kiss. Not good-bye then, but adieu. My heart leaped against the pain in my ribs. He pointed to the top of the hill, urging me to go on.

'Come!' Margaret commanded me, almost tearing my arm out of its socket. 'We have no time to waste. We cannot save the Fae. We must fly.'

'Fly?' I thought wildly amidst my panic. I'd never flown before, not for real, only through my mind. I shook my head. 'You go, save yourself.'

'I'll not leave without you. Come, then, I will fly you.'

She stood still, then her feet left the ground and she was five feet over my head. Still she reached her hand to me. 'Come little fledgling,' she said. 'It's time for you to find your wings, too.'

'Save yourself, Margaret!' I said. 'I'll... I'll fight from the ground.'

'No, Dara, you have the power,' she urged. 'The moon is still full, even if we can't see it. Let its power run through you.'

But I could feel nothing right at that moment except the adrenaline racing through my body and the pain which kept me grounded. Any moon power I might have had dried up in the face of my fear and my inability to choose between which foe to face.

'Come on, Dara,' she urged, hovering fifteen feet away and reaching out her hand. And she urged me again. 'You know you can! Jump off this cliff, it will be much easier that way.'

Could I? Could I trust that I could fly, real true actual flight, not just a journey with my mind? I teetered, unable to push myself off the cliff, as if there was a physical wall preventing me from doing this unnatural act of throwing myself into the void. Everything in me, every mortal cell in my body screamed against this act.

I had to try, so against every natural instinct I had, I took a deep breath and threw myself into the abyss.

All I could see were the houses and trees of Inverness rising toward me, far too fast, but then Margaret filled my vision, her smile expectant and triumphant.

'Believe.' I couldn't hear her but could read her lips as the air rushed past me, lifting my hair. The world stopped rushing to greet me, and we dangled there for a moment. I was flying, it was possible!

I was about to lift myself onto the breeze, let it carry me as I found these new wings when felt a tug on the chain still wrapped around my waist, anchoring me to the ground. It was Willem, bleeding and gasping but holding on to the silver chain and not letting go, weighing me down.

'Get off me!' I screamed and I dodged and feinted but his grasp was true.

'Save me, Dara! We need to work together,' he called. 'If we turn in Meg, then we have a chance with the Kin!'

The lights of the city were a long way down, and there was nothing in between to cushion a falling body. With a great effort, I flew out over the empty space, taking Willem with me.

'Yes, Dara!' Willem panted up to me. 'Carry me away to safety. We are true kindred spirits – remember the good times we had! Look at what you are now – that is because of me.'

I hesitated in mid-air. 'Good times? You mean like the time you drugged my friend Brin in order to coerce me into working with you?' I called down to him bitterly. 'Like when you tried to overthrow the Kin by making me carry the Crystal Charm Stone?'

'You would never have had the nerve to do it yourself,' he screamed. 'I did you a favour! You owe me so much!'

'Favours like that I can do without,' I hissed at him. I was beginning to sweat with the effort, but I moved further out so that nothing lay between us and the city. 'I should just drop you right here.'

He turned pale and wriggled like a worm at the end of the chain, but there was nowhere for him to go.

'But I'll have mercy on your pathetic soul,' I continued. 'I don't think you'll get what you deserve, but you'll get something, that's for sure.'

With that, I struggled, but pushed myself till I was directly over where the Kin stood in order to make my delivery. Cromwell was being physically restrained by his own officers, a light of madness in his eyes. For added satisfaction, I strove higher into the air before giving Willem a mighty last kick and watched him fall, landing directly on Cromwell with a thump and a squashing sound. My aim was true.

I didn't have time to linger enjoying Willem's fall, for I could hear Margaret calling me.

'Over here,' her voice came through the still air. She hovered over the trees, just out of sight of the Kin, like a child uncertain of their invitation to a party.

Much lighter now I'd dumped Willem, I floated over to her. 'What now?'

She grimaced. 'I don't trust my chances with that lot.'

'Where can we go?'

'We won't know until we get there,' she said. 'But we'll have to lie low till we see which way the wind is rising politically. Come, I know of a place where we can rest and hide.'

I thought hard about this, weighing the pro's and cons of a life, possibly on the run, with Margaret. I could learn so much from her, practical stuff, not like old Ven's theorizing and history. I glanced over to the Kin contingent, where Willem was being trundled to the army van with his hands cuffed behind his back, not going gracefully into the dawn but kicking and squirming and yelling about his rights all the way.

Johanna sternly watched the proceedings, her arms crossed across her chest. The Venerable Nachtan, looking livelier than I'd ever seen him, busily smoking his pipe and pontificating while wagging his finger in the air. I couldn't hear him over Willem's noise, but he seemed to be having a blast.

And Hugh. He must have felt my gaze on him, for he turned, searching the sky, not stopping till he found me. His face softened and he smiled, shaking his head.

Don't leave me. His voice filled my head, a presence familiar and dear.

I'm in deep shit, I told him.

He paused before thinking to me again. *Trust me. We can make it right.*

I'd freed Auld Meg from the dungeon. It had been a judge-ment from the last century and her transgressions might no longer be relevant today, but still, I was technically an outlaw in the eyes of the Kin, and certain factions would use this against me. I'd caused the biggest breach of the Pact between Fae and Kin in hundreds of years, and there'd been blood shed on my account, all because of my actions. Even worse to some, I'd exposed the huge rift within the government of the Kin. No one could ignore this elephant in the room anymore, not after Cromwell had set his Uncommon Forces onto Tomnahurich against Johanna's direct command, and this alone ensured my unpopularity. I had a lot to answer for, and I doubted even Hugh or Johanna could smooth this over.

Margaret's offer was more than tempting, but I knew I had to face the music sometime and clear my name, and if I didn't do it now, this taint would follow me for the rest of my life.

I wasn't ready for Margaret. Not yet. Slowly I turned back to her, still hovering in midair. I knew I had to face the music, but there was no need for me to take her with me. I held out the Chronicle.

'Does the curse allow you to take this?' I asked.

Her eyes widened. 'We can but try,' she whispered over the air, then floated down by me. She reached out and took the heavy book from me. It stayed in her arms and didn't pull me along in her path. She held it like she might a baby, cradling it in her arms and bending her head to smell the leather.

'Au revoir, then, dear one,' she said to me. 'I'll keep in touch. And... tell Nachtan that Margaret sends her regards.'

With that, she let herself drift off on the air currents up to the North. I didn't know where she would land, maybe Shetland or the Orkneys, the isles off the coast, or perhaps even Russia, where the Kin had no treaties. It would no doubt be somewhere isolated where she could lay low until she knew which way the Kin were blowing.

I floated down to land beside Hugh and Nachtan and Johanna, my head bowed. This was the moment of truth. I even held out my hands slightly, ready to be cuffed. Not that I was offering myself as a sacrifice, but I wanted to do this with the most dignity I could muster.

Hugh silently appeared at my side and placed his arm around me. It was warm inside his grasp.

'I'm sorry,' I said to Johanna. My voice was low.

She brushed my apology aside. 'Dara de Teilhard Martin, you are under arrest by order of the Kin for... for just everything.' I'd never seen her so flustered before.

Johanna looked at the pair of us, and then over to where Cromwell was being subdued. She brushed her blonde hair off her forehead and sighed. 'Christ. What a mess,' she said. 'Time enough to talk tomorrow,' she continued, her voice weary. 'Hugh, don't let her out of your sight.'

I would have to face the music, but she was giving me a grace period. As I was escorted into the army vehicle, I sent a last glance skyward. Margaret was no longer in sight, but the Venerable Nachtan still stood rooted to the spot, gazing upward in the direction she had gone, a misty tear forming in his eye.

I slept solidly for the whole drive back to Edinburgh, nestled snuggly within the safety of Hugh's arm.

CHAPTER 33

Johanna sure was right about the whole thing being a mess. I had almost single-handedly stirred up a huge stinking pile of wasps' nest.

Willem, well, I'm still pretty proud of that. It felt so good to drop him in the middle of the Kin, and Cromwell had a black eye for the next week. The Kin are interrogating him for terrorist activity, but it's also tangled up from a lawsuit with the Sorcerer's and Practitioners Society (SAPS) because they think they should have first dibs on Willem as he was practicing sorcery without a license, despite the terrorism charge which should be at the forefront. Sorcerers are a bunch of entitled buggers, even worse than the Kin, and I'm just hoping they don't give him a legal loophole to escape custody. That's one magical being who should be kept in the deepest, nastiest, smelliest dungeon of the Edinburgh Vaults, but they transported him to the Tower of London. I truly hope he rots there.

A small East European country is also trying to get their hands on Willem, but the Kin suspect this is the hub of the terrorism, Willem's boss and cohort of the Ice King. That fearsome creature is temporarily out of the picture, with his court being destroyed by my action, and that is another good thing that came out of all this mess. He and his dimension were always a touchy subject politically for the Kin, as there were strong suspicions he was looking to come into this world, aligning with said small Eastern European country to overturn the Kin.

Trevor – I still think of him, and I feel guilty about his fate. Yes, he was a goblin and a pretty treacherous one at that, but it was a rotten way to die. I'd never seen anyone murdered before, right in front of me like that, I still have nightmares of the goblin blood oozing onto the stone floor. Hugh said he deserved what he got, for Willem had paid him to befriend me and lead me to Auld Meg. But still. He was only being a goblin trying to better himself.

Johanna and the Kin are trying to sort everything out. Cromwell, after a short stay in a 'recovery' centre, is back on the scene even though he broke the Pact with Aonghas by sending his Uncommon Forces onto the hill and then having the temerity to fire shots over the border. If it had been anyone else, I'm sure he would have been locked away for this unreasonable use of force, but Cromwell still has the support of the Covenanters section of the Kin behind him and he is Baron of Something-or-Other so Johanna has to use kid gloves when handling this one, even though Aonghas is demanding retribution. Cromwell and his cronies give me the hairy eyeballs whenever they see me around Edinburgh Castle, and I make sure to stay out of their way.

The Kin have their hands so full that there hasn't even been repercussions for me yet. Mrs Mac wouldn't take me back, she claimed I lowered the tone of her establishment, so they found a secure place for me in the Regimental Headquarters on the grounds of Edinburgh Castle, far away from Cromwell's offices.

And Mom, well, we were allowed to spend a few days together, catching up on all those missed years, and honestly, one part of me is relieved she wasn't around for my teenage years. We would have driven each other nuts. I was sad and not-sad to wave her off at the airport when she returned to Canada, sharing the Kin jet with Dad who had been summoned over to help deal with all the political mess. Now that must have been an interesting flight back home. Fortunately, magic is forbidden during flights as it screws up the electronics of the plane, so they had to talk out their differences. What with all the excitement, and its aftermath, I never did get the whole story of why and how Mom was in the Ice Kingdom, but maybe, just maybe, I'll be allowed to go home for a visit later next year, and I'll make her tell me all then.

Hugh is allowed to visit me, though, and he spends a lot of time here, ostensibly ensuring that I don't escape and also that Cromwell doesn't have another lapse in judgement and attack me before the trial.

There will, of course, be a trial. Or should I say Official Inquiry. I dread the thought of the days and weeks this will consume, sitting on those hard benches at Inverness Castle watching the dour faces of the Kin as they take apart every single thing that happened over the month leading up to the Incident, and then muckrake into my past while they're at it. However, that's in the future, for the wheels of bureaucracy turn excruciatingly slowly. Hugh strongly believes my case can be argued that although I removed Margaret from her dungeon and used magic when I was expressly forbidden to, I mitigated the damage by handing over Willem and disrupting the Ice King's plans to move in on Kin territory.

I'm thinking of structuring my story to paint me as the hero, letting them believe that I lured Willem up to the Ice Kingdom, and that it was all a carefully laid trap in order to deliver him back to the Kin. Well, it was all planned out – just wasn't me doing the planning and luring. That was pure Willem. Hugh scolded me when I told him that, said I wouldn't be able to keep up the lie. And I'm afraid he's right. He knows me too well.

Surprisingly, I'm still under his and the Venerable Nachtan's tutelage, which has to be a good sign for my future. That old witch has warmed up to me a lot since the early morning on Tomnahurich. I think it did him the world of good to be out in the fresh air, to lose the stink of the tower, and he holds me responsible. He walks with a lighter step, there's a gleam in his eye, and although he still smokes just as much, at least all the crap in his lungs has loosened a bit. I even saw him at Starbucks the other day with his beard brushed and in a clean robe drinking a chai latte. I passed on Margaret's regards, as I promised her, but he went all silent on me, with a faraway look in his eyes. There's another story there, between those two, and I'm going to find that out one day, too.

Oh, and he rescinded the curse on Margaret, much to the dismay of many in the Kin. But no one could argue with him on that, because after all he is the Venerable Nachtan and is accordingly revered, and also because he was the one who placed the curse on her in the first case. No one else in the Kin had the power to do that, or to remove it either.

After all we went through, Fergie's decided not to speak to me anymore, she's not answering her phone or my texts. No surprise there, although she wasn't arrested that night. Not really. The handcuffs were just to keep her in one spot till they figured out what was going on, then she was let go within a couple of hours and given a limo ride back to Edinburgh. You'd think she'd thank me for adding a bit of excitement into her humdrum life, but no, Fergie really meant it when she forswore the Kin life and decided to stick to Hedge Witchery. She prefers to add temporary glamour to people's lives, make wedding days and hen nights special and leaving it at that. I heard through the grapevine that she's at the top of her class, and I'm happy for her.

And Hugh, well...

'Writing again?' He's found me in my favorite spot, the little stone balcony at the end of the hallway. The low walls are crenellated, I guess that was to make it easier to shoot at enemies from this height, and they're so ancient they're covered with gold and orange lichen. From here, when I look down to the west, I can see Fergie's apartment if I crane my neck. The days are getting longer and warmer, and we're coming into the full moon phase again. Hugh has hardly left my side this whole week.

I'm looking forward to working within the Kin some day for real, if they'll let me. With their power and influence, they can do anything they put their mind to. Sure, they're not all good guys, and I know this level of power can be corrupted, (and as the VN says, 'Absolute Power Corrupts Absolutely') but it's going to be a hell of a ride. If they'll take me, of course, but Hugh says the general consensus seems to be they want me inside the organization where they can keep a close eye on me.

We'd talked about that night at the foot of Tomnahurich, when I'd overthrown him with such strength. He'd been shocked.

'Shocked that you could, yes, though intellectually I knew that anything was possible with your powers at their height,' he admitted. 'But I was more shocked that you *would* do it, that you would turn your force on me when thwarted.'

'Yeah, me too,' I confessed with a grin. 'But then again, you were in my way.'

'Remind me never to do that again,' he said dryly, rubbing his shoulder where the bruise was fading from purple to an interesting greenish blue colour. He looked at me with a new respect these days.

Our relationship has matured since that night, perhaps because I feel different these days. When he'd met me the previous year, I'd still been a child, really, still stuck in resenting my father, resenting his rules which I can now see made perfect sense for him. Dad had thought that by denying my magic and hiding it, I would avoid the exact kinds of things that had happened because I meddled in magic. I can see from my new standpoint that he hadn't made the wisest of decisions, like Margaret pointed out. But I no longer hate him for it.

'Don't forget to mention going back to Lewis and Harris,' Hugh adds. He's looking over my shoulder, how dare he? I quickly cover the paper with my elbow and glare up at all delicious six feet of him.

No, I'm not going back to Scarp, no one feels comfortable about that yet. When all of this is over and done with, providing of course that things go as Hugh predicts, we're going to visit his family estate so I can meet his folks and siblings and cousins and the menagerie. Don't ask me to pronounce the name of the place, let alone spell it.

'Mum is eager to give you the ring,' he reminds me.

'Oh right, the famous family heirloom ring, passed down to the wives of the Earls of Garmoran since the time of the Stewart Kings.' He'd shown me a photo of the jewellery the other day, it's a huge hunk of gold with an egg of a ruby stuck in the middle. Not attractive, but fortunately it only comes out for formal occasions. The ring is supposedly the property of the reigning Countess, but it's a family tradition to offload it on to the wife of the oldest son at the first opportunity.

'You could sound a little more enthusiastic.' That's a pretend scowl on his face.

'Well, you haven't asked me to marry you yet,' I point out very reasonably. 'And besides, I'm way too busy for that. I have a career to think about.'

'So perhaps sometime in the next decade?'

'Maybe, we'll see. That'll give you some time to work on convincing me.' I grin up at him, and offer him my cheek to kiss. He bent down and lingered, his soft breath minty and mixing with the smell of the potted roses blooming in my sun catching, heat-trap private balcony. I wriggled my toes with pleasure. 'Now, go away, I'm writing.'

'The next Chronicle?' He placed his hand on my notebook.

'Sorry, that's out of bounds,' I said as I closed the journal and held it against my chest with both arms. I stood up. 'Did you make fresh coffee after taking the last cup?'

Of course he hadn't. I followed him back into my room to oversee the brewing of a fresh pot, for I couldn't trust him not to just whip up a cup of instant. Hugh had many talents, but none of them were evident in the kitchen.

Speaking of Chronicles, my mind often goes back to that night. Margaret flew off north into the dawning day, and she got off easy. The Kin aren't looking too hard for her, for it turns out that her transgressions of one hundred and more years ago aren't very serious offences in this day and age of equality of women, and Johanna could hardly lock Meg back in her dungeon without another big Inquiry. I really don't think the Master of Scarp wants to set that in motion, for she has enough on her plate.

The Covenanters feel differently about the whole matter, of course, but they're a miserable bunch of traditionalists and nobody else really cares much what they think.

Most importantly for Meg, now that Nachtan has lifted the curse, she is free to return and get her trust sorted out.

I want to hear the rest of her tale. In fact, I want to see her again, I want to learn from her and work with her. She's my hero, and I have a strong feeling that this story is not finished yet.

When I return to the balcony, there's a dragonfly resting on my journal. A twinkling, jewelled brooch. Margaret's brooch. I search the skies above and all around, yet they are empty of clouds, not even the crows are flying on this gorgeous day. No sign of Margaret but I know she's around, and I smile.

I hold the brooch up to the sun, the better to see the colors of the gems which make up its wings.

Hugh, returning with my coffee, moves into my patch of sunshine, his shadow causing the bright prisms to blink out as he lays the cup on the table.

'Who's that making you grin from ear to ear? A text from your mother?'

Without even realizing it, my hand silently closes over the brooch. I move my arm to shield my eyes from the brightness surrounding his outline. For some reason, I'm unwilling to share this evidence of Meg with Hugh, my dearest and beloved.

If at that moment I'd had an inkling of her future betrayal, if I could have known the depths of deceit that witch was capable of, perhaps I would have shared more with Hugh. Would it have made a difference to the outcome of the events to come? Would Hugh have stopped me from becoming ensnared in Cate's web?

Perhaps. Or perhaps not. At any rate, I chose to keep the brooch's sudden appearance to myself.

'Nah.' I keep the smile pasted on my face as I squint up at him. 'Just thinking about the future.'

I didn't realize, then, just what our futures would hold. The intrigue. The falseness. And tied to all of it, the re-emergence of Cate, my father's wife, into my life.

The end

....

The story of Dara and Hugh, and Margaret of course, continues in *AN ENIGMATIC WITCH*, Book 5 of the Witch Kin Chronicles.

Available for purchase direct from Liz Graham's shop here or from all other retailers!

A darkness emerges from within that threatens to shatter her world.

Dara's poised on the brink of her new life. She's finally won her place in the ranks of the Kin and her ambition steers her ever upward. Yet what she finds here is falseness and intrigue — Hugh, her father, Meg — all are revealed in their true colors, until the only witch she can trust is her worst enemy. Cate.

A larger peril looms for the Witch Kin, one that has been brewing beneath the surface for centuries. In order to help, she needs to travel back to her home land and find herself while facing the demons of her own past and future.

Yes, Dara can attain her deepest desires, but is the terrible price of her ambition worth the cost to her soul?